I0831257

VALKYRIE ACADEMY DRAGON ALLIANCE

COLLECTION BOOKS 1-5

KATRINA COPE

Valkyrie Academy Dragon Alliance
Books

Marked Prequel
Chosen
Vanished
Scorned
Inflicted
Empowered
Ambushed
Warned
Abducted
Besieged
Deceived

KATRINA COPE

CHOSEN

VALKYRIE ACADEMY
DRAGON ALLIANCE

BOOK 1

EDITORIAL REVIEW

Cosy Burrow Books

Valkyrie Academy Dragon Alliance
Book One

CHOSEN

"Asgard has two kinds of Valkyries, winged and wingless. The wingless Valkyries are treated like slaves, but headstrong teenager Kara is determined to change that, and with the help of a powerful dragon, she just might get her chance." Susie D., Line Editor, Red Adept Editing

Chosen
Ebook first published in USA in August 2019 by Cosy Burrow Books
Ebook first published in Great Britain in August 2019 by Cosy Burrow Books

www.katrinacopebooks.com

Published by Cosy Burrow Books

ISBN: 978-0-6486613-0-6
ASIN: B07TRK3KNM

Created with Vellum

Dusk ~ For your endless love and dedication ;)

CHAPTER ONE

A horn blares, and I run outside the academy walls to watch the ascension of the winged Valkyries to the rainbow bridge. There could only be one explanation for the horn–a war in Midgard, and warriors are falling. The winged Valkyries flock to Heimdall's post, the entrance of Bifrost, seeking departure from Asgard and entrance into Midgard. Envy stirs deep within when I think about their mission–to find the brave warriors of either side and reap their souls to send to Valhalla in preparation for Ragnarok. It is a mission that is denied to me and my kind. Awe envelops me as I watch them take flight with their beautiful majestic wings flapping and raising them high.

A piercing alarm bell rings throughout the school, and a sense of urgency flutters through my body. I pull my eyes away and rush past Asgard's harsh landscape to the center hall, where we're expected to gather every time the alarm sounds. This is my third year at Valkyrie Academy, leaving one year to go. After receiving a formal education, the Valkyries are sent to the academy from ages fifteen to eighteen to finish their training for their duties, which they will undertake for the rest of their immortal lives.

"Wait up, Kara. What do you think they need us for?" Eir moves in beside me. She pulls a hairband off her wrist and ties back her long light-brown hair, securing her wavy locks neatly out of her face. Her kind face creases, and her light-brown eyes fill with worry.

"Perhaps for once, they are giving us something important to do." Hildr joins me on my other side, clasping the hilt of her sword, looking ready for action, even though we're not going to war.

"I doubt it," I say, and her green eyes focus on me with such annoyance that I think I see her short spiky red hair stand on end. "Hey, don't kill the messenger." I hold my hands up in defense. "You know where I stand with the bias against our wingless kind."

She huffs as we enter the academy hall. We scurry to find a seat around the outskirts, watching our mistress stand in the middle.

The winged Valkyries file in and sit in the reserved seats in the rows closer to the mistress. On one hand, I loathe that they are treated like royalty among the

Valkyrie, but on the other, I long to be part of what they can do.

My eyes narrow as my nemesis enters the room, flanked by her two accomplices, Mist and Prima. They look as though they were made from the same molding cast. Rota's perfect waves of blond hair fall to her shoulders, and her slim figure in her tan leather jacket and tight blue pants is framed by her beautiful, majestic white wings. She is beautiful in every way, as a Valkyrie should be. I don't despise her for this. Even the wingless Valkyries are known for being beautiful. My distaste for her is based more on how she treats my kind, me in particular. It isn't unusual for the winged Valkyries to pick on the wingless ones, as we are seen as lower class, but this particular one has taken it to another level with me. For some reason, she has taken an interest in tormenting me in my daily life in the academy right from my very first day. Perhaps it is because she knows that I've strived to be one of the winged Valkyries and how I long for the myth of how Brynhildr got her wings to come true.

Rota is holding her head high with an air of superiority as the three take the prime seats, directly in front of the mistress. Deep-green envy runs through my veins. I wish that, for once in my life, I could wipe the smug looks off their faces.

As everyone scrambles into the room, the ruckus of the hall is overbearing. The mistress raises her hands.

"Now, Valkyries, students, quiet down." When the hall remains noisy, she raises her voice some more. "You must be silent this instant. We have an urgent matter to discuss." The noise in the hall remains the same. Her voice crescendos. "Valkyries! Be quiet now!"

The hall falls silent. It is surprising that the hall remained as loud as it did for so long. We all know that if we do not listen to the mistress, the punishment is severe. Shuffling shoes echo through the hall as some straggling Valkyries hurry to their seats.

A flicker of annoyance passes over Mistress Sigrun's face before being washed away by control. "There is a war on Midgard, and we do not have enough Valkyries to reap the brave warriors. As you know, we need these courageous warriors to train here so that they will be ready to defend Asgard when the day of Ragnarok arrives." Her eyes land on the winged Valkyries, and a sense of pride fills her face. "My top students, it is now your time to undergo your first reaping."

A murmur echoes through the hall, and the mistress raises her hands again, causing the hall to fall silent. "We knew this time was coming, and for the senior students, your opportunity is now. You have trained hard and trained well."

Without meaning to, I look at my nemesis, and I can't help glowering. Her face is overflowing with pride and arrogance in knowing that she's about to have her first reaping. She knows that soon, her name will be honored among the Valkyries and spoken of in the halls of Valhalla. I don't think it is possible for me to loathe her any more than I do right at this moment.

The mistress raises her arms again, calling for attention. "Valkyries, let us leave and head to Heimdall's point. Time is of the utmost importance."

A rustling of feathers echoes through the room as the winged Valkyries stand and exit the hall, leaving the wingless Valkyries in their spots, and a potent disappointment tarnishes the atmosphere. Because we are not winged, we are not permitted to go to these battles.

Pausing at the entrance of the hall, the mistress spins around to add insult to injury. "Oh, and don't forget to clean the hall of Valhalla. I'm sure the claimed warriors had a large party last night and have left it a mess after drinking too much mead. The hall must be cleaned and ready for the new group of warriors so that they may be impressed by our hospitality."

Although she's the mistress, I can't help but glare at her with all the hostility I can muster. I want to prove my worth, and I am sure we have special gifts as well. My sword's sheath rubs against my black leather pants as though reminding me it is there.

Without another word, the mistress spins around and follows her prize possessions up to the bridge in a sea of tan leather jackets and blue leather pants—their Valkyrie uniform.

"I want to punch someone!" Hildr's feet are planted

firmly on the ground with her knees shoulder width apart. She sits forward, and her black leather pants squeak as her elbows twist into them.

Eir reaches over me and places her hand on Hildr's back. "Chill. There is more to life than fighting."

Hildr's voice explodes with aggression. "Just because you're willing to go with the flow doesn't mean I can't be angry about our role. Are they ever going to let us fight with them? Kara and I are incredible fighters. Even you are, too, when you put aside your peace-keeping intentions."

I rise and head for the door.

"Where are you going?" The anger in Hildr's voice remains, but I ignore it. I know it is aimed toward the winged Valkyries and their rules.

I turn around to look at her. "I'll meet you in the hall soon. I'm going to watch them ascend."

Hildr huffs. "Do you think I need any more salt rubbed into my wound? There is no way I am going to watch them ascend into glory."

Eir gives me an understanding smile. "Don't do anything stupid. They would love to give you more menial jobs, I'm sure, if they catch you at Heimdall's point instead of cleaning the hall."

Turning, I cast her a smirk over my shoulder. "I'll be stealthy." I quicken my pace and stop at the weapons wall outside of the hall, grabbing a bow and throwing a quiver full of arrows over my back before heading straight to Heimdall's.

The sky lights up with a rainbow of colors then dulls again as Bifrost straightens. The first lot of Valkyries is released into Midgard. A few moments later, another large flash goes through the rainbow colors filling the sky, and I know that the next lot of Valkyries has gone—the Valkyries from the academy. It is only seconds before Bifrost straightens, lining the sky in a nice neat rainbow.

I head in that direction. Maybe I can find a way to sneak past Heimdall and help the winged Valkyries reap the souls with or without their approval.

CHAPTER TWO

By the time I reach Bifrost, my legs ache. It's far away from the academy, and the journey ends with an extensive climb, a feat that the winged Valkyries don't have to accomplish. They land with ease, using the power of their wings, an option not available to me. Instead, I had to climb the rocky terrain, ascending to the point of the tower.

Placing my hands on my hips, I catch my breath and study the rainbow bridge stretching far and wide. I observe the straight lines and follow them all the way until they reach the small tower where Heimdall stands with his legs in a ready stance. His towering bulk is covered in armor, a horned helmet protects his head, and his hands are planted over the hilt of his sword while he guards the entrance to the other worlds, scanning with his all-seeing eyes. I'm sure he is also watching the Valkyries' progress into Midgard.

Ignoring my exhaustion and the pain surging through my legs, I approach Heimdall. His eyes slowly turn, and he gazes at me as the distance between us closes.

"Young Valkyrie of the wingless kind. You have traveled far. What is your purpose?" His eyes bore deep into my soul, as though he's reading my intentions. From what I have heard, he is not able to read our thoughts, but he does know what we do.

I square my shoulders and step forward with confidence that I don't feel, doing my best to steady my breath. "Heimdall, I wish to join the winged Valkyries and help them reap the brave warriors for Valhalla."

The corners of his eyes twitch up, and his eyes dance for a moment, as though he is about to break into a smile. He quickly pushes his mouth into a flat line. "Young Valkyrie, you are courageous, but this is not your destiny. You must turn around and go back."

"But I believe I can help." The words come out faster than I intend, sounding urgent, almost desperate.

"Your intentions are good, young Valkyrie. But this is not permitted. It is the Asgard way. You must return to your academy. I will inform your mistress that you are willing to drop everything to help the cause."

My mistress's likely response flickers through my

mind, and my heart sinks. Her face would break into a smile, and she would laugh despite my wanting to help and my intentions being good. I know if anything, it will just be a joke to her.

"No, don't bother. This can remain our secret." I let my eyes trail to the tower, the entrance of which I can use to leave this realm and go into Midgard. And my heart longs to enter there. I can feel his eyes studying me, taking in everything that he is seeing, and I'm sure it is an unforgettable memory that he will store away. I so badly want to go and help. Surely I can be of more use than cleaning the halls and being almost a slave to the winged Valkyries.

As I stare at the entrance, a voice enters the depths of my mind, deep and rumbling. *Go, young Valkyrie. Despite what he says, it is your destiny. You are more important than what they make you believe.*

I look at Heimdall to see if he's the one talking in my mind. Perhaps it is a gift he holds that I don't know about. I search the depths of his dark-brown eyes, which peer out from under the canopy of his large horned helmet, and see no sign lying in them that it is him. Maybe this is a joke he plays when faced with someone opposing the rules of Asgard's borders. He is the watchman of the gods and the gatekeeper to Bifrost. *If he is not the one that is telling me this, then who can it be?* I cast a brief look around but cannot see anyone else.

A deep, searing pain shoots from my shoulder and down my right arm. I flinch and clutch at it, grimacing.

"Young Valkyrie, what is wrong?" Heimdall moves forward, concern in his eyes.

I yank back my black leather sleeve, revealing my shoulder, and peer down at the initiating point of the pain. The scar that I received a couple of years ago has turned bright red and is burning. I place a hand over it, protecting it, as though that'll help the pain go away, but it does not feel any better, so I rub it, trying to work away the pain.

Heimdall's eyes are wide. "Where did you receive this mark, young Valkyrie?"

After seeing no new damage, I cover my shoulder. "Some beast attacked me one day when I was in the dragon fields. I had stumbled across a nest of dragon eggs. It was trying to steal them, and I went to stop it. I managed to scare the beast away from the dragon eggs, but it clawed me as it took off, leaving me with this scar." I rub the spot harder through my clothes. "It has never burned like this before."

"What kind of beast?"

At first, I am shocked by his question, until it occurs to me that he wouldn't know, as he doesn't watch what happens in Asgard all the time. Instead, his eyes are focused on outside threats.

"I don't know."

His brow furrows, and something flits over his shoulder. It takes an effort to peer around his bulky form, and my eyes widen as they land on the same beast that caused the mark on my shoulder. I hadn't seen it since the day it injured me.

"It was *that* beast," I say, pointing past Heimdall.

He spins and lifts his sword a split second before the beast lunges for him, managing to block the beast's attack. The beast lunges at him again then maneuvers back before the mighty protector of Asgard can strike.

Even though my shoulder is throbbing, I am still determined to make my way to Midgard to see if I can help the winged Valkyries. The thought of helping the great gatekeeper fight off the beast passes through my mind, but as I watch him, I am confident that he will be able to defeat it. He is an extremely large warrior.

While Heimdall is distracted, I run to the tower, the entrance to the portal. Behind me, I can hear the beast continuing to attack the great guard of Bifrost, yet neither seems to be successful in striking the other. No cries of pain come from either one.

I reach the portal entrance and hold the knob with both hands. When I turn to see Heimdall, the beast is moving in for another attack. He spins and swipes his sword at it but misses as the beast flaps its wings and darts away. The creature's beady eyes land on me, and a piercing squawk fills the air before it flaps away.

Heimdall's distraction is disappearing into the

distance, and I am about to miss my opportunity. I brace myself, ready to turn the key, when Heimdall spins and spots me at the portal.

"No, young Valkyrie!" His large form takes enormous steps as he runs toward me, closing the gap between us quickly.

I have to act now. With my heart thumping quickly, I twist the knob. Heimdall is only seconds away from me as a bright, colorful light surrounds me, and I feel myself being sucked into a vacuum as though I am on a slippery slide twirling downward. Dizziness engulfs me, so I close my eyes, knowing I can do nothing other than go with the flow until I land with a thump.

My butt aches from the rough landing. I place my hands on either side of me and feel a solid surface with something rough tickling my palms, then I open my eyes and blink a couple of times before gazing down to see green strands protruding out of the hard, grey dirt. It is some kind of foliage that softens the hard earth, and I notice that it covers nearly every part of the ground. Midgard almost looks green. It is beautiful.

I gaze into the distance to see large brown trunks reaching for the sky, and branching out of them are limbs covered with green foliage framed by a crystal-clear blue sky. These must be what they call trees. And from what I see, they are more beautiful than how they were described.

A soft rustling surrounds me as the wind whips my

black hair away from my face. I breathe in deeply, taking in the fresh air. It smells beautiful, almost sweet, unless that is the pale-pink flowers I spot not too far away. Instantly, I know I am in love with Midgard. But a scream that pierces the air stops my daydreaming.

CHAPTER THREE

I spring to my feet, spin around, and run up the hill. As I reach the crest, I am devastated by the scene playing out before me. Massive amounts of men and women are fighting each other, and brave warriors are dying in all directions. I watch as the winged Valkyries fly above them and land in certain spots, fighting off the angels of death before reaping the bravest warriors that they can find. The soldiers that they reap will be another mark of honor against their name in aid to Valhalla and a proud contribution to the mighty warriors that will fight in Ragnarok. A twinge of envy pierces my heart as I watch them undertake this honor with their graceful wings.

A rumble rolls across the sky, and I think that perhaps Heimdall is searching for someone to come and retrieve me. I spring into action. I'm not going to miss out on this. It's my chance to prove that the wingless Valkyries are worth more than what the winged Valkyries give them credit for. We have trained to fight and are spectacular warriors on the ground.

The soldiers push forward toward a massive wall, stepping over their fallen comrades, and the Valkyries gracefully swoop down one by one and land next to the fallen and reap their souls. The ones that they do not reap are left for the angels of death.

A group of soldiers hunkers down and aims a cannon at the wall, lights it, fires, and watches the explosion destroy the ramparts. Even from this distance, screams rumble across the plain. A Valkyrie swoops down to the wall to claim the souls of the brave soldiers before they pass away. As she lands, a dark-winged male swoops down and lands next to her. I've learned about them at the academy. These winged beings are the angels of death—the largest threat to our victory.

The Valkyrie unsheathes her sword and starts to fend off the angel of death, who is eager to grab these soldiers and take them back to the underworld. She slices at him, and he dodges with nimble feet, narrowly missing her blade. A dark shadow passes over the corner of my eye, and I turn to see another angel of death hovering over a wounded soldier that has not been spotted by a Valkyrie.

I pull an arrow from my quiver and nock it then

draw it back and aim the tip at the angel of death. "Stand back. This one's mine," I call across the distance.

The angel of death halts. His black eyes peer through his strands of dark hair that have fallen over them. These angels have been our lifelong enemies, and we need to defend our future soldiers against them so we can train the soldiers to fight in the final war of Ragnarok. But as he peers at me, I am taken aback by how young his skin looks and how striking the lines are in his chiseled jaw. He flicks his head, and the hair moves out of his eyes. I think I see amusement in them.

He stands planted on the spot. His black leather pants cling to his legs, and a fitted black T-shirt hugs his chest, defining the muscles of his torso. My teachers told me a lot about the angels of death, but they never discussed how attractive they were. This is the first one I've seen face-to-face.

Trying to wipe the sight of his body out of my mind, I focus on his eyes, but he is rather distracting, and an amused smile gleams from his eyes.

"What do we have here?" His voice is so deep and smooth that it almost sounds like he is singing his words.

Slowly, I move toward him with my arrow remaining pointed at him. He keeps his hands raised, watching me as I continue forward, ignoring his question and taking my time assessing the situation.

"What are you?" he asks. He peers over my shoulders as though looking for something. "You're not a Valkyrie. That's for sure."

Anger heats my face, but I bite my tongue. As much as I want to shoot my mouth off at him, I don't want to give him any information he doesn't already have.

"What's wrong? Did I say something wrong?"

My heart catches in my throat. I never thought a voice could sound so beautiful yet taunting at the same time. Within a few moments, he has found a way to get under my skin.

After weighing up my choices, I answer him without bothering to hide the spite in my voice. "I'm a Valkyrie. And if you don't shut up, I'll shoot this arrow through your arm."

His smirk grows wider. "A Valkyrie? But you don't have any wings."

My eyes shoot daggers at him, and I shake the arrow slightly, pulling his attention back to it. "Remember, your arm?" I aim the arrow directly at his arm again.

"I was merely saying." He shrugs. "No need to get so irritated over it. I've never seen the likes of you before. Every Valkyrie has wings."

"No. Not every Valkyrie has wings. A large amount of us don't." *So much for withholding information.*

"Well, in that case, my name is Harut. It is nice to meet you." His smile broadens. "Your name was?"

"I didn't say."

"No, you didn't. But I was trying to make friends. We don't have to be enemies, you know."

Movement catches my eye, and I see a Valkyrie fighting off an angel of death over the potential warrior. I glance back at him. "Yeah, it really looks like we can be friends," I say with sarcasm.

"Why can't we be friends? You're the first Valkyrie I've seen without wings. Where do they keep you if there are so many of you?" His intentions seem innocent enough, yet I can feel the rush of blood to my face again.

"That good, is it?" He cocks his head. "I guess they don't treat you well, looking at your reaction."

"They treat us like second-class citizens," I snap.

"So how did you end up here?"

"I snuck past Heimdall and traveled Bifrost when he was distracted by some creature."

"That's daring." He raises an eyebrow.

"I'm dying to prove that we are worth just as much as the winged Valkyries. I want to reap a soul for Valhalla–to prove the point. We train as warriors just as much as they do, but they never let us on a battlefield because we lack wings."

He indicates the soldier, who is still groaning on the ground, only moments away from dying. "In that case, be my guest."

I look at the soldier then back at the angel of death. "Really?"

He nods.

"Thank you." I'm about to squat when a guilty rush hits me. He's been kind to me, and I haven't even told him my name. "I'm Kara."

He smiles broadly again, showing many straight white teeth. "Nice to meet you."

I feel a different kind of redness flowing to my face. Quickly, I dart my eyes down to the warrior dying on the ground and squat before him.

I haven't done this before, although I believe that when we touch humans, this is what happens. My heart thumps rapidly as I reach down to touch the soldier's skin. I hope this works. So much is riding on it.

CHAPTER FOUR

Bracing myself, I take a deep breath. This is breaking new territory for me and all the wingless Valkyries. After composing myself, I place my hand on his skin.

"What are you doing?" A voice booms over my shoulder.

I balk and turn to find Rota standing beside me. Her hands are on her hips, and she stands with her feet firmly planted. "You shouldn't be here. What in Vigrid do you think you are doing?" Her gaze travels from my hands to the wounded soldier. "You should be back in Asgard, cleaning the Valhalla hall and getting it ready for us to celebrate, not standing here wasting time. They're our soldiers to reap, not yours. You will never be a reaper."

Harut opens his arms. "Give her a chance. Everyone

must be able to prove themselves at some point. Why should she go back and clean the halls?"

"Stay out of this, angel of death. This is none of your business."

He takes a step toward her, and she pulls her sword from its sheath. The sound of sliding metal rings through the air. A breeze passes from the angel of death's direction, and a putrid smell fills my nose. I breathe it out and try to search past him over the grassy plain, right up to the edge of the trees. It smells like bodies decaying. I frown. This war field is too new for any bodies to be decaying. A dead animal that I cannot see must be lying in that direction.

A high-pitched whistle screams, and my shoulders slump. Rota has called for the mistress. Shortly, I will face punishment. I have to make this worthwhile.

A groan distracts me from my imminent demise, and I gaze down. The man is so close to death, and I touch his skin. I have only seconds before they will pull me away. Looking deep into his eyes, I stroke his forehead with one hand, and with my other hand, I clasp his.

Hovering over him, I whisper into his ear, "I release you from your pain on earth and send you to Valhalla to serve amongst the bravest of warriors." These are the words that I have heard the winged Valkyries being taught to say as they reap their warrior. I hold his hand and stroke his forehead, but he remains in front of me, still laboring to breathe, his face distorted in pain.

The seconds tick by slowly, and I wonder when he will be sent. The uneventful moments turn into what seem like hours. Deep despair fills me as I watch him remaining in pain, his spirit not leaving, and I feel like I have betrayed him, all the wingless Valkyries, and myself. Not only that, I have also managed to look like a fool in front of the handsome angel of death and my nemesis.

"Oh, get out of the way."

Roughly, I'm nudged aside, and I stumble on top of the soldier. He cries out in pain, making my despair dig deeper, twisting the horrible guilty knife into my heart farther. I couldn't take away his pain as I promised him. It didn't leave.

"You will never be able to reap the warriors," Rota sneers. She kneels beside him and clasps his hand while holding his face, saying exactly the same words I just said to him.

I watch as peace fills his face, his ragged breathing stops, and he lies perfectly still. For him, deep happiness fills me, but at the same time, I want to tear at my enemy. I want to push and shove her. I want to take out all my aggression on her, all my disappointment in myself that I did not prove that the wingless Valkyries are just as valuable as the winged Valkyries. Deep embarrassment sits deep within my soul, causing these urges to be even stronger. I move toward her to play out the actions in my mind when two feet hit the ground right next to me.

My eyes dart up from the form and land on a face with terrifying blue eyes that pierce deep into my soul. Mistress. She is certainly not pleased. Horror whirls in my stomach, and I grit my teeth, knowing what is about to happen.

A hand, gentle but firm, lands on my shoulder, and strange sensations of warmth and cold fill me.

The mistress's eyes dart to my side. "Angel of death, leave."

I turn to realize that it is Harut's hand on my shoulder.

He nods curtly at the mistress once then leans forward and whispers in my ear, "Don't give up. You may find a way." And with that, he pushes off the ground and takes to the sky. He flies with all the grace of a winged Valkyrie in the opposite direction, looking for another warrior that needs to be sent to the underworld.

"You shall return to Asgard now, Valkyrie." The words are spiteful, and it takes all my willpower to face my mistress. "You will be on dragon-stall-cleaning duty for the rest of the month on top of your other cleaning duties."

I groan, and my shoulders slump. As much as I love being around the majestic beasts, it is horrible cleaning up their muck–cleaning out the bones and the rotting flesh and the undigested remnants in their waste. I cast my eyes to the ground. "Yes, Mistress." I see no point in arguing, because I would end up with worse duties.

"How did you even get here, Valkyrie?" Her eyes scrutinize me.

"I snuck past Heimdall when he was distracted by some creature."

"What kind of creature?" It surprises me how everyone is immensely interested in this creature. Either that, or they are trying to find holes in my story.

"I don't know. I've only seen it once before when I stumbled across a dragon's nest, and it was stealing the eggs. It has a hideous look, and it almost seemed like it has some dragon in it because of its wings, yet at the same time, its body is fluffy and misshapen. It struck me that day, and when I saw it today, a deep burning sensation went through the scar that it gave me a couple of years ago when I chased it away from the rare dragon egg."

She raises an eyebrow at me. "You shouldn't have been so foolish as to go into the wild dragon wastelands, anyway. Where is this scar it gave you?"

I pull my sleeve over my shoulder from the neckline and expose the scar that runs from my shoulder and down the top of my arm. She strokes her finger along it.

Her brow furrows as she studies the scar. "There doesn't seem to be anything out of the ordinary with it that would cause it to burn again after such a long time. Are you sure you didn't just imagine it?"

"That would not be possible. The burning was very intense. And it was right here." I indicated the point on the scar. "Like the scar had just been caused again. There is no way that I could have imagined that pain." I am almost insulted by her suggestion.

Her shoulders stiffen, and she tilts her chin upward. "You must tell me if you see this creature again. We cannot have this creature going through Asgard."

After her comment that I might have imagined it, I wasn't in the mood to share any information. But to keep up appearances, I nod. "Yes, mistress." Although deep inside, I can feel the rebellion rising. I would rather learn what this creature is myself than let her find out this information. I will prove our worth as wingless Valkyries.

The rainbow colors of Bifrost open and point down to where we are. I step into its rainbow and am sucked up into the colors before landing flat on my feet in the tower with Heimdall. His scowl is the first thing I see as he regards me with distaste, and I flinch. I am in for it now.

CHAPTER FIVE

"Heimdall." Nervousness seeps through my voice. "So nice to see you." I smile broadly, showing off as many teeth as possible.

His scowl deepens, and he steps closer to me, his bulky form towering over me. I am considered average size, and I cannot compare to his bulk. I lean back slightly to look into his eyes, and I try to hold my smile, but it slowly fades from my face.

"How dare you sneak past me, Valkyrie. You have violated many rules of Asgard. You are not allowed to pass these borders without permission or without being accompanied by a winged Valkyrie." He grabs me roughly by the shoulder and turns me toward the bridge, stomping that way. "You are coming with me to visit Odin."

My hands turn clammy, and I lose all feeling in my face. I am definitely in for it now. Though I'd thought cleaning out the dragon stalls for a month was a bad enough punishment, this is worse. My primary goal is to become a reaper and a proud warrior for Asgard and to impress Odin, for myself and the other wingless Valkyries, but my idea is quickly flowing down the sewer.

The walk across Bifrost couldn't go any faster. Each step seems to be a giant leap bringing me closer to the palace gates. We reach the steps and walk up. My heart thumps against my rib cage, wanting to abandon this sinking ship as I am dragged toward the palace. I really don't need this kind of attention from Odin. Heimdall hauls me across the marble floors, past the towering marble walls and sculptures, and pauses in front of the throne. Odin is sitting on his throne, his cloak draping over his shoulders and tumbling down his back. He glares at me with his one eye, the other covered in a patch from the time he traded it for wisdom. In a sick sense, I am glad that he can only stare at me with one eye. It is intimidating enough. No words are needed from Heimdall.

"What do we have here?" Odin's eye narrows on me. It is evident that he knew instantly by the way I am being handled and dragged by the gatekeeper that I have caused mischief.

Heimdall pushes me closer to Odin. I feel exposed with nowhere to hide. "This one has defied the laws and snuck behind my back, leaving Asgard without permission. I do not know why you have created these Valkyries without wings. They are no use to us and cause nothing but trouble."

Odin's glare is so intense that I fold to my knees, only sparing a glance through my eyelashes with my chin tilted. "Forgive me, great Odin. I was merely trying to prove my worth on the battlefield. I hope that I have a higher purpose than cleaning halls and dragon pens."

Odin stands, clasping his staff in one hand, and towers over me when he approaches. "Why? Why do you feel like you need to be more? All places are of high importance. And your place and your kind were brought here to serve the winged Valkyries and the gods–to make their living smoother and give them more time to fulfill their duty."

"Yes, great Odin." I know that I should leave it here, but I can't help myself. "I understand, but I would like to be more than just an ordinary slave." When his scowl deepens, I say quickly, "I think that we would be of great service to you."

"Could you reap any?" he asks while pulling his shoulders back, giving him a mightier appearance.

I drop my gaze to the floor and shake my head. "No. I could not."

"Your kind has not been given the talent to reap the souls for Valhalla."

"But there must be a way that we can serve better. Something else we can do in the field to help."

He tsks then huffs a short laugh. "No. There is not." He turns to Heimdall. "How did she escape?"

The mighty gatekeeper tilts his head downward. "I was distracted by some kind of beast. It came and attacked me at the same time that she approached. It's almost as though they were working together."

When I gasp, Odin casts me a warning look before returning his focus to Heimdall. He rubs his chin between his thumb and index finger. "What kind of beast?"

"I don't know. I've never seen it before. It had dragon-like wings and a furry body. It was hideous. It must be a creation—perhaps some kind of witch or god has been mucking around with the creatures of the world. The timing of her escape was too perfect not to suspect that they were working together."

"Oh no." I start to rise until Odin shoots me a glare, and I stop halfway and slowly return to a kneeling position and bow my head. "I was not working with the creature, mighty Odin. I do not know where it came from. I have only seen it once before when it was stealing dragon eggs."

"Stealing dragon eggs, you say?" The eyebrow over his one eye lifts.

"Yes. The egg of the emperor dragon."

"The rare, vicious breed that nobody can get near?"

I nod and ignore the disbelief in his eyes. "I managed to scare the creature off, and it dropped the egg. It also scratched me at the same time."

Odin held his stomach and gave a deep, rumbling laugh. "A creature of some sort stealing the vicious dragon eggs, the golden ones. That is one game creature. What would it be doing with dragon eggs?"

Heimdall says, "I have seen some dragon eggs being traded on the black market. I believe they are being bought and raised as weapons of war, trained to fight, and the golden dragon would be the leader of the pack, able to control all the other dragons. If a commander were to get their hands on one of those dragons and tame it, then they would be in charge of all the dragon world. This could lead to a massacre."

I look at Heimdall with disbelief. "Do they ride these dragons?"

"Of course they ride them. What else would they use the dragons for?" He looks thoughtful for a moment. "I guess other than their vicious fighting skills where they can demolish any being in no time, including giants, and turn them into a meal." He shrugs.

"Then why don't we use dragons to fight?" I look at Odin. "Couldn't the wingless Valkyries join in and help fight for the good warriors alongside the winged Valkyries by riding the dragons? We have been trained as warriors. It would make sense if we were given the opportunity to ride something with wings to help fight for the time that Ragnarok comes. You will need us as well as the few Valkyries you have to help fight in Ragnarok for Asgard and Midgard. We could become protectors rather than servants." A new sense of worth is flowing through me, and before I realize what I am doing, I have half risen to my feet again.

"Do not stand in my presence, Valkyrie. I have not permitted you." Odin's gaze turns vicious again. "You are being ridiculous. Wingless Valkyries are only good and created for what you are doing now. You are nothing more."

A strong voice rumbles through my head. *Do not listen to him, young Valkyrie. You have much to prove.*

My head shoots up, and my eyes dart everywhere. "What?"

"What's wrong with you, Valkyrie?" Annoyance is written all over Heimdall's face. I am staring at him because he is the only other person in the room.

"Did you just say something?"

"No, I didn't."

Odin stamps his staff on the ground, and a crack echoes through the large room. "Your nonsense has caused enough trouble today, young Valkyrie. You must leave and clean the stalls. I have enough to deal with over the rumors of frost giants entering Asgard without permission."

I look at Odin in shock as he points to the door of the hall. Heimdall grabs me by the shoulder and leads me out again. As I am escorted across Asgard, my eyes dart everywhere as I search for the owner of the voice. *Who could have spoken to me, especially when it appears that the two men didn't hear the voice?*

CHAPTER SIX

Argh! The smell is disgusting. The potent odors of regurgitated flesh follow me around as I scoop it up from the floor of a dragon's cave. The solid rock walls have successfully managed to trap the smell within the enclosure. Heimdall commanded me to grab my shield and get changed into my oldest clothes, and pointed to the dragon stall that I had to clean first. Naturally, it was the most potent. Without any extra hands, I sling my shield over my back and shovel up the muck and carry it toward the chasm. The dragon stalls are built within the solid rock of the mountains in chasms or cliff faces.

The current occupant of this particular stall is a blue dragon that despite being smaller than other dragons, still towers above me. When I look at this specific breed, it is hard for me to believe that all dragons are classed as aggressive. The blue dragon has a smaller snout and lacks the horns of the other breeds, and its eyes have an innocent look. Its scales are a medium-blue color edged with white, making its overall color seem lighter than it is.

This young male's blue eyes watch me intensely as I clean out his mess. Despite his look of innocence, I make sure I keep my eye on him. I have been warned to regard all dragons with caution at all times. As I walk toward the edge of the cave to throw the pile of trash over the mountain's side, he runs at me, breathing out a plume of fire.

I dart forward and trip on a rock, dropping the shovel and falling flat on my stomach. My face narrowly misses the pile of manure that I just gathered. Something warm and gooey wraps around my arm, and I realize that my arm was not so lucky. "Yuck!" I shake my hand, trying to rid it of the horrible smelly slop.

A strange sound comes from the dragon. I managed to miss the plume of fire, and remembering it, I suddenly jump to my feet and turn to face the dragon, who has just proven that despite his looks, I must treat him with caution. The winged Valkyries are raising these dragons to be aggressive so that they can be fighting practice. Despite knowing this, I am curious as to why this dragon has had a go at me. Except when I face the dragon and meet his blue eyes, his head is jerking up and down, and his teeth are showing.

I blink a couple of times, trying to clear my vision, because I am having trouble believing what I am seeing. Cocking my head, I ask, "Are you playing with me?"

The dragon pushes his shoulders back and spreads his wings wide, showing off the decorative white dots that resemble stars across the blue membranous wings. He looks much larger than seconds before, and he wipes the smirk off his face and gazes at me with his big eyes. Suddenly, he narrows his eyes and shoots out a long plume of fire. I move aside with my back toward him, narrowly missing the edge of the cliff. When I spin around and look at the dragon again, he is doing the same thing as before, sitting on his butt, making a funny sound, bobbing his head up and down, and showing off his teeth.

I observe the dragon for a moment. "You are playing with me, aren't you?"

He can't come any closer to me because of the chain around his rear leg. I have not cleaned out this particular dragon's stall before. In fact, I haven't had much to do with the blue dragons, so I am surprised when this one stands up and starts to wag his tail.

"Okay. I will play. But can you stop throwing plumes of fire at me? I prefer not to be seared." I stand ready with my legs shoulder width apart, braced for the next move.

The dragon's eyes widen. He seems to realize what I am doing, and his tail wagging increases speed, knocking aside scattered bones behind him. My arm still stinks and feels disgusting, but I'm not about to turn my back, in case he throws another plume of fire at me.

I look for something on the ground that I can throw, so that maybe he will chase it like a dog. As I do this, I see a bright-orange light coming in my direction, and I dodge. I have no time to grab my shield, and I block it instinctively with my arm that is covered in manure.

As I feel the searing pain from the fire, I curse myself for my stupidity, though it isn't a direct hit because I dodged far enough away. Yanking my arm away, I stare at the damage. I am surprised to see that the manure has protected my arm from damage, and all that my arm suffered from was the extreme heat. I expel a breath. "That was close."

Next time, I won't be so stupid. The muck around my arm has dried, and I peel it away. The dragon seems to be laughing again, and his back legs jump up, and his tail starts to wag.

Instantly, I brace myself and throw up a hand while the other reaches for my shield. "Stop. No. Don't do that. You're going to hurt me. I would love to play, but I don't want to be hurt." I feel ridiculous talking to a dragon, but maybe he can understand me. After all, the emperor dragon I ran across a couple of years ago could. I can only hope.

Yet his neck vibrates like he is about to send out another plume of fire. I dart forward, as is often recommended when attacking a larger opponent, and manage to duck under the plume of fire, then I grab him around the neck and swing my leg over him. I fling my arms around his neck and sit up straight with my legs bracing his torso and clasp onto his scales. "There. Now I've got you."

He cocks his head and peers at me with one eye. At first, his eyes widen with surprise, then they seem to do that funny smile again, followed by the noise I have worked out to be a chuckle. Suddenly, my whole body tilts forward as the dragon rolls onto his back. I tumble quickly to the side, land on the ground, and somersault to my feet. The dragon lies on his back with his big eyes staring at me and that chuckle jerking his torso.

"You like that, do you? What about this?" I dart forward and sit on his belly, trying to tickle his underside. The funny gurgling sound continues, and he rolls from side to side. It must be a lonely life, living in this cave all by himself. He seems to be enjoying any interaction. I can never understand why they keep dragons. They don't need them as fighting opponents. It seems like a waste, having them cooped up like a prize within these caves.

A deep, velvety voice bursts through my head. *You seem to have a way with the dragons.*

I freeze and sit up straight, looking around the cave for the source of the voice.

"Heimdall? Is that you?" I could swear it is the same

voice I heard back in Odin's hall. I search everywhere, except as I am doing this, I'm knocked off the dragon as he sits up straight, as though standing to attention, looking toward the entrance.

No. This is not Heimdall. It is a shame to see these dragons cooped up like this, with nothing to live for.

I continue to search everywhere for the source of the voice but find nothing. "Yes. It is a shame. This one seems quite playful. Who are you?"

A deep rumble sounds, and it almost sounds like a chuckle. I don't know what to make of it–if I should be insulted or not.

Let's just say I'm someone who's been watching you for a little while. You treat the dragons with more respect than others. You do not mistreat them like your winged kind. They treat them as though they are nothing, disposable, like beasts to be pushed around and injured–something to practice their fighting skills with. For this, I shall reward you.

I'm confused, my feet rooted in place. I look at the dragon and notice that he has remained at full attention, almost as though saluting a corporal. "I don't understand. Why would I treat dragons any differently than any other animal?"

They are higher than any animal, but you treat them with respect and friendliness.

A strange noise sounds at the cliff entrance of the cave, and I look but can't see anything. My gaze darts to the blue dragon, and it is also looking in the same direction. So I start to search the area again, following the sound, only to see that the massive form of a golden dragon has appeared out of thin air right in front of me. Its eyes are golden and vicious and looking directly at me.

CHAPTER SEVEN

It suddenly dawns on me where I have heard this voice before. This is the mother dragon that gave me one chance to escape her wrath a couple of years ago, and I took it. I cannot for the life of me think why she has sought me out. As I look into her deep-golden-brown eyes, they feel as though they are boring into me. I try to swallow the lump in my throat. The dragon seems aggressive and intimidating, and I want to hide. I back up, ready to dart behind the blue dragon, when I realize that he's also backing up to hide behind me, and whenever I try to dart around the back of him, he somehow moves quicker. I observe him and wonder what his deal is.

Right as I do this, the golden dragon commands, *Bow!*

I spin around. "Me?"

At the same time, the blue dragon shuffles behind me, and I turn to see him bowing toward the golden dragon. His front legs buckle underneath his weight, his chest touches the ground, and he casts his eyes down. He is in a complete form of submission.

I refocus on the mother dragon. "I-I disappeared as you commanded." My fear rises when I feel her anger. "Why have you pursued me?"

I have been watching you.

"How?"

The emperor dragons have the distinct ability to become invisible, and after you caught my attention, I have been watching you. You have proven to be different from the others. And I have heard your plights to be great.

"Why would you be watching me?"

The dragons have become factious due to this pact with the Valkyries in which we give over one of our clan every year to seal our alliance. It has caused great distrust amongst the dragons, and it is time for the emperor dragon to rule again and unite the dragons. You can only hear my voice because I have allowed you to. Nobody else can hear what I am saying except for the dragon beside you because I have chosen it to be so.

"What do you want of me?"

I am going to lend you this. Beside her, another dragon appears. The dragon is almost identical to her, only smaller. It is young, but its body is at least the size of the blue dragon behind me, and stockier. I stare at the dragon with an open mouth.

"You're going to lend me a dragon? Why?" I can't hide the surprise in my voice.

This is not any dragon. This is my daughter, the egg that you saved from the creature and that you saved from being enslaved in the black market. For as long as you respect her and treat her well, I will lend her to you.

I frown. "Is she a slave to me? Because that is not how I work."

The scowl from the mother dragon's face lifts, and I think it is the closest expression she has to a smile. *No. My daughter and I have discussed this, and she has agreed.*

I look at the smaller dragon, and she nods slightly.

But mark my words—I will be watching you, and she will be reporting back to me. She turns invisible, and I hear the push as she takes off, followed by the flapping of her wings fading away. She has left before I can react.

I call to the empty space, "Thanks."

As I look at the dragon, I'm not quite sure what to do. She studies me with her golden-brown eyes in return. Her horns point menacingly out of the top of her head, and her size is intimidating, even if she is smaller than her mother. Her scales capture the sunlight, and it sparkles off the yellow gold.

Um, hello, Kara. I'm Elan. Her voice is uncertain and sounds much younger than the mother dragon's.

My mouth drops open. I can't believe that they even know my name.

She continues with the uncertainty still in her voice. *It's nice to meet you. I've heard a lot about you. Please excuse my mother. She is rather a stick-in-the-mud.* She chuckles slightly then stops abruptly. *Oops! Don't let her know that. You know, because I'm supposed to show her respect all the time. After all, she is the leader of the dragons.*

"You're nothing like what I expected." I frown, thinking.

Yeah, no. I'm not like what my mom would expect, either. I do tend to chat a bit–just as a warning. Sometimes I drive my mom crazy. I hope you don't mind. It gets rather lonely out in the fields as a dragon. I see you met my friend Naga. She nods toward the blue dragon. *It was my idea about him playing with you. Sorry about the plumes of fire and all. He doesn't seem to understand that they can hurt you.* She looks at him affectionately. *He's not the brightest of dragons. But I know that he had fun with you.*

I spin around and raise my eyebrow at the blue dragon. He's now sitting up straight and looking eager, not intimidated like when the mother was here.

He's only young, like me. He was the one that the blue dragons sacrificed this year for the treaty with the Valkyries.

"What is this treaty with the Valkyries?" I ask.

Don't you know? She looks dumbfounded.

I shake my head.

Hmm. That's odd. I would have thought that they would have taught you in Valkyrie school. She cocks her head.

"Sorry, I have no idea."

She folds her legs and lies on her stomach. *The Valkyries and the dragons used to be at war all the time, and the Valkyries made weapons and managed to kill off many dragons, and the dragons used their many gifts to retaliate against the Valkyries. As numbers diminished on both sides, they made an agreement. The dragons would hand over one baby of each clan to the Valkyries as a peace treaty for the Valkyries to stop attacking the dragons. Because of this, the dragons have increased in population. But recently, the dragons have caught on to how the Valkyries are using these sacrificial dragons, and much distrust is building within the dragons and they are becoming factious.*

"Why?"

Because they don't like how the Valkyries are treating their babies, and the dragons selected are not chosen by their own tribes. Another tribe chooses them, with the final decision coming down to my mother. She doesn't say much, but I know it tears her up inside to have to give away the baby dragons. It is also unfair, as we don't have to give up one of the emperor dragons. This is because we are the leaders and our breed is seen as rarer than the other breeds, as we do not have as many eggs. But our breed is known to be more vicious and have more talents. The sacrifice of an emperor dragon is not written in the agreement.

"It seems like a strange sort of agreement. If you

don't have to come to live with the Valkyries, why would you want to be lent out to me?"

Oh, I don't want to have to make the decisions of who has to go when I get older and my mom dies. Some of the dragons get quite hurt. Some even die. Being used for target practice with no protection can make them quite aggressive, naturally.

"So why isn't this dragon aggressive? He wanted to play." I indicate Naga, who remains behind me with a vacant look on his face.

That's because he hasn't been put under their tests yet. He's still young and new to the Valkyries. There is still hope that he will remain this way if we can stop them. The other dragons are quite vicious.

"I wouldn't blame them. I would get quite vicious, too, if I kept getting attacked and used only as a weapon and were constantly injured." When I stroke Naga's neck, he nuzzles into my hand, then I turn to look at Elan again, but she has disappeared.

"Where did you go?"

Just then, the stone door slides aside, and in walk Eir and Hildr, my wingless Valkyrie friends from the academy.

"We found you." Eir walks into the cave hesitantly, her eyes on Naga.

After Hildr closes the stone door, she follows, also being wary of the blue dragon. "We've been looking for you forever." Her gaze darts around the room while her fingers twitch over the hilt of her sword. "Who were you talking to?"

I give them a guilty look. "Oh, nobody. I was just muttering to myself as I clean out the pen."

Eir screws up her nose. "It stinks in here. Are you done yet?"

"Almost." I grab the shovel and throw the rest of the mess over the edge of the cliff, then I approach Naga and stroke him briefly on the nose. His eyes widen then dance with excitement.

"That's odd," Hildr says, her hand still twitching over her sword's hilt. "It almost looks like it likes you. I've heard these are dangerous creatures, not friendly ones."

I turn to leave. "I think we're about to find out that that's all wrong. The Valkyries mistreat them. Perhaps they would be different if we treated them with respect."

"Jeez. Did you hit your head while you've been in here? You sound delusional." Hildr grunts as she pulls the stone door open.

I turn around to search the room for Elan, but I still don't see her. I'm about to leave when I hear her in my head.

Meet me at the edge of the cliff above the dragon pens at sundown.

I nod and help Hildr close the door behind us.

CHAPTER EIGHT

"Have you been listening to me at all?" Hildr's runs a hand through her spiky red hair.

I swallow a mouthful of food then cast her a guilty glance. She only has my attention because she nudged me in the ribs. My mind is still focused on the dragons and why they would pick me. As I look around the dining hall, I nod. "Sure. You keep going on and on about how I shouldn't have raced off and gone to Midgard and how I got myself into trouble. Blah, blah, blah." I'm pretty sure this is not what she's been talking about, but I thought I would add it in as a bit of humor.

She rolls her eyes. "It's not all about you, you know."

"I know. I was just adding it in to make it seem like I was listening to something. I'm sure that comment came in somewhere." I shrug and smirk.

"Where is your mind? Have you not been listening at all?" Eir's usually calm face clouds with concern.

I expel a loud sigh. "Listening to what?"

"There have been rumors that the frost giants are trying to invade Asgard and take the throne from Odin," Eir says.

"They will never be able to do that." I scoff. "They have to get past Heimdall." I take a gulp of orange juice.

"Well, *you* did." Hildr fixes her gaze on me. Her freckled face is pale with concern.

I place my glass down. "That was just a fluke. That creature had arrived just in time. It distracted Heimdall, and I have no idea where it came from."

"Maybe the creature works for the frost giants. Maybe it was testing out how Heimdall can be distracted." Eir flicks her fork against the peas in her cottage pie.

"No. Heimdall will be on high alert now. I've made sure of that. See, not everything I do is bad." I smirk.

Hildr groans and stabs her steak with a knife. "There you go again. Making it all about you."

I gaze around at the other Valkyries in the academy and spot all the winged ones sitting in the best corner. Rota glares at me from the other side of the room.

"You certainly made her a stronger enemy," Eir says before finally shoveling some of her food into her mouth.

"No. If anything, I've embarrassed myself. I couldn't

reap the soldier. Though I had the best opportunity ever, I couldn't do it. We're clearly not gifted for that line of work. Still, there must be something we can do to help them in the field."

"Young Valkyrie." The stern voice comes from behind me, and I can't help the shivers that run down my spine.

I spin around. "Mistress Sigrun," I say with the sweetest tone I can muster. "What can I do for you?"

"You haven't finished cleaning the dragon stalls. Hurry up and finish your dinner and go and finish the job. We need these dragons healthy and feisty."

"Yes, Mistress." I have finished my meal, and I am about to get up when I halt. "Mistress, why do we mistreat the dragons?"

If I thought I was in trouble before, that was a mistake. Her voice turns even colder. "The dragons are a vicious breed, and it is in our best interests to learn to fight them to protect ourselves. We do not mistreat them, and it is none of your business as to how we treat them. Your only business is to clean out the stalls." She abruptly turns and walks off.

I sigh then grab my plate and stand, pushing back from the table. "I'll see guys later, okay?"

"Have fun," they say in unison.

"Yep. Because bailing out poop is a whole barrel of fun." Disappointment taints my voice.

I MAKE MY way to the next dragon stall, push back the solid stone door, and enter. This one is in the corner. Its shackle is firmly pressed around its back leg, chaining it closer to the wall, and a muzzle is over its mouth. Its red eyes glare at me, and it puffs out plumes of smoke. This one does not look anywhere near as happy as the last dragon.

I hold up my hands in surrender. "Peace, my friend. I am here to make your living quarters more pleasant. I will not hurt you."

The dragon stomps toward me then stops when its chain runs short. The chain clatters and clangs a few times and quiets when the dragon gives up trying to reach me and slumps in resignation, still glaring at me.

"I'm sorry they treat you this way. I'm going to try to stop them from doing this. I hope you trust me with that."

The dragon says nothing, and a growl rumbles deep within its throat. Keeping my distance, I clean out its water, scoop up its droppings, and throw them over the edge.

This is really not a very nice way for them to live. I do this with a few other dragons and have the same response as I did with the red one. It is breaking my heart to see them like this when I had such a close interaction with Naga and Elan earlier today. They have more to them than being our target practice.

After walking down a stone corridor, I enter another dragon's stall. This one doesn't seem quite so old, but it isn't as playful as Naga. Instead, it cowers in the corner and eyes me suspiciously. It doesn't have a muzzle, but I make sure I stay out of reach, just in case. It has a tremendous ugly sore running down its leg that looks to be made by a sword, and my heart sinks because of how the dragon regards me.

I finish quickly and look out the opening to see the sun setting. Not much light remains in the sky. I promised that I would meet Elan at the top of the cliff, so I have to run, and I scurry out of the dragon's enclosure. Just as I exit the rocks, a high-pitched scream fills the air. Increasing my speed, I search for where this has come from. When I reach a small hill, I climb up it and look around. Another scream fills the air, and my gaze darts in that direction. At a distance not too far away, I can see Rota being thrown around like a rag doll by a frost giant. Other winged Valkyries flock in, ready to attack. As much as I despise them because of how they treat us, I'm not going to let any of them die by a frost giant's hand. They are too crucial to the cause of Valhalla and the future of Asgard with the coming of Ragnarok. I run toward them, unsheathing my sword.

"Wingless, what are you doing here?" Mistress Sigrun glances at me out of the corner of her eye, and I see the annoyance on her face right before she pushes off the ground.

"You have trained us to fight. I am here to help," I call to her as she flaps above me.

"Go and get help instead." She glares down at me. "You cannot fly, and you haven't trained to fight against frost giants."

"No, Mistress. I'm staying to help," I say with determination in my voice while I survey the situation.

Her eyes are like daggers when I chance a look at her. "You have been given an order."

I ignore her final statement, and when I notice the frost giant is distracted by the Valkyries overhead, I charge toward him and dig my sword into his shin. He bellows in pain, and before I can dart back, his hand swings wide and whips me away from his leg, knocking my sword from my hands and toward the cliff. It clatters several feet away, stopping just on the edge of the cliff, balancing precariously.

Though I long to dart for it, I have second thoughts when the frost giant's large hand swoops down at me again. I dodge the swipe and stand just out of its reach. Something flickers in my peripheral vision, and I look to see Rota's limp form being shaken like a rag doll in front of the different Valkyrie swords. Each time one of the Valkyries attacks the frost giant, they halt only inches away from Rota's body. I have to try something else. Backing away, I search for a hand-sized rock and unclip my sling from the leather strap at the back of my pants. I slide one of several perfect-sized stones I find into the sling and let it fly, aiming at the frost giant's head, and hit him firmly in the temple.

He roars, and I slip another rock into my sling and let it fly before the giant works out where these rocks are coming from. This one hits the giant in the left eye, and he roars louder, holding out Rota's body, almost getting her stabbed by one of her comrades. I step back in shock, trip over a small boulder, and land on my backside. Sharp pain jolts up my torso and down my leg. I glance down to find a place to push off the ground to stand, only to see the giant taking a leap toward me and knocking me firmly off the ground and over the edge of the cliff.

As I fall, I let out a scream and gaze up at the mistress in time to see her eyes widen in horror. While she is distracted, the frost giant swipes at her as though she is a little fly. She too goes flying, except she has her wings to brace her from any fall.

I continue to fall, calling out and wondering what good it will do. I am certain that this is my end. I have achieved nothing, and this will be my fate.

CHAPTER NINE

U*h-oh.* A voice sounds in my head. *Quick! Turn around!*

"What?"

Flip around so that your stomach faces the ground. Impatience leaks through the voice.

The wind roars in my ears. This is insane. I attempt to flip, and after several tries, somehow, I manage to face the ground instead of falling back first. A golden dragon appears right underneath me just as I slam into her back. I fling my arms around her neck and cling for dear life as Elan glides forward.

Oh, yay! You finally worked it out. It was cutting it fine, though. The ground is only a few feet below.

I peer over her shoulder right as she tilts her wings, narrowly missing a pile of boulders protruding from the ground. When I realize I had only a few more feet to fall before I would have hit the ground, I feel like I want to pass out on her back. She must feel the shift in my mood, because she gazes over her shoulder at me.

"Thank you." After a few seconds of resting on her back, the memory of why I was falling suddenly hits me. "We have to go back and help them," I say with urgency.

You want to save the Valkyries that always belittle you? She gives me a strange look.

I nod.

You're mad. But here we go. Suddenly, she veers in a different direction. I grip her neck tighter, clinging to her scales and feeling their sharp edges digging into my skin. Something gleams in the afternoon sun. It is my sword, which has fallen part of the way down the cliff and is resting precariously on the edge of a rock protruding from the cliff.

I point at it. "I have to grab that first."

She looks at where I'm pointing and maneuvers directly at it. *Get ready!*

"For what?"

For this. Despite me holding on to the scales around her neck, she flicks her body, knocking me off her back and making me free-fall. Panic grips me right down to my core.

"What are you doing?" I scream through gritted teeth.

Before she answers, Elan flips around and catches me in her claws. *I can't get you close to the cliff face with my wings. I have to hold you out and hover while you grab the sword.* She flaps her wings until I line up with the surface of the boulder sticking out of the cliff face.

Hop on. She pushes me forward. I land on the rock, pick up my sword, and slide it into its sheath. She spins around the other way, facing out, and looks over her shoulder at me. *Now jump and grab on.*

Too scared to breathe, I brace myself and back up a few steps then sprint and jump off the edge of the boulder, aiming for her head and intending to grasp on to her large horns, but they are just out of my reach, and I start to fall. I reach out, barely managing to wrap my arms around her neck. My body weight pulls me down, and I clasp my hands in front of her throat as I feel myself slip. When I jolt to a halt, I gasp then breathe a sigh of relief when I realize that I am secure. Elan straightens and flies ahead, taking me away from the side of the cliff face. At the same time, she disappears.

"What are you doing? I can't see you."

No. And neither can the frost giant.

"But it will still see me."

You are much smaller than I am, and you will have more of an element of surprise. My body rises and falls as she labors to lift us higher up the cliff face.

We rise high enough to hover above the frost giant and the Valkyries still trying to attack it. I watch as they work in vain. He is much larger than they are, even the tall Valkyries. They are managing to injure him, but with each injury, he is becoming more aggravated and lashing out more. Each time a Valkyrie flies toward him, he continues to hold out Rota's limp body, blocking the attack. They will not cut one of their own.

Grab your sword. Elan pulls my focus back.

"I hope you know what you're doing," I say as I reach with my right hand and pull the sword from its sheath. The sound of metal grinding against metal is blown away by the wind in the opposite direction of the frost giant.

I'm staying downwind so the frost giant can't smell me, either. Their noses are quite sensitive.

"Okay. I didn't know that. What's the plan?"

I'm going to remain invisible and aim for his neck, and you aim with your sword straight down into his heart.

"Sounds vicious. I like it."

She circles to the front of the frost giant, and if he looks my way, he will see me gliding alone in the air, no wings or anything. It will be strange. The Valkyries, on the other hand, are too busy fighting him off to turn around to see me. Elan flies directly toward him and dodges by a few inches when he flicks his arms to fight off another Valkyrie blocking the view to his neck.

Hook your legs around my neck, and hang on to my scales with your spare arm.

I take her advice, and she flips upside down, dodging his arm. I hold my sword firmly in my right hand.

Moments before we hit, his eyes focus on me, and they widen in surprise. By then, it is too late. He can't even see the dragon and is looking right through her.

As her teeth clamp around his neck, I thrust the sword deep into his heart. I may be upside down and hanging on for dear life, but I still manage to pierce his skin. His knees buckle, and his hand clasps my sword hilt, which is protruding from his chest. He drops the unconscious Valkyrie, and her comrades fly in and catch her up before she hits the ground. They all look confused as to what was happening and are only reacting to the motions of the giant.

The mistress's gaze darts everywhere as she tries to work out what has happened and why the frost giant has fallen. Eventually, she spins around and spots me flying alone in the air with no wings, and watches with wide eyes as I land not far from the ring of Valkyries. Confusion is written all over her face.

Elan giggles. *Look at her face, would you? She still looks annoyed, even though she has no idea what is going on.*

"Young Valkyrie, what are you up to? What have you done? And how on earth are you flying? You don't have wings."

As I feel the thump of the ground underneath Elan, a smile spreads across my face. I watch the gold fill out underneath me as Elan exposes herself. The Valkyries immediately pull back and ready themselves for a fight, their swords aimed directly at my dragon.

"Put your swords down," I say. "She's a friend. She is the reason why the frost giant has fallen. Can you not see the big bite mark around his neck?"

They look too scared to take their eyes off the dragon, but one of the Valkyries quickly looks at the frost giant and sees the large puddle of blood staining the soil beneath him, then she looks at the hilt of my sword, which can just be seen protruding from the frost giant's chest. She regards me with a look of confusion and hesitation before returning to the other Valkyries surrounding Elan.

Apprehensively, the mistress steps toward the dragon and me. Her sword is still half raised, not far from being ready to defend. She looks at me, then back down at Elan, then back up at me.

Elan sits back on her haunches, and I slip down her back and climb off. Then I approach the mistress.

"And why are you sitting on the most dangerous dragon in all of Asgard?" She lowers her sword as I approach.

"This is my friend. She has chosen to be friends with me because I saved her from the creature I told you about when she was an egg. The creature that distracted Heimdall and allowed me to escape past him to Midgard."

"Why didn't you tell me about this? This is a dangerous dragon to have in our area," the mistress barks.

"Yes, she's dangerous. She killed the frost giant and protected you." I don't hold back my spite, even if she is my mistress. "You should treat her with more respect."

"The only respect to treat dragons with is with distrust. They are dangerous. You will end up getting yourself killed."

I back up and place my hand on Elan's broad golden-yellow snout. She leans into it and brushes herself against my hand like she is used to being petted.

"Yeah. She's extremely dangerous," I say sarcastically. "I'm keeping her with me, and you're not going anywhere near her unless you treat her with respect. If you mistreat her, look out. Not that I need to warn you." I glance over my shoulder. "I'm sure she is more than capable of fending you off better than any dragon you have captured in your caves."

With that, Elan snarls at the mistress, and my instructor backs away.

"Then you must keep her locked away in the cave," the mistress commands. "She must be chained."

"No. She will not be chained. She will sleep where she sees fit, and she will remain free. She came to me of her own free will. I am not going to bind her."

The mistress of Valkyrie Academy eyes Rota, who is still lying unconscious. "We will finish this later, Valkyrie. We must get her to a healer."

CHAPTER TEN

The darkness of the night has overtaken the sky, broken only by the beauty of the full moon. After saying goodbye to Elan, I wash off the frost giant's blood in the bathroom and trek toward my dormitory. I am elated over becoming friends with the dragon and managing to take down a frost giant with the help of the dragon. At the same time, my spirits have been knocked down–the mistress still doesn't see me as a warrior and one that could help in the battles. She treats me like a child, and I am not a child. I am almost a grown woman that has been trained in combat. When I reach my room, I kick off my boots beside my bed and flop face-first onto the soft mattress and bury my head in my pillow for a moment.

A shuffling sounds at the door. "Oh Vanir! There you

are. I've been so worried about you." Eir rushes to my bedside.

"We've been looking everywhere for you." Hildr stomps in after her. "Where have you been? There has been so much turmoil around. A frost giant has been just outside the academy. It's attacked the winged Valkyries."

I groan, roll onto my side, and prop my head up with my hand as I look at them. "And what would you say if I told you I was there to fight the frost giant?" I study each of them in turn.

Eir clasps her hands and does a little jig. "Were you really?"

Hildr looks at her and shakes her head then nudges her with her elbow. "Of course she wasn't. She can't fly. What's she going to do? Run around and take him out at the knees?" She rolls her eyes.

"Actually, I took him out with a sword straight into his chest. And the dragon that I was riding tore open his throat."

Hildr makes a guttural noise in her throat in a held-back laugh, but her eyes don't leave my face. I nod and smirk while her mouth drops open and eyes widen.

"You what?" Hildr sits on the edge of my bed, looking as though she is about to fall off.

This time, Eir nudges Hildr firmly in the ribs with her elbow. "See? I told you. She said she would, and she did. And you doubted me!" She poked Hildr in the arm to emphasize the point.

I nod as Hildr continues to stare at me open-mouthed.

"So what did the mistress say?" Eir raises Hildr's jaw with her hand, closing her mouth. "She must be bowing down at your feet, asking you to join them."

"Nope," I say, shaking my head. I push myself up into a sitting position and rest my head in my hands with my elbows on my knees. "She still wants to give me another talking-to."

"What?" Hildr squeaks. "She should be begging you to join them. And what about this dragon? Did you free one and go and ride it?"

"No. It was the strangest thing. This dragon decided to be my friend because I saved her when she was an egg."

"You mean the one you've been bragging about for the last couple of years?" Eir asks.

I nod.

"I thought that was just a story," Hildr says.

"Well, that just shows how much faith you have in me. Do you think I have just been wasting my breath, telling you fibs about my adventures?" I shake my head at her and smirk. I don't blame her. It did seem like a pretty tall tale.

"But wait—wasn't that dragon an emperor dragon?" Hildr asks.

"Yes."

Her jaw slackens.

"Won't they eat you for breakfast?" Eir asks.

"They could. But they promise not to eat me."

"That's a plus. So what now?" Eir secures a lock of her hair behind her ear.

I shrug. "I don't know. The mistress is still determined to keep me in the bad corner. I would have thought my defeating the frost giant with the help of the dragon would have boosted her confidence in me. I hoped that it would show that we are more than just scrubbers and cleaners, more than ones to pick up after the winged Valkyries, but she seems stuck in that mindset. I am still planning on changing this."

Kara! Elan's voice calls clearly.

"What is it?" I ask, and I stare at the wall as I concentrate on her voice.

It looks like you have a problem.

"What do you mean?"

"Who are you talking to?" Hildr's voice breaks through my thoughts.

My eyes focus on the room, and I remember that Hildr and Eir are with me. "Oh, don't worry. I'm not going mad. I'm just talking to Elan, my dragon."

"It talks to you?" Eir asks.

"She," I correct her. "And yes."

"Where is she?" Hildr searches everywhere in the room, and tension stiffens her body.

"Not in here. Shh. She is trying to tell me something important." I hold my index finger up to my lips. "What's the problem, Elan?"

Odin is coming your way, and boy, he looks cranky.

My shoulders slump, and my dormitory door flies open. The mistress and Odin block the entrance. My eyes land on Odin. Elan was not exaggerating.

THE END

Did you enjoy this book?
You can make a big difference.

HONEST REVIEWS of my books help bring them to the attention of other readers.

IF YOU'VE ENJOYED this book, I'd be grateful if you could spend a few minutes leaving a review (it can be as short as you like).

The review can be left on Amazon and Goodreads.

Thank you very much.

KATRINA COPE

VANISHED

VALKYRIE ACADEMY
DRAGON ALLIANCE

BOOK 2

Cosy Burrow Books

Valkyrie Academy Dragon Alliance
Book Two

VANISHED

"As a wingless Valkyrie, Kara strives not only for her own importance on Asgard but fights for justice for all creatures, even creatures that spout fire. This fast-paced read will inspire readers to fight for justice and maybe even acquire their very own dragon." Jessie B., *Proofreader, Red Adept Editing*

Vanished
Ebook first published in USA in August 2019 by Cosy Burrow Books
Ebook first published in Great Britain in August 2019 by Cosy Burrow Books

www.katrinacopebooks.com

Published by Cosy Burrow Books

ISBN: 978-0-6486613-1-3
ASIN: B07VF2Q8GT

Created with Vellum

My family ~ For your never-ending support

CHAPTER ONE

Sitting on the edge of my bed, I wait with a churning stomach. If Elan is right, Odin is about to storm through my door. Hildr's squeaking leather pants don't ease my tension as she paces the room. I gaze at Eir. Even the calm one is sitting on the edge of her seat and fiddling with her fingers.

The door swings open, and Mistress Sigrun storms into the room. Her face is long, showing off her picture-perfect beauty, yet the expression on her face portrays something to be feared. In her annoyance, she has stretched out her majestic white wings, making her appear more intimidating.

Odin brushes her wing aside and pushes past her. Elan was right. He looks irate. His eye not covered by a patch glares at me with the look that he gave me not that long ago when Heimdall dragged me to his palace.

I don't understand what I've done wrong. If anything, he should be thanking me for Elan's and my assistance in saving the winged Valkyries and our academy from danger. We saved the day. *Doesn't that at least deserve a smile and thanks?*

He stomps farther into the room and stands in the center. His eye bulges as he glares at each one of us individually. I didn't know that Odin did house calls. He must be furious over something.

Hildr abruptly stops pacing and stands still in the middle of the room, not far from Odin. Odin's eye rests directly on me. A lump forms in my throat, restricting my airflow. I attempt to swallow and struggle to move the lump an inch.

Odin places his hands on his hips, and his red cloak drapes gracefully over his elbows, making him appear broader and more intimidating. He tilts his jaw higher and glares at me. "Young Valkyrie, of the wingless kind. Mistress Sigrun has informed me that you have refused to hand over your dragon."

My jaw drops as I stare at him, dumbfounded. We have just protected Asgard, and this is how he treats us. I thought he would be thrilled with our efforts and would be rewarding us. Despite feeling intimidated, I straighten my shoulders and look him square in the face. "Yes. I believe she deserves to remain free. She helped save us where the winged Valkyries failed. I think that letting her remain free is the least that we can do to thank her. After all, she did come of her own free will. She is not one of the sacrificial dragon young."

His glower deepens. "The dragons have made an alliance with us. They must give us one of their young dragons. The Valkyries and our warriors need to practice their fighting skills against such beasts in case any of them decide to turn against us. And this dragon is an emperor dragon. We do not have any of them. They have not honored the alliance by giving us one of them." He moves to tower over me.

Holding my ground, I broaden my shoulders farther. "It is my understanding that the emperor dragons are not required to hand over one of their young because they are a rare kind, and their existence is endangered." I can't help raising my chin as I say this. Though I regard Odin with all the respect he is due, I can't stand this injustice.

"Did you not say that the nest you saved this egg from consisted of three eggs?" Odin's eyebrow lifts as he gazes down at me.

I don't know how he knows, but clearly, someone has told him my story. "Yes. I did. This was a couple of years ago."

He has a twinkle in his eye as though he thinks that he has outsmarted me. "Three eggs are a large amount for a dragon to have in one batch. This would make it evident that these dragons are not endangered anymore.

So now, they must honor their agreement and hand over a young one every year."

My mouth falls open. "I don't know if these other two eggs survived and hatched. I have not asked."

Odin chuckles. "*Asked*. You act as though they can speak to you."

"I-I-I guess I mean that I haven't asked the other Valkyries if they have seen the three babies." I curse myself for my mistake. It has become clear that they don't know that I can speak to the dragons and that the dragons are capable of speaking to us. A thought runs through my head, and I frown. "How did you make a treaty if you can't speak to the dragons? There must be some way you can communicate with them to form an agreement."

Odin puffs out his chest and starts to pace the room. "An emperor dragon made the agreement many years ago. Loki managed to shape-shift into a dragon form, and he then communicated with the dragons, and this is how the alliance was agreed upon."

"Loki can shape-shift into a dragon?" Hildr blurts.

Odin gives her a strange look. "Do you not know anything about the gods?" Without waiting for an answer, he shakes his head and continues, "Yes, Loki can. He's a shape-shifter, enabling him to transform into many different shapes and sizes." He stops pacing and focuses on me. "Back to the subject. The emperor dragon owes us a baby, at least, if not two. This is a good place to start. The dragon that you've been riding is ours. It's vicious, and you must turn it over to the Valkyries. Do you understand?"

"Yes, I understand." I nod once.

"And if anyone deserves to ride an emperor dragon…" He puffs out his chest. "It will be the gods. We are the only ones who deserve to ride the leader of the dragons."

Eir clears her throat, and hesitantly, with a small voice, she says, "Great Odin, that doesn't seem fair. This isn't a just repayment for the good that this dragon has done for us. The dragon does not wish to harm us. She wishes us peace. We should let her remain free."

Odin glares at Mistress Sigrun. "I didn't know that you are raising dragon sympathizers within this Valkyrie Academy. This must stop right this instant!"

The mistress's face pales. She shakes her head and holds up her hands. "This is not of my doing or the doing of any of the instructors. This purely comes down to Kara." She throws me a glare out of the corner of her eye and crosses her arms.

"I am not here to listen to blame games. If I don't have a dragon delivered to me within the week, other measures will be executed."

"What other measures?" I can't hide the worry in my voice.

"Pray that you do not find out, young Valkyrie. It won't be pleasant." The great god spins around and glowers his disapproval at Mistress Sigrun before he exits the room.

Mistress Sigrun straightens her shoulders in a way that reminds me of a duck shaking its body. "Well, Valkyries, you heard him. You must follow his instruction." She lifts her chin and follows Odin out the door.

CHAPTER TWO

Hildr slams the door behind Odin and Mistress Sigrun. "That's ridiculous." She spins around and places her hands on her hips. "They can't take a dragon away. And besides, it's you who's bonded with the dragon."

"You don't have to tell me." Crossing my arms, I say, "I don't care if he's a god. I'm not handing my dragon over. I'm going to tell Elan."

"Can we come?" Eir asks. Her usually calm eyes look anxious and keen at the same time. "I've never known that they can be peaceful creatures, and this one sounds interesting."

"I'd love to come too." Hildr's freckly face is loaded with enthusiasm.

"Okay. I don't know how she'll react. It's not like

she's an animal in a circus. No chains or cages are holding her away if she wants to attack."

I open the door to the hall to make sure that there is no sign of Odin or the mistress. When I'm sure that they are gone, I quietly make my way outside, with Hildr and Eir following closely behind. It feels ridiculous to be sneaking around the halls of the academy, but I have to go and see Elan and warn her of what Odin's intentions are.

The corridor branches off, and something catches my eye along the alternative pathway. Peering around the corner, I see Rota being aided by her winged Valkyrie friends, Prima and Mist, down the end of the hallway. Despite Valkyries' fast-healing bodies, she is still bandaged in many places. I'm not surprised after the beating she received from the frost giant. It probably broke most of the bones in her body from the way it was throwing her around.

After the reception from Odin and Mistress Sigrun, I don't know what her reaction will be, so I make sure we tiptoe quietly past her down the hallway. The last thing we need is for Rota and her friends to hear us while we exit the building.

We sneak around the back of the lounge chairs in the lobby, avoiding as much attention as we can. It is not prohibited for us to leave the building during the night, but I want as few eyes as possible seeing where we are going.

When we reach the main entrance, I release my pent-up breath and step into the darkness. Bright stars twinkle in the night sky, and a long line of light cascades from the full moon across the rugged land. The sharp peaks have an eerie glow under the moonlight, yet at the same time, it brings me a strange comforting feeling. This is my home, and it's what I've known all of my life. Under the moon's glow, the land almost looks like it's covered in snow. Tonight, it is only an illusion.

"Elan, where are you?" I say in a normal voice after we have passed hearing distance from the academy building. I figure she must've remained close as she was talking to me only minutes before Odin arrived.

A few moments pass before a golden glow catches my eye, and I turn to see her golden scales bathing under the full moonlight. I am awestruck by the beauty of her colors under the moon. She is a creature that has the potential to be so dangerous and a face that is hard and vicious to look at, yet she has chosen me.

She lifts her head and peers in our direction. Her face is set in a menacing expression, and her large horns protruding from the top and back of her head are daunting and even frightening for me to look at. I hear a gasp, and Hildr halts her footsteps while I continue toward Elan. Her golden-brown eyes focus on my two friends then back on me. For a moment, I almost think that it is her mother, not Elan, who lies in the moonlight.

Unpleasantness plasters her face, and those golden-brown eyes hold a warning.

"Elan?" Even I sound hesitant as I call her name.

She nods once, and a puff of smoke exits her nostrils. She looks intimidating, and I had forgotten that I have only known her for such a short time. In her friendliness toward me, it didn't even occur to me that I may need to ask her for permission to show her to my friends.

"She… she looks like she's going to eat us." Hildr's voice sounds unusually meek behind me.

"Perhaps this was not such a good idea." Eir sounds equally intimidated.

As I look at the angry expression in Elan's eyes, the lack of thought slaps me across the face. I curse my ignorance. "My friends would like to meet you," I say hesitantly.

She snorts, and more smoke shoots out of her nostrils. Her large split irises hold no compassion. The silence is painful as she stares at me for a moment longer before she eventually nods once. *Very well.* A serious tone dominates her voice, and my steps falter. She looks so much like her mother when she does that.

I am no longer confident about my actions. "Are you sure that's okay?"

She exposes her teeth, vast and menacing, and I flinch. A strange sound exits her mouth, and her tone changes. *I'm just kidding. Sure. They can come over. I don't mind.* Humor dances in her eyes. *Did you like my mother's impression? Was I intimidating?*

With the sudden release of tension, I almost collapse to my knees. I can't imagine what Hildr and Eir have gone through. "Very." I steer confidence back into my steps as I approach her and raise my hand to stroke her nose.

She leans into my touch. *You know, it's very unusual for us to like being touched like this.*

"You are a very unusual dragon," I say and smile. My hand travels along her snout and up to her horns, and I pull at them playfully. "You rascal! You scared the soul out of my friends."

Did I? Elan giggles, and her head jerks with the movement. *I know I did. I can see it on their faces.*

Hildr and Eir keep their distance while watching us interact. They would only be able to hear my side of the conversation as Elan speaks in my mind.

She stops giggling, and with her teeth still showing, she focuses on my friends cowering in the distance. Her eyes narrow. Looking like this, she is more intimidating. A voice deep and menacing projects through my head which I'm sure she is making sure the others hear as well. *What are you staring at?*

At first, I think she is still only talking to me, but her eyes are still focused on my friends. She stands abruptly and stomps toward them. *If you keep staring at me, I'll eat you for supper.*

Hildr and Eir back away from Elan's approach. Eir's foot catches on a rock, and she grasps Hildr as she stumbles, pulling her to the ground with her.

Refusing to take her eyes off Elan, Hildr reaches for her sword, and metal sliding against metal rings through the air as she pulls it from its sheath. The dragon has taken it too far.

"Elan!" I call, trying to stop her.

She throws her head back and cackles, the strange sound filling our surroundings and rumbling through our heads. Hildr's and Eir's jaws drop, and shocked relief washes over their expressions.

A second later, Hildr's relieved expression turns to anger, and she glares at Elan. "That's not funny." She aggressively thrusts her sword back in its sheath.

Eir's hand covers her heart. "Oh Vanir! I almost peed my pants."

Elan looks at me. *I thought you said these guys are warriors.* Her face fills with disbelief.

I raise my eyebrows. "We are. But I said you are friendly, and they weren't expecting you to attack. You need to be realistic. Look at the size difference between us. You are enormous. Besides, we haven't been taught how to fight dragons. It is only something that the winged Valkyries are allowed to do. But don't get me wrong… now that I have met you, I am glad that we haven't been fighting dragons. Perhaps we can work together differently."

Hildr has regained her composure, and she stares at Elan. "Can I climb on your back?"

At first, Elan looks startled, then she bares her teeth, and a hiss escapes her mouth.

"Elan!" I chastise her.

She glances at me out of the corner of her eye, and I see the mischief there. Then she pulls her lips over her teeth and buckles her front legs. *Sure. Be my guest.*

Excitement dances in Hildr's eyes as she observes Elan's posture when she tilts down so that Hildr will have an easier time to climb on. "Really?"

Absolutely. I don't see why not. After all, it is my body and my choice. Elan tilts her shoulder down closer to Hildr's height.

Eyes sparkling, Hildr approaches Elan, grabs her scales, and yanks herself up. It takes a lot of effort because the dragon is so big. Using her warrior strength, Hildr reaches into her core and uses her stomach muscles to pull her legs and torso over the dragon. When the struggle is over, she sits up straight on Elan's back and runs her hands over the golden scales along the dragon's shoulders.

Are you holding on? Elan peers over her shoulder at Hildr.

Hildr reaches forward and circles her arms around Elan's neck, clasping her scales. Elan bends her knees and pushes off the ground, flapping her long membranous wings until she reaches a decent height then soars through the air. Hildr's screams of enthusiasm reverberate through the valley while Elan flies a short circuit. After circling a few times, she spreads her wings and glides down to stop, landing stably on all four feet directly on the spot she ascended from. Her wings spread wide, and the spikes on the edges of her wings narrowly miss us as she tucks them away in time.

"Oh Vanir! That was awesome!" Hildr remains on Elan's back, transfixed to the spot, staring at the scales, her face full of awe. "We can't let Odin take her. She's amazing."

What? Elan's eyes widen with surprise, and she looks at me. *What is she talking about?*

"That's why Odin came to visit me. He is furious that I won't hand you over to Mistress Sigrun. He has demanded that I give you to him within a week."

Elan bounces to her feet, and the process knocks Hildr off her shoulders. When Elan realizes what she's done, she holds out her wing just in time to catch Hildr and stop her falling to the ground. She tilts her wing, cupping Hildr within it, and places her gently on the ground. *You can't be serious, can you*?

"Unfortunately, it's true," Eir says with a placid voice.

"Don't worry. I'm not going to let him take you. I'm certainly not handing you over," I say, placing a hand on her snout again. After a few strokes, she seems to relax slightly.

Hildr moves beside me. Her face is still awash with excitement as she looks up at Elan. "I will never let that happen. In fact, I would love a dragon of my own. Do you think you have a spare one somewhere?"

Elan giggles and nudges Hildr with her snout. *You're funny. Like my mother's going to do that. She will never hand over another dragon to the Valkyries other than what the alliance requires.*

My mind races with ideas. "Wait. What about one of the new dragons that have been received this year? What about the blue dragon, Naga? He is one we already have access to."

Hildr clasps her hands together. It is the most excited I remember seeing her. "Brilliant idea!"

Elan looks thoughtful. *To be honest, I think he would love to have someone to be with. He's rather playful.*

"Fantastic! A lively one," Hildr says excitedly. "Perhaps he can bring down frost giants too."

Maybe, Elan says. *I'll talk to him.*

"Sounds great! Just keep away from Odin. Okay?" I give her a warning look. "We should get back before someone notices we are gone."

We turn to leave, and she heads toward the dragon stalls.

CHAPTER THREE

The next morning, I hear from Elan, and I run to Hildr's bed and shake her awake.

She rolls over and smacks me in the face.

"Ow! I'm doing you a favor." I chuckle with disbelief. "You're always such a grouch in the morning."

"Yeah, you know I'm not a morning person." She flings her body into a sitting position and plunks her feet on the ground. "Why are you waking me up so early anyway?"

"Elan has spoken to me. She talked with Naga, the blue dragon, last night. He is keen to meet you. So we'd better get out there before anyone notices we're missing."

"Really?" Her face suddenly comes to life, pushing aside all signs of drowsiness. She runs to the basin and splashes water over her face then grabs her sword from her bedside and straps the sheath on her belt.

"You won't need that. This is a friendly dragon."

Her eyes set in determination. "You never know what might come up. You should know that from training."

"You're right." I throw my quiver of arrows and my bow over my back and latch my sling over my back pocket. It has come in handy in the past when I have least expected it.

Eir hears the commotion, and her eyes crack open a sliver. "What's going on?" She rubs her eyes and slowly sits up.

"Hildr is going to meet Naga, the blue dragon. Did you want to come?" I adjust my quiver into a better position.

"Sure." She splashes some water on her face and follows us.

We weave our way through the boulders and over the rugged landscape until we reach the dragon stalls. It is a fair walk but nothing for our fit bodies.

The sun starts to push up over the horizon, and Hildr breaks into a jog. "I don't want to miss this. I want to see what it's like to have a dragon."

In an attempt to keep up, Eir and I break into a jog behind her.

When we reach the dragon stalls, Hildr pauses. "Which one is it?"

"It's in the one you found me in the other day when I was cleaning the stalls."

"The one that you patted on the snout?" she asks, peering at me over her shoulder.

"Yes, that one. Under the instruction of Elan, he had been playing with me just before you arrived. But I don't think he needed the instruction from Elan. He seemed to enjoy it anyway. He's like a big dog."

We run down the corridor, and she leads us straight to the door where they had found me the other day. In a combined effort, we slide the door across and see the dragon facing the door and standing to attention in the middle of the room. When he sees me walk in, his eyes widen, and his tail starts to wag.

I walk in cautiously, waiting for the plume of fire to shoot my way. I hold up my hands. "Remember, no plumes of fire. Okay? They hurt us."

The dragon nods enthusiastically, his flat head a symbol of friendliness.

"He's tiny compared to Elan," Hildr says, walking in cautiously behind me.

"Yes, but I'm sure he can still carry your weight." I spot Eir following Hildr into the room, then I go up to Naga and put my hands around his neck and lean over his head. I carefully rub him on the snout and tickle his forehead. A strange bubbling comes from his neck, and I pull my face away from his head before he jerks it upward and shoots it down, snorting out a plume of fire.

"Vanir!" Hildr cries. She darts out of the way just in time. Her eyes flick to the dragon. "Is that what he calls friendly?"

"He must have forgotten that plumes of fire can hurt us." I look up into the blue dragon's eyes, and they are wide with shock. "It doesn't look as though he meant it."

Hildr eyes him suspiciously as though trying to read his face for understanding. She approaches him hesitantly before being cut off by Eir as she rushes forward.

Eir stares at the dragon with wide-eyed amusement and strokes him on the nose. "Oh, the poor thing! He definitely didn't mean that." Then she strokes him down the neck.

Hildr takes another step toward him and rubs his nose. I hear another rumble in his throat and pull away. Before I can shout a warning, his head jerks up then down again, and he spits out another plume of fire in Hildr's direction. She jumps aside, and the plume narrowly misses her.

The blue dragon's eyes are wide. He almost looks regretful.

"What is wrong with him?" Hildr protests. "It's the second time he's nearly got me with a plume of fire. I thought he was supposed to know that it's dangerous to us." Her face fills with annoyance until she sees that his is full of regret. "He looks uncertain. Why is he not speaking to me? Does he not understand us?"

"I don't know," I say. "I guess after being with Elan, I just expect them all to speak English. If he can understand what you want but doesn't speak the same language, does that matter?"

Suddenly, a puff of smoke shoots out of the dragon's nose, this time shooting just a few feet away from Hildr.

"Vanir!" she cries.

I search the dragon's eyes for the reason. "Wait. I think the poor guy has a cold." I pet him on the nose and around the holes for his ears. "Do you have a cold, my dear little dragon?"

His big blue eyes dart my way, and he nods. *Yes, I'm sorry. I is sick. My English not good. But I still play.* His eyes widen with enthusiasm.

Eir shuffles over to him and hugs his nose. "He's adorable, Hildr. You have to give him another chance."

Hildr stands poised in front of him for a few moments, her eyes fixed on him in contemplation. Then her shoulders slump. "All right. I'll give him another chance." She approaches him, and his tail begins to wag.

Yeah. Yeah. I can play! I can play! His voice passes through all our heads at the same time.

A smile almost breaks across Hildr's face before being interrupted by the dragon's head suddenly tilting up then down again. Another plume of fire shoots right at her. She jumps to the side. "Vanir! This one is going to keep me on my toes."

I sorry. The dragon gives her a wide-eyed look. *I didn't mean it.*

Hildr dusts her leather sleeve and looks at him. Her eyes are full of distrust and annoyance. But after a few moments, she pulls herself together and says, "That's okay. We shall try again." Her voice isn't joyful, but I can tell that she's willing to give him another go, especially seeing as she's determined to ride a dragon and have a formidable partner with her in battle. She looks up at him and spreads her arms wide. "Let's play."

The blue dragon stands and wags his tail, and I get out the way with Eir following my example. Naga's whole backside is swaying with the motion before he pushes off and sprints toward Hildr. At first, I think he is moving in for a cuddle—until I suddenly realize that he's not about to stop. He slams straight into Hildr, knocking her onto her back.

"Vanir!" She slowly climbs to her feet, rubbing her backside to get the feeling back into her rear end while glaring at the dragon. Then she holds up her arms. "I can't do this today. I've had enough. I'll try again later." She turns and promptly exits the stall.

CHAPTER FOUR

I pet Naga on the nose and scratch him behind his ears. "It's okay. I'll go talk to her."

Eir strokes him on the nose and follows me out of the stall, and we close the big solid rock door behind us. As we walk down to the stone hallway, we see no sign of Hildr. She has stomped off so quickly that she has completely disappeared and left us behind.

I turn to Eir. "I'm going to talk briefly to Elan. I'll meet you at the breakfast hall."

Eir nods and makes her way back to the Valkyrie Academy building, and I head off, looking for Elan, but I can't see her golden scales glimmering anywhere in the rising sun. I travel to where we met her last night, and I can't see her there either. I call loudly enough to be heard by her but not so loudly that the academy can hear me. "Elan?" I wish I could speak to her directly in her head. It would be much easier to hold a conversation without being noticed than having to say everything out loud. "Elan?" I call again when I don't hear an answer. I continue to search for her, hoping to spot some sign of her. While continuing to call her name, I travel a full circle of the academy but with no luck. After fifteen minutes of searching, I shrug and head back to the hall to have breakfast.

When I arrive at the hall, I search for Hildr and Eir and spot them at a table in the far corner. Their plates are loaded with food, and they have started eating. I grab a plate, pile food on it, and go sit with them.

"What did Elan say?" Eir asks.

"I can't find her."

"What?"

"I kept looking and calling to her, but she never responded and never showed."

"Is she all right?" Hildr's eyes cloud with concern. The short visit with Elan has apparently impacted her significantly and made her fall in love with the dragon.

"She should be. I don't see why she wouldn't be. She's probably just gone for a little trip off the grounds and will be back later. Or maybe she's even gone to tell her mother a few things. I don't know. She's a free dragon." Tingles run down my spine, giving me the feeling that someone is watching me. I glance around and see Mistress Sigrun staring at me with a conceited look on her face, almost victorious.

Hildr and Eir follow my gaze.

"She looks rather happy this morning." Hildr grunts.

"Is there such a thing?" I ask. "Especially when looking at us." Coldness creeps over my shoulders as I stare back at the mistress. I try to shrug it off. "It's probably just a warning look that she is coming to take my dragon if I don't hand her over. Well, she can wait, and she can die waiting. It is not going to happen." I take a mouthful of food and swallow it without chewing. "I'm so annoyed. I could really do with something to work out some of this aggression."

"Perfect timing." Hildr says. "We have combat training next, and we are fighting against the winged Valkyries."

"Perfect!" I say, then I scoff the rest of my food and rise to my feet. "I'm going to sit in the hall. This is one lesson I don't want to wait for." I march down the hall and to the combat room to find that the mistress is already there.

"You're early, Wingless."

I roll my eyes then squint at the mistress, dying to say something snarky back. Though I have been here for three years, she still doesn't call me by my name. "I didn't want to wait for combat, Mistress. I am keen to work off some aggression."

Her mouth straightens into a thin line. I think it is meant to be a smile that she has forgotten to turn up at the edges of her mouth, but with her, I'm not quite sure.

"Well, this is the perfect place," she says. "Why wait until class starts? You can start with one of the winged Valkyries."

I glance over and see Prima, one of Rota's friends. And even though I saved Rota the other day, her face is still covered in a sneer. The disdain for the wingless Valkyries is evident on her face, no matter how I tried to prove our worth that day.

She grabs a baton off the shelf and swings it threateningly against her bare hand. "Come on, Wingless. Let me help you with that aggression. Or wait… maybe you can help me with *my* aggression."

Without even waiting for me to collect a baton, she starts swinging hers and whacks me. I don't try to lunge for a weapon—I won't get there in time. A second later, she is already swinging the baton at me from the other direction. I dodge the hit, sliding down to the floor, and swing out my leg, which flicks around in a circle and knocks her feet from underneath her. She crashes to the floor onto her backside, and her weapon falls in her lap then clatters to the ground. She cries out from the impact but dusts herself off quickly and rises to her feet at the same speed as me.

I try to edge my way to the back of the room while keeping an eye on Prima. Even with her face screwed up into that horrible sneer, she still looks like a beauty queen. That beauty is skin deep, I'm sure. Underneath, she is as ugly as anything.

She holds the menacing stare and looks annoyed that she has already landed on the ground so early in the fight. When she swings the baton at me again, I dodge it. At the same time, I throw a fist at her face, and it connects with her chin. A loud crack sounds, and I can feel her jaw disconnecting from the force. She grimaces in pain as she labors to pull herself together and swings her baton at me. It connects with my forearm, and I hear a small snap. Pain shoots up to my head and down my fingers. I am sure that she has managed to fracture my arm. Thankfully, we have quick self-healing powers, one of the gifts that we have as a Valkyrie along with being immortal, but still, healing takes time. I have to pull myself together and prepare for another attack and get ready to retaliate. Putting the injured arm behind me, I skip in and deliver a roundhouse kick to the head.

I spin backward at the same time she swings the baton, and it collides with the shoulder of the same arm that is injured. I hear the snap as my collarbone breaks, and my arm goes limp. The pain is more intense than before, and I see stars. Before I know it, she raises the baton again, and she cracks it down on my head, which jerks and throbs with a splitting headache. I'm fortunate that I'm not falling to the ground, passed out. Though it is almost impossible for me to hold myself together and not to focus on the pain, I spin around and do a roundhouse kick to her head. I manage to knock her out, and she falls to the ground, her baton clunking to the floor.

Blood pours down my face and over my eye, and I wipe it away, leaving a smear on my forearm. It takes all my effort to remain on my feet, and I stumble. I place my legs shoulder width apart with my knees bent to hold me steady. Prima is still slumped on the ground, unmoving. My knees buckle, and my head lands cushioned in her white wings, before I pass out and dream of lying in white clouds.

CHAPTER FIVE

I am brought back to consciousness with a bucket of cold water.

"Wake up, sleepyhead." Hildr stands over me, the bucket still in her hand.

My head hits the floor with a thump, and I grimace then turn to realize that I was still lying on Prima's wing, and my cushioning disappeared when Rota pulled her up. I roll up into a sitting position. "Who won?"

Hildr huffs. "You were both knocked unconscious. I'm pretty sure that means you're about even."

I almost let out a cheer. My fighting skills have come a long way since I started at Valkyrie Academy. "That's a nice change." Stars circle my head, and I rub my forehead. "I always used to get my butt handed to me by those three."

"I don't know—I wouldn't really call that a victory." Hildr drains the last of the water in the bucket onto the floor.

"Yeah, but I knocked her out too. It wasn't just me being the unconscious one. To me, that's an improvement since the last time I fought against her, about a year ago." The stars diminish, and I look around the room some more. "How long have I been out?"

"Long enough for the class to start and for them to walk in and find you two passed out on the floor." Hildr huffs a laugh.

"Where is Mistress Sigrun?" I search the room, looking for the hard-faced mistress.

Hildr's eyes hold disbelief. "She left the room, leaving you two on the floor."

"I saw her leave just before we came in." Eir holds me by the shoulders to help stabilize me. "It's rather disconcerting that she would leave you both here and not put you somewhere better or try to help you recover quickly. We should take you to the wall."

I rub the spot on my head a bit more and wipe away some of the blood. "Yeah, well, I'm not surprised."

"It is shocking, as far as I'm concerned," Eir says as she and Hildr help me to the side of the room.

They lower me to the floor to sit against the wall while ignoring all the stares and sneers from the winged Valkyries. Despite it being an even match, they still see it as though I am less than them and will never have the fighting capability that they have. Considering we don't get as much combat training as they do, I am ecstatic.

"Take another beating, did we?" I look up to see Rota mocking me as I walk past.

Mist giggles. "Ha-ha. Yeah, the floor jumped up and beat her."

Rota glowers at Mist and her stupidity.

Hildr slides between us and puffs out her chest. "I would call it an even match, actually. Prima even had the advantage of wings, and she still can't beat her."

Placing a hand on Hildr's arm, I say, "Just leave it, Hildr. It's not worth it."

"I just so want to teach these winged imbeciles that we are greater than what they give us credit for. The fight was even. It's the only way to describe it. It's about time they learn this," she says through gritted teeth.

I rub my head where the wound is bleeding. Weariness is catching up to me. "I know."

Hildr hooks her arm under my shoulder. "Come on. Let's get you to the nurse."

Eir hunkers down and takes my other side. Together, they assist me down the corridor and into the nurse's quarters.

OUR HEALER STANDS with her back toward us and her head bent over a bench as she studies the things lying on top. It is a beautiful sight to see and a comfort that she has no wings. Her auburn hair falls in tight curls to her shoulders. Hearing our approach, she spins around to look at us. Her face is slightly weathered, the faint wrinkles around her eyes the only signs of her being older than the students. Yet she is still a picture of beauty.

"Hi, Anita," Hildr greets her as though everything is fine.

As her green eyes focus on us, her face softens. "I see you've been trying to teach the winged Valkyries a lesson again." Her voice is authoritative, yet a tone of understanding seeps through.

"It's about time they learned the lesson." Hildr escorts me to the nearest gurney then crosses her arms.

"This war between the winged Valkyries and the wingless has been going on for years, even before I was at the academy. Which, I must admit, is an extremely long time ago. I can't even remember the number of years." Anita chuckles. "The curse of an immortal life!" She shakes her head. "Never have the winged Valkyries given us more than menial duties."

Gawking at her, I say, "But you're a healer. You don't clean. You don't chase after them."

"I am a healer, yes, and I love doing what I do. It was an enormous effort that took a great deal of time and patience for me to get this far, and I only managed that because I had a natural talent. Eventually, after a lot of persisting, they allowed me to pursue my interest. I'm not sure that I am the highest-ranking wingless Valkyrie in the way that jobs go." She grabs a vial off the bench and starts to stir the contents with a glass spoon. "Don't get me wrong—I love what I do, but there was a time when I wanted to join the winged Valkyries and help reap souls for Valhalla. Never has the wingless Valkyrie managed to achieve that." After placing the vial down, the healer grabs a cloth and wipes the blood off my face and cleans my wound. She then grabs the vial and smooths the newly mixed paste over the sore before placing a butterfly closures over the split.

"Even so…" I gasp as she presses hard on either side of my sore to get the bandage to stick and seal it back together. "You have achieved great things by getting this far. It still gives us the inspiration to try to change their ways."

She lowers her face to my level, and sadness mixed with softness and understanding manifests in her eyes. "I have seen many come through who would like to prove them wrong and prove that we are worth more. But none have managed to succeed to that level." Anita turns around and places her equipment on the bench, and the glass spoon clatters against the vial. Then she turns back to me. "I wish you luck in doing that. I honestly do. It will be a breath of fresh air for that change. I am much older and enjoy my medicine too much to go into the fighting scene again although I will certainly support a cause. And, besides, I hear you did a great job yesterday fighting off a frost giant not only by yourself but also with a dragon." A question lies in her eyes.

"Yes, I did."

"I hope you know what you're doing. Dragons are very wild, unpredictable creatures. I would hate for you to become their dinner."

My mouth pushes up on one side. "Yes, I keep getting that message. At the moment, I think I will be more likely to become the mother's dinner than the dragon that I ride. She really is something else. I will take you to meet her if I find her today."

"What do you mean, 'find her'?" Her brow furrows with confusion.

"She seems to have disappeared. But I'm not so worried at the moment. She's probably just gone to visit her mother or take a break. It is not like she's welcome here. On top of that, Odin wants to capture her and enslave her."

Hildr's eyes widen with enthusiasm. "Yes, she really is something else. I wish I had a pet dragon. One that will let me ride it and fight with it."

"We tried that this morning, remember? But you got too impatient and stormed out." I shake my head at Hildr.

"He kept shooting fireballs at me!" Hildr flung her

hands up in exasperation. "He wasn't the brightest of creatures."

Eir looks at her with disappointment and pouts. "He was cute. You should have given him more chances. He had a head cold."

The healer observes Hildr and says, "I imagine you would have to get used to a little aggression if you want to deal with a dragon. Does Odin know that you are doing this, or Mistress Sigrun?"

I shake my head. "No, and please don't tell them. I don't want them to know. It could ruin everything for our plans. And besides, there is no guarantee that Hildr will bond with the dragon."

"I'll help where I can," Anita says.

"Thank you." A thought shoots into my head, and I gasp. "Hildr, I think there is another dragon we could try."

Hildr's body straightens, and her wide eyes focus on me, her face a mask of shock. "One of the dragons? Aren't they all vicious in there?"

"There was one that didn't attack me, and it still looked quite young. There is a chance that we could try that one."

CHAPTER SIX

"Hildr, wait up!" Eir calls, holding her chest and puffing.

Though we are just as fit as Hildr, we are both puffing, trying to keep up with her. She has left us behind in her excitement to meet this new dragon.

I'd forgotten that they hadn't had to clean out the dragon stalls, as they were mostly given other menial tasks like housekeeping or scrubbing the floors. It is rumored that cleaning the dragon pens is the most disgusting job and the most dangerous, making the majority of the Valkyries afraid to go near the stalls. Because of my fascination with them, I push aside these concerns so that I can interact with them.

I call to Hildr, "Do you even know which stall you're going to?"

Hildr slows down slightly. "Sure, one of the ones with a dragon in them."

"True, but there are hundreds of them." I don't hide my disbelief.

Her excitement doesn't waver. "Then one of the ones in the newer area."

"There is a new area?" I ask in a mocking tone.

Hildr slows her pace and keeps in step with us. We all pant while we continue forward down the stone corridor until we reach the door to the dragon stall that I believe holds the dragon. I help Hildr roll the door open, and she sticks her head inside. A massive roar bellows through the door, and she pulls her head back just before a plume of fire shoots her way.

With wide eyes, Hildr faces me. "Is this the one? Because it doesn't seem too friendly. Even the old dummy down the hall has friendlier plumes of fire than this one."

Cautiously, I quickly stick my head around the corner to make sure it is the right dragon. Inside is a massive yellow dragon with horns pointing upright. It lacks the golden tinge of the emperor dragon and is thinner in size, but this one still appears quite intimidating. When it sees me, it points its horns in my direction, ready to charge. It peers defiantly at me with a look threatening death.

I pull my head back and duck behind the door, slapping my hand over my panting chest. "Well." I pant some more. "That's not the stall."

Hildr rolls her eyes, and they help me move the door across the entrance.

Looking down the corridor, I calculate the doors in my head, trying to remember which one is the correct one. I point to each one, counting silently in my head. "Actually, I think it's that one." I chuckle slightly. It is the stall next to the one we just opened.

We approach the door and pull it open. This time, Hildr sticks her head in more cautiously.

When she doesn't pull it back within seconds, I stick my head around the corner as well and peer in. Leaning against the far wall, with his big brown eyes looking sad and sorrowful, is the same brown dragon with the big gash down his leg and no muzzle over his nose.

"Yes, this is the one."

His scales are the color of mud. Two large horns protrude from the crown of his head with a mane of smaller horns covering the back of his head and the top of his neck.

Eir sticks her head around the corner. "Oh, the poor thing! Look at his leg. That's a horrible sore."

The gash looks worse than it did yesterday. A red circle surrounds it, and it appears bigger and puffier. It is showing all the signs that it is infected.

"I can't believe how they mistreat these dragons.

They're living creatures. They deserve to be looked after." Hildr pushes into the stall.

The dragon's eyes are wide with caution and distrust as he watches us. I don't blame him after the way the winged Valkyries have treated him. He remains pressed against the stone wall, watching me. It is the same thing that he did when I entered to clean the stall yesterday.

As we move closer, he spreads his wings, which are attached to his front arms like bat wings. I have not seen this on the other dragons.

"Don't worry," I say in a soothing voice. "We're not here to hurt you. We're just here to see if we can make friends." I take a couple more steps toward him while holding my hand up, palm facing the dragon. "I don't know if you can understand me, but I have just made friends with an emperor dragon."

Though I'm not sure if it's me or my imagination, I think I see a flicker of disbelief in his eyes.

I edge farther forward. "No, no, it's true. I really have, and she's allowed me to ride her. Together, we are working on building the trust between the Valkyries and the dragons. We are starting with my friends. They want to make peace with the dragons and get to know them."

The dragon still looks at me with disbelief in his eyes. He must understand me, and he has a level of intelligence that Naga, the blue dragon, doesn't seem to have.

Hildr pushes forward, bypassing me, and the brown dragon pulls back and watches her with curious eyes. When she steps within a few feet of the dragon, a low rumble rolls up his throat.

"Careful," I warn her. "That was a warning rumble that it is about to shoot fire."

Hildr braces, ready to move, but her excitement is pulling her toward this dragon, even after the warning that she is approaching too quickly. She must be able to see the intelligence in his eyes compared to Naga's. She slowly moves a step closer. "Hey, big guy. I am just trying to make friends. I'm not trying to hurt you at all. In fact, I want to help."

The dragon shifts his head to the side, spits out a small plume of fire, then looks back at Hildr. It is almost like he is telling her that he doesn't believe her. The intelligence outweighs the age.

"It's true, big guy. This is one of my friends. She is not like the winged Valkyries." I move in line with Hildr. "This pact that has been made between the dragons and the Valkyries is not fair, especially to you and the other sacrificial dragons handed over. Perhaps if we work together, we can break this alliance and live in peace together."

Hildr extends her arm slowly toward the dragon at the same time as taking a cautious step forward. The dragon's chains around his ankles clank against the stone floor as he pulls away.

When Hildr goes to take another step, a voice rings in my head.

Stop. The voice is loud and clear.

"Did you hear that, Hildr?" I ask, warning her before she takes another step forward.

"Yes," she says, looking disappointed.

"I heard it too." Eir moves to stand next to me.

The dragon continues to watch Hildr. It hasn't sent out a plume of fire yet, so I take that as a good sign.

Hildr moves her feet a few inches forward, and the dragon tilts his head up in annoyance.

Hildr balks. "I promise I'm here to be your friend."

The dragon raises his head higher as though to emphasize his dominance.

Then stop. The voice rings through our heads again. *You must come no farther. I do not trust your kind, and if you wish to gain my trust as a friend, you must do as I say to prove yourself.*

Hildr pauses, doing what the dragon commanded. She doesn't look as though she is about to make another move forward and is listening to the dragon. This is good.

A horn blares in the distance, and instantly, my ears prick up. "I'm off, guys. I'll catch you later."

"What?" Hildr looks dumbfounded.

"You've got this. You don't need me. I bonded with my dragon on my own through communicating. This is good."

"Yes, but where are you off to?" Hildr asks, not taking her eyes of the dragon. A wise move.

"I'm off to find Elan," I say.

"You'd better not be chasing after that horn," Hildr says.

"You know me too well." I smirk at her over my shoulder.

"They're not going to let you through," Hildr calls back.

"I know. But perhaps I can get through with Elan."

"And how do you expect to pull that off?" Hildr asks.

"Perhaps I can fly through at the same time as the winged Valkyries."

Eir shakes her head.

"Don't get into mischief," I call.

"I wasn't about to run off and get myself into trouble like you are," Hildr calls back.

"They have to catch me first," I say as I run out of the enclosure.

CHAPTER SEVEN

While hurrying away from the dragon stalls, I search everywhere for Elan. I can't see her anywhere. I call, "Elan? Where are you?" It would be so much easier if I could speak in her mind as she does in mine. I run around until I reach the spot I saw her last night. "Elan! Where are you?" I call again between the blare of the horns.

A flock of Valkyries flies over me and heads straight for Heimdall's point for the entrance of Bifrost. I wish I could find my dragon and join them. Searching high and low, I run around the academy another time. I am constantly distracted by the Valkyries flocking to the entrance of Bifrost. I spot Rota and her friends flying together toward the departure spot. Again, it pulls at my heartstrings. Even though I helped save Rota and stopped her from being harmed any further by the frost giant, they still do not see me as equal and still want to belittle me. Searing pain shoots through my shoulder and my arm, and I peek at my scarred shoulder and rub it.

Another shadow passes over me, and I glance up, expecting to see another winged Valkyrie. Instead, I spot the creature that attacked Heimdall—the one that scratched my arm. I'm about to drop to the ground and hide behind a boulder when I realize it isn't interested in me. It is flying in an odd direction away from the bottom of Odin's castle, away from the depths of the mountain. I can't help but think that this is odd. It is a mystery to me how it is flying around so freely when I have been telling people about it. Surely, they must've gone to look for it now, and I'm not the only one who has seen it. Heimdall has also seen it and told Odin about it. I rub my shoulder and keep searching for Elan.

Another horn blares, and I give up my fruitless search for Elan. It's incredible how much I miss her, even though I've only known her for such a short time. She is so amazing, and the fact that she's chosen me makes my longing for her more like an addiction.

I have little time left to catch the opening to Midgard before the blare of the horn stops, so I start the climb up the sheer face of the mountain. I claw, push, and drag myself up until, finally, I reach the edge of the cliff, where I hook my fingers into a crevice and throw a leg over the side, yanking myself up. My back arches as I crouch on all fours. Slowly, I stand and regain my breath, only to be met with Heimdall's glare of disappointment.

"Young wingless Valkyrie! What are you doing back here?" His feet are shoulder width apart, and his fists are on his hips. His horned helmet casts an eerie shadow over me. "You know you cannot be here."

My shoulder aches some more, and I instantly start looking for the creature, but it never shows. I rub my shoulder then look back at Heimdall. "Please, I just want help to prove myself. I helped with the frost giant that entered Asgard. I thought that they would also let me help in Midgard."

Sympathy and compassion flash across his face, unlike the first reception I got when I tried to get through the gate. It is only for an instant, then that expression flees. The huge gatekeeper pulls his shoulders back and stands to attention. "No. I cannot allow you to pass."

My shoulders slump. "Are you serious? I have worked so hard for this."

"I'm sorry, young Valkyrie. I cannot let you pass. It is forbidden."

Something flickers, and I turn to see a black silhouette forming in the middle of Bifrost's lights. At first, I frown, then my eyebrows rise. It's only seconds before I can feel my cheeks burning. Standing within Bifrost's light is a young male wearing all-black clothes, and two beautiful black wings protrude from his back.

"Harut," I whisper in confusion. I forgot how good-looking he is.

His eyes land on me, and his mouth presses into a smile. He looks as though he is in Asgard, yet at the same time, he doesn't seem to be here. Almost as though he is a hologram.

"What are you doing here?"

He remains in that spot, still smiling. I move toward the entrance of the building, and Heimdall blocks my way with one big step.

"My friend Harut, an angel of death, is here." I point at Harut. "I want to go see him."

Heimdall crosses his arms. "You are not going to distract me that easily."

I pout. "But I'm telling you the truth."

"Whatever you say. I'm not falling for it." Heimdall shakes a finger at me.

I shake my head then try to go around him. Again and again, he maneuvers and blocks my way.

"Return to the academy, young Valkyrie. This is not a place for you."

When I peer at the portal of Bifrost, Harut is gone. I stop trying to push my way past. I couldn't be more downhearted than I am right now. I am denied entrance into Midgard, I'm not allowed to talk to my unusual friend, and I can't find my beautiful dragon. Feeling dejected, I turn around. My journey back to the academy is a lot slower than my way there.

I stop at the academy, looking for my friends. They aren't in the room, so I try the mess hall and classes. When I come up empty-handed, I try the dragon stalls and head back to the one I left them in. It's open, and I stick my head around the corner before I enter. Hildr is still trying to get through to the dragon. She doesn't seem to have made any progress since I was there. She is still standing the same distance away.

"How's it going?"

"You're back early. How did it go?" Eir asks.

"The usual story."

The dragon's back is straight, as though he's standing at full attention. Every so often, he casts a warning look at Hildr. He isn't moving any closer, nor is he backing away.

"He won't let me in any farther, and he won't move," Hildr says, sounding annoyed and disappointed. As though to emphasize the point, she moves her feet a few inches forward, and a deep growl rumbles out of the dragon's throat.

"What's his name?" I ask.

"How am I supposed to know?" Hildr snaps.

Eir smiles softly. "She's been too busy trying to get closer and hasn't asked him too many questions."

"You could start with a conversation to build up

trust. Perhaps after the dragon gets to know you, he might relax a bit."

I notice a mess that is new since I cleaned his stall yesterday. "Another way to help him out would be to clean up his stall." The dragon's sore is weeping and looks to be getting worse. "And perhaps you could show that you care by going to get something to help ease the pain of the sore and help it heal faster," I suggest.

Hildr slaps her palm on her forehead and groans. "Argh! I've been so stupid. Of course, all these things would help. I've been so busy trying to get close to him and pet him that it completely wiped all these other ideas from my mind."

I shrug. "In the meantime, I'm going to try to find Elan and ask her if she has tips or can come and talk to him. I'll talk to you later." I walk out, leaving her and Eir to clean up the stall.

A fair amount of time has passed since I last looked for Elan. Perhaps she has come back. I cling to hope and spend more time walking around, calling to her, but I still don't find her. It is just my luck to have a dragon that can disappear and turn invisible. I wish she were always visible to me.

Passing through a group of jagged mountains, I hear something up ahead. I follow it around the curve of the mountain and turn left when something catches my eye. A clatter sounds as I approach the place, confirming that

I didn't imagine the first sound. After all the calling to Elan I did before this, I have hopes that she is here. Maybe she has finally heard me.

I weave my way around the cliff faces of the jagged mountain and turn another corner only to stumble across an old lady. She looks haggard and worn as though the years haven't been kind to her. It is an unusual sight after living at the academy for so long. All the Valkyries look so young, even the old ones. The gods have blessed us with beauty and long life.

Studying her, I move a little closer. "Who are you? I haven't seen you around."

The woman comes close to me and raises a gnarly finger lined with too many wrinkles to count. They even cover her knobbly knuckles, which bulge so much that they look deformed. "There are many people on Asgard, my dear." Her eyes are dark, and they have a strange intelligence behind them. "And many that you will not know. I am just one."

Though I don't argue because I know it is true, I struggle with her age. It is such an unusual thing. I would think that I would remember someone so different from the majority of people of Asgard. I can't pull my eyes away from her. "Are you lost out here?"

"I could ask you the same thing." The old woman smiles, showing her gappy brown teeth, then reaches out and touches my shoulder, and I pull away. She gives me a strange look then shrugs and points at my shoulder. "What is that?"

I look at where she is pointing and notice that some of the scar that the creature gave me is showing. A strange sensation runs through the scar. I shrug. "It's just an old scar."

She studies it for a few moments. "It looks to be tainted with magic."

Frowning, I say, "I have no idea what you are talking about."

Her faded brown eyes continue to study me, and she arches an eyebrow with a look of amusement. "This may bring you many interesting things."

It occurs to me that she must be some kind of witch. Perhaps she has dark-elf blood running through her veins, but I have not heard of any living in this part of Asgard.

Breaking the silence, she says, "I heard you call for something. What was it?"

Trying to assess whether I should tell her, I stare at her for a moment. I'm not sure how much I should tell her about the dragon.

She must spot my hesitation because she places a hand on my forearm. "Don't worry, dear. You can tell me. I am a friend of your mother."

I can't help frowning. I didn't think my memory of my mother was that bad. It has only been a few years since I permanently left home and moved to Valkyrie

Academy. After careful consideration, I give in. I am sure that the rumors would have already started to spread. "I am looking for my dragon."

"A dragon, you say." She removes her hand from my forearm and clasps her other arm in front of her. "What an interesting thing. And what does this dragon look like?"

I think I see a gleam in the old woman's eyes, but I push it aside. "It is one with golden scales. The emperor kind."

She raises an eyebrow, exposing her faded dark eyes more.

I interpret this as her not believing me, and I blurt, "The dragon is only young." I wave a dismissive hand at her. "It's all right. You probably haven't seen it around here." The temptation to leave is great.

The woman raises a finger. "Ah, yes. Yes. I have. I have seen one of these dragons."

The hurry to leave has diminished for the moment. "Where? Was it recently?" My shoulders sag. "Or was it back when you were young?"

The woman chuckles. "It was recently." She leans in as though she is about to tell me a secret. "In fact, it was only today."

"Really?"

She nods. "I saw one at the bottom of Odin's castle. It is surrounded by guards and is deep down in the depths of the castle's grounds."

I gasp. "Really?"

Nodding with more enthusiasm, she asks, "This wouldn't happen to be your dragon, would it?"

"It better not be." But deep down, I have a suspicion that it may be Elan. I haven't seen her all day, and no other emperor dragons are in the area—unless Odin was lying. He made it clear that he didn't have his own emperor dragon. He must have found her and stolen her, even though they gave me a week to hand her over. "I have to get her back."

"Ah!" She nods once, her eyes full of understanding. "Good luck with that."

I spin around to leave then change my mind because I have another question I want to ask her. "How—" When I turn around, she has disappeared. Briefly, I search for her without success.

Around the next corner of the mountain, something catches my eye, and I glance over just in time to see the beast that tried to steal the dragon's egg take off into the sky. I dash to the side of the mountain and push my back up against it, trying to hide within its shape. Holding my breath, I watch as the creature flies away.

CHAPTER EIGHT

The hairs on the back of my neck rise as I watch the creature fly away. Only when I'm sure it's gone do I allow myself to move, contemplating the old woman and how this is a strange place to find her. I hope she makes it to her destination without the creature finding her.

With the creature gone, I leave my hiding spot and head back to the dragon stall. I search for my friends in the academy but come up empty-handed until, eventually, I find them in the dragon stall where I left them. Some progress has been made since I left, for when I enter, Hildr is past the barrier that the dragon had set for her, and she is now rubbing some cream over his leg. This is progress. As she rubs on some of the ointment, the dragon throws his head back then brings it forward. The salve must have a kick to it when applied. Hildr's face beams as she works.

"Is it starting to help?" Eir moves slightly closer.

"Of course. Did you expect it to do anything else?" Hildr places the lid back on the salve and looks at the dragon. "Does that mean I can pet you now?"

Don't push it. The dragon's brown eyes fill with warning.

"You can't blame me for trying." Hildr pulls her head back and grins at the dragon.

"You seem to be making some progress." I step farther into the stall, and Hildr and Eir jump then turn around to look at me.

Eir throws a hand over a heart. "You scared me. Where did you come from?"

"Sorry."

"Back so soon? Didn't you find her?" Hildr looks shocked.

"No. But in my search, something else came up, and I need your help."

"What is it?" Eir asks.

I glance at Hildr sitting close to her dragon and notice that he has dropped his guard some more. "Actually, it doesn't matter."

I turn to run off, but Hildr calls after me. "Where are you going?"

"I have to go and check something out."

"What?" Eir looks at me, concerned.

"Well, on the way back, I ran into an old woman."

"An old woman?" Hildr asks.

"Yes, an old woman. It was a strange meeting. She came out of nowhere, and she was extremely old. I don't remember seeing someone so old. In any case, she told me a dragon is tied up underneath Odin's castle. She didn't know if she saw my dragon, but she said it was a young emperor dragon that was tied up underneath the castle. I'm going to take a look."

"Are you mad?" Hildr almost yells at me.

Worry fills Eir's eyes. "It is definitely pushing the boundaries, going to Odin's castle uninvited to check out one of his prisoners."

"Yeah, but if it's her, he took her without my permission. Whether he likes it or not, she's *my* dragon, not his, and she is a free dragon."

"I'm coming with you." Hildr backs away from her dragon, and he gives her a funny look.

I shake my head. "No, you can stay with your dragon. Besides, it is going to be too dangerous, and I could even get myself expelled or worse. I'll meet you back here."

"Are you sure?" Hildr asks.

I nod at the dragon. "Spend some more time with him to see if you can bond some more. Hopefully, I'll find Elan."

~

MY HEART THUMPS rapidly as I head toward Odin's castle. With the mistress distracted by a mission, I don't have to worry about her interfering when she discovers that I am gone. The walk to the castle seems to take a long time. I am eager to see Elan again. On one hand, I hope it is her, but on the other hand, I hope it isn't. Either way, I have to find out.

It takes some effort to skip past the guards and avoid their attention as I sneak down the halls. My arm has been giving me funny sensations ever since the old woman touched me. I shake it, trying to get rid of this odd feeling, but it doesn't go away.

With my back pressed firmly against the wall, I manage to sneak past the guards at the entrance of the castle, and head for the lower levels. I have never been down here before, though that is a good thing—it means that I haven't been locked up in the palace. I have heard they're quite nasty to the imprisoned.

It takes quite some time to pass the kitchen and the laundry and wind farther down into the dark, windowless depths of the palace. If Elan is down here, it must be so drab and dreary for her after coming from the wild.

I make my way down the corridors, dodging past more guards and holding my breath until I am confident they are gone. After a while, I notice that I haven't seen a guard for some time. I take a deep breath in and decide to risk it. I say in a normal voice but not too loudly, "Elan." Pressing my back against the wall, I rest my head against the solid form, wanting to capture some of its security. I try to still my thumping heart. I don't hear any scuffling of guards coming my way, so I take a deep breath and try again, and this time, my voice is slightly louder. "Elan."

There is no answer. I let out a long breath. I had hoped that the dragon would hear me and respond. Though I still don't know if she's the one that I am trying to rescue and risking my freedom for.

Moving along the halls, I reach a lower level with all kinds of creatures in it. As I stealthily move past the creatures, I keep an eye out for one that looks like the creature that marked me. Perhaps it isn't the only one. But nothing like it is locked up here.

I push through until I see several guards run into one of the stalls with spears aiming forward. A steady rumble shakes the solid foundation of the floor, followed by an enormous roar. A large plume of fire shoots through the bars at the guardsmen standing menacingly outside. From the intense flames that burst through, I know it has to be a dragon.

Peering through the bars, I spot a large and intimidating golden dragon. Its screams of rage promise demise to all who approach it. A couple of bloodstains on its chest weep from holes large enough to be caused by spearheads. They don't appear to be deep, just enough to let the dragon's blood flow. Its face is so full of anger and threats that it reminds me of Elan's mother.

Perhaps they have a different dragon. After all, Elan had other siblings. I'd never asked if they had hatched.

The dragon's slitted golden-brown eyes narrow, then it shoots out another massive plume of fire, narrowly missing the guards. A guard wipes the sweat away from his forehead as he backs a couple steps away. At first, I can't understand why the guards are trying to combat this captured dragon, but I spot another guard lying unconscious in the back corner of the room. I retreat around a corner and wait, listening to the guards' struggle.

After quite some time, a guard calls, "Retreat. We'll have to try again later. Maybe when she is asleep. There is no way she is going to let us through to get him."

After they pass, I peek around the corner and into the cage. The dragon stomps over to a pile of meat lying on the floor and devours several pieces. Her scales on her forehead are bunched together into a frown, and her eyes hold a look of aggression.

My body shakes as I move on silent feet to stand in front of the bars. The uncertainty is rocking me to my core. I hold my breath and brace myself, ready to dash to the side. The dragon is uncannily like Elan, and with this expression, she looks very much like Elan's mother.

After watching for a moment, I decide to take the risk. "Elan?"

The dragon stops eating, and the golden-brown eyes focus on me, her jaw still hovering over another piece of meat. The intense stare she is giving me makes me want to back away. Eventually, she blinks. *Kara?*

My breath releases with a loud gush. I would know that voice anywhere. "Yes. I'm so glad I found you."

Me too. How did you like the impersonation of my mother? Did you like it? Did you like it? I think I had the guards convinced. They were certainly running for their lives. She approaches the cage, and I reach out my hand, and she nuzzles it.

"You nearly had me running for my life. I started to think a different dragon was down here."

She laughs heartily, the noise rumbling up her throat. *So it worked then! I even had* you *fooled.*

"Yes, you even had *me* fooled. Now, though, we need to get you out of here." I pull my hand back and angle my body so I can slide through the bars. My black leather clothes squeak against them.

I approach the unconscious guard and search his pockets. "What happened to him?"

She looks at the ground. *Um. He kind of ran into my tail. Is he all right?*

"Ran into your tail, huh?" I say with sarcasm then feel for a pulse. "He'll be fine. Probably just a concussion."

Oh. Phew! I didn't mean to hurt him. Honest.

I continue searching his pockets until I finally hear the rattle of metal and pull out a loop of keys and set to work on the lock. It takes several keys before the lock finally pops and the door opens slightly.

"Got it." I leave the keys hanging from the lock and open the door wider.

Oh, you're awesome! Elan stoops her head down and nudges my chest. It is only then that I notice the big metal collar around her neck.

"I've been so worried about you. You just disappeared. I didn't know where you were. I thought that you might have gone to your mother's and decided not to come back."

Yeah, I forgot to make myself invisible after you left. I was snoozing, and they pounced on me with a tranquilizer and a net. It was a massive net, too, and I got all tangled up in it when they dragged me here.

"That makes sense." I hug her head, avoiding her horns, then retrieve the keys from the door and unlock her collar. "I was wondering how they managed to find you." Pocketing the keys, I set the collar on the ground.

We make our way out of the cell and down the corridor.

"Don't forget to turn invisible this time. We need to get you out of here."

CHAPTER NINE

The passageway of the palace is enormous, except its size is nothing in comparison to the size of Elan. Although she is treading softly, the floor still shudders with every step. It is going to be extremely difficult to bypass all the soldiers with her massive bulk rocking the palace. Up ahead, some guards block the way, and I halt. A crunch sounds behind me.

"What are you doing?" I whisper.

She responds with a groan. Instinct tells me to turn around and have a look, but this would be pointless. Elan is still invisible, and it would be impossible to see what she is doing.

Sorry. I'm still drowsy from the dart that they hit me with. It was some potent stuff. It's taking a while to wear off.

"Do you mean the tranquilizer they shot you with?"

I listen to the noise of the guards, hoping that they didn't hear the crash. It seems to have gone unnoticed.

Possibly that's what I mean. She giggles. *How stupid. I can't even remember what it's called. Whatever it was, it made me sleep really quickly.*

I push back against the wall and hide behind a pillar as the guards patrol in front of me, moving to the next section. When I can't hear their footsteps anymore, I stick my head around the corner to check that all is clear. Only one of the guards is going in the opposite direction, but his back is toward us.

After calling back softly, "Clear," I tiptoe through the corridor and cringe as the walls vibrate behind me. "Can you step any lighter? You're making the whole floor tremble."

Are you serious? I thought I was super light.

"Yes, I'm serious. You could get us busted."

I cast a glance over my shoulder at the guard going in the opposite direction. He halts and starts to turn. Scooting backward, I press myself up against the wall, hoping that he won't see my slight form or that he will think that it is part of the pillars. I suck in a breath and hold it as his eyes scan the area. The few seconds he studies the corridor feels like hours. Finally, he turns, and I let my breath escape.

That was close, Elan's voice echoes in my head.

I jump, holding a hand over my heart. I'm not keen to answer her in case my whispers echo in the corridor.

A light shines in the distance, and I quicken my pace until I spot the entrance. Two guards stand on patrol outside the open door. I turn to Elan and indicate for her to go out the door.

Do you want me to go ahead without you? she asks, sounding surprised.

I nod. She will be able to leave without being noticed while she's invisible. I stand on my tiptoes and pace in front of her then look at where I think she is.

Yeah, yeah. I get it. Walk quietly.

I bob my head up and down enthusiastically.

The ground still shakes slightly as the dragon paces to the door. Stealthily, I continue forward, keeping an eye on the guards and their reactions and doing my best to stay out of sight. Something grabs a guard's attention, and he moves slightly from his spot, searching the area. Elan must be outside by now, and I'm guessing that the rumble of her footsteps or something similar must have alerted him.

I pause and look for something to use for a distraction, but the palace floor is spotless, and I curse silently. Quickly, I search my pockets, and I almost cheer when my hand grasps the keys to the dragon stall. I thought I left them in the cell. I fling them in the opposite direction of the entrance, and they clatter against the marble floor. Instantly, both guards spin to look, and they trot off in that direction to investigate. Using this opportunity, I sneak past and out the door then duck around the palace corner, out of sight, before they return. I pant heavily, happy that my plan worked.

Something brushes against my skin. I jump and spin around to see nothing.

It's all right. It's just me. Elan's voice pierces my thoughts, and I breathe a sigh of relief.

"Oh, thank Vanir!"

Jump on my back, and let's get out of here.

"Um. That's a good idea, except I can't see you."

She giggles. *Of course. Here.*

Her golden form appears in front of me, and I climb on, grabbing on to her neck tightly. "I think I'm going to have to make a saddle or something so that I can hang on to you better. Your scales can get quite slippery at times."

She turns invisible and pushes off the ground, and my hands slip. Quickly, I dive forward and embrace her neck. "Not to mention, it's challenging to grab on to you properly when I can't see what I'm grabbing."

Then a saddle is probably a good idea, she says.

"Where are you taking me?"

I'm taking you back to the academy. Then they won't know that you were missing and that you're the one who broke me out of the palace.

"Actually, can you take me to the dragon stalls instead? I need you to talk with the brown dragon that was injured. Hildr is trying to make friends, and so far, I don't think she's succeeding. Although she seems to be able to get a bit closer when she wants to put the ointment on his wound."

Do you mean Drogon?

"I don't know. He hasn't told us his name because he was too hurt and angry over his leg. But he is much more receptive than a lot of the older dragons."

Yup, sounds like Drogon. He is actually really nice. He hasn't been attacked too much, but he is a little bit bitter toward Valkyries of the winged kind. But I have hope for him. Let's go and chat with him. She veers around and heads straight to the dragon stalls.

When we get there, she lands on the cliff entrance of Drogon's stall. Instantly, I spot Hildr closer to the dragon and talking with him, and Eir is standing not far away.

Eir spins around, eyes wide, searching for what caused the noise at the entrance of the cave. Her shoulders relax when she sees me sitting in midair.

Drogon stands upright and Hildr peers at him, looking confused. "What's wrong with you?"

Elan turns visible. *It shows that he knows I'm here. That's all. Stand at ease, Drogon. It's just me, not my mother.*

The young dragon relaxes his shoulders and looks down at Hildr.

Elan is looking at the dragon. Her head is moving, and her eyes are twitching, and the brown dragon is responding likewise. I assume that they are having a private conversation.

Drogon looks at Hildr then back at Elan. It takes a moment before resignation and acceptance flash through the dragon's eyes.

Elan turns to me. *Can you remove his shackles? He promises to be good. And to remain here despite the fact that he hates the enclosure and being a captive. I said if he stays and cooperates, he will be treated well by Hildr.*

"Of course he will!" Hildr almost yells.

Elan tilts her head at Hildr in acknowledgment. *He has agreed, for now. He also said that if you can remove his shackles, Hildr can climb on his back. Despite his leg hurting, he can fly.*

Hildr stands, her eyes full of enthusiasm and excitement. "Really?"

Elan's teeth show in a threatening display that I have learned means a smile. *Yes, really.*

Hildr thrusts her hands into her leather pockets and pulls out a skeleton key and sets to work on his chains. After a few seconds of fiddling with the lock, it pops open, freeing Drogon. And true to Elan's words, Drogon folds his front legs so that he is low enough for Hildr to climb on.

Without a moment's hesitation, Hildr climbs on, throws a hand around his neck, and clasps onto his scales, ducking to avoid the spikes protruding from his head and upper neck.

"Hang on tight, Hildr!" I call as Drogon pushes off into the air.

CHAPTER TEN

Hildr takes off on Drogon, and I clench my teeth when he flops sideways, weaving unsteadily all over the place. Eir moves to stand next to me, just in time to see Hildr flick to the side with one of the jerky movements of the dragon. Only her arms being secured tightly around his neck stops her from falling to her death.

Eir gasps loudly, and my teeth clench tighter. We can't do anything for her other than hope that she manages to stay on the dragon's back. The dragon peers over his shoulder, sees what is happening, and jolts around to try to catch her on his back again. It takes several nail-biting attempts with Hildr flicking from one side to the other. Her arms wrapped around the dragon's neck is her only stability. Eventually, one of the flicks flings her body the right distance so that she can hook a leg over his side and dig her heels into the dragon's ribs again.

"That was close." Eir continues to watch the progression with a horrified expression.

"Yes, it was."

It's okay. I know he can look after her like I looked after you. You should organize those saddles though.

Hildr and the dragon become more synchronized with each circuit they execute over the area. Strange pride fills my chest, and I have more hope for the future between dragons and Valkyries.

"It looks like a perfect match." Awe radiates in Eir's voice. "Hildr seems completely satisfied with this one. I think they will work it out and get along well."

"If that's the case, then that's two of us joined with dragons. Perhaps we can slowly build this up into a private army. One to fight against the alliance that is enslaving the dragons and also to fight against the discrimination against the wingless Valkyries and help protect the future of Asgard."

Elan looks down at me. Her mouth is broad, and her teeth show. It's that scary smile again. *That sounds like a plan. Except I don't think Mother will give over any more dragons. We will have to do it ourselves.*

"Do I get a dragon?" Eir asks, a hopeful expression in her eyes.

"As far as I remember, only one more friendly dragon is in this enclosure. And that's the simple dragon. Naga's not the brightest, but he has a sweet personality."

Eir's eyes light up. She clasps her hands together and bobs up and down excitedly. "I love him! He's so cute! I will certainly give him a go."

Then it sounds like you will have a dragon, Elan says.

"He has a kind heart, just like you. You should be a perfect match."

She jumps up and down with excitement. "I can't wait! Actually, I'm going to check on him now."

I'm about to say something when she cuts me off. "Don't worry. I'll avoid his sneezes." She spins to leave then halts.

"What's wrong?" I turn to look when something catches my eye—a soldier.

"Sire," he calls.

Eir turns to face me, a horrified expression on her face. A second later, my expression imitates hers.

Odin's bulk has filled out the entrance to the dragon's pen. He points at me. "Seize her! And capture that dragon."

I jerk Eir's arm and climb on Elan's back. "Come, Eir. It's time to get out of here."

She jumps on Elan's back and loops her arms around my waist as I lean forward and clasp mine around Elan's neck and secure my hands on her scales. Then Elan pushes off into the sky while turning invisible. I don't know what the plan is, but I'm not willing to be seized by Odin at this moment. I am pretty sure he has worked out what I've done.

~

THE END

Did you enjoy this book?
You can make a big difference.

HONEST REVIEWS of my books help bring them to the attention of other readers.

IF YOU'VE ENJOYED this book, I'd be grateful if you could spend a few minutes leaving a review (it can be as short as you like).

The review can be left on Amazon and Goodreads.

Thank you very much.

KATRINA COPE

SCORNED

VALKYRIE ACADEMY DRAGON ALLIANCE

BOOK 3

Cosy Burrow Books

Valkyrie Academy Dragon Alliance
Book Three

SCORNED

"In *Scorned,* Katrina Cope takes us on an adventure with Kara, who is on the run from Odin and must enter a dragon world and figure out how to survive. It's a tightly wound story with a surprise ending. Recommended!" –Kate B., Line Editor, Red Adept Editing

Scorned
Ebook first published in USA in September 2019 by Cosy Burrow Books
Ebook first published in Great Britain in September 2019 by Cosy Burrow Books

www.katrinacopebooks.com

Published by Cosy Burrow Books

ISBN: 978-0-6486613-2-0
ASIN: B07VR7MDX5

Created with Vellum

Colin & Glenys ~ Thank you for the peace you supplied (with a view)

CHAPTER ONE

Wind thrums against my face, and I twist my head to the side to relieve my eardrums from the consistent pressure and noise. A frustrated groan carries across the void of land. Gazing over my shoulder and down the golden scales on the back of the dragon, I focus on the point we left behind. Even in the distance, I can see Odin's open mouth as he yells his disapproval. I've really done it this time.

I look back to Eir, and guilt rocks me to my core. I hope I haven't doomed her as well. I hadn't been thinking when I grabbed her arm to leave with me—it was a-spur-of-the-moment decision. My thoughts were only on removing everyone I cared about from the immediate threat.

I face front, and the wind blows noisily against my eardrums again. Goose bumps prickle down my arms and back as Elan takes us higher. The mountains shrink below, and crisp air fills my lungs as we rise and fall with the rhythm of Elan's wings.

On the left, far into the distance, Hildr rides her dragon. I hope that her actions and the timing of Odin's visit haven't endangered her too. She was only supposed to be going for a short flight then returning Drogon to his enclosure. The timing of Odin's appearance had spoiled the sneaky first flight. No one was meant to know that the dragon had left his stall. This could jeopardize the alliance with the dragons if Odin decides to rule it a breakaway. I contemplate what our next move should be.

The monotonous drone of the flapping wings calms my nerves, and I breathe in the crisp air only to have the calmness ripped away when Elan suddenly nosedives toward the ground. Eir presses her head into my back and clasps her arms around my waist more securely as I bring my legs forward and hook them around Elan's neck.

"What are you doing, Elan?" My words fall slightly short of a scream.

She peers over her shoulder at me, and I glimpse amusement in her eye. *Stop stressing! I've got you.*

My eyes are leaking tears from the pressure of the wind. "Yeah, but a little warning would be nice. And besides, there are two of us. It's a little harder to catch two of us if you fling us off your back," I retort.

She rolls her eyes. *Then you will just have to get working on the saddle, won't you? I'm not going to let you fall. You should have more faith in me. I'm great at catching.* She swerves off her path as if to prove a point. *You should know that. I have caught you a few times.*

"It still doesn't put me at ease," I say through clenched teeth.

You stress way too much. Have a little faith in your dragon. Elan sounds upbeat as usual—at times, it borders on annoying, and at the moment, it's leaning that way. My future—and possibly my friends' future—at the academy is at stake, all because I rescued Elan. If I had to relive my actions, I wouldn't have done anything differently. It doesn't stop me worrying, though.

I glance over my shoulder but can no longer see the stalls or the academy through the mountains that stand in the way. A small jolt rocks through Elan's body as she softly lands on the ground. Hildr's dragon circles a few moments later then lands next to us. I kick my leg over Elan's neck and slide down from her side, hearing a thump behind me as Eir follows.

Hildr's face beams from her flight, yet traces of worry crease her expression. "Odin's timing stinks!" she says. She pets Drogon gently on the nose, and the dragon nestles his chin into her hand—their bond grew stronger during the short flight. He sits on his haunches, and I notice that the swelling and redness of his injury is clearing, and the weeping has reduced. "What are we going to do?" Hildr's face puckers into a frown. "Eir and I had nothing to do with helping Elan escape. Although I completely support you in your actions. And I wasn't taking Drogon. I was only borrowing him for a quick flight before returning him until I needed him again." She crosses her arms. "Odin couldn't have chosen a more inconvenient time to come."

"I know. I'm sorry that you've been dragged into this. They were quick to chase me. They must've discovered Elan's absence in no time at all. I didn't think they would miss one dragon from the dungeon that quickly." I move back and prop myself against Elan's side. Her scales warm my back.

Perhaps it was that unconscious guard. Maybe he woke up and saw that he was alone in the dragon cell, and he alerted everyone else, Elan says. *Maybe I should've knocked him harder.*

I gasp. "Elan!"

Oh, don't get your tail all twisted. I'm kidding. You saw how I reacted to hurting him. I don't like hurting people. Besides, he ran into my tail, remember?

"Aha," I say, crossing my arms over my chest. "You seemed to be having a lot of fun back there, acting like a big bad dragon."

Oh, I was. Her front feet shuffle with excitement.

I glance at Eir and notice that she looks pale. "Are you okay, Eir?"

She nods with a vacant expression, staring over the

wastelands. "Yeah. I'm just worried about what to do next." She pauses and twists one of her wavy light-brown locks. "Actually, I'm more worried about what Odin will do to you." Her brow pushes together in a frown, and she looks at me. "Hildr and I can go back at any time. We had nothing to do with Elan's breakout. And Odin's reasonable, right?"

I can't help but laugh. "Um, not that I've seen. I would be more likely to class him as unreasonable unless you can somehow manage to get him to see your way. It's something I haven't yet achieved."

"It's not like Hildr and I have done anything wrong. She took a dragon for a flight, but she was going to return him."

"Odin is not a peacemaker like you are," I say, "although the dragon does have to go back to the stall."

Drogon stomps his foot and shakes his horn-covered head. *I don't want to go back to my stall.*

"But you have to." I push off Elan's back and stand in front of him.

But I don't want to. He stomps the other foot. *The food in there is disgusting, and I shouldn't be held captive.*

"How is the food disgusting?" I raise an eyebrow at him.

They give us meat that is already dead and cut up. It's not fresh and running around.

Eir screws up her nose in disgust then turns the other way.

You have to return, Drogon. Elan pushes her shoulders back and uncoils her wings, giving off the impression that she is larger.

Drogon plunks himself on his backside, and a deep frown sets on his face. *Why?*

Because it is part of the alliance. If you don't go back, then you can disrupt the treaty, and it could cause a war between the Valkyries and the dragons again. We could lose many. You don't want that on your conscience for the rest of your life, Elan says, her golden-brown eyes flooding with compassion and sympathy.

But I don't want to. Drogon's bottom lip protrudes and droops slightly.

Elan stands on all four feet and towers over him. She huffs, and tendrils of smoke escape her nostrils. *You made a promise to me that you would go back. You have had your fun, and now you will go back. That is an order*. Elan's voice booms with authority, and I almost mistake her for her mother again.

Drogon's large brown head tilts forward, and his gaze falls to the ground as his front legs crumple in an act of submission. *Yes, Elan. I will go back.*

Elan sits back down and folds her wings. *Good.*

I am dumbfounded. It is the first serious act of aggression and authority that I have seen from Elan, and this time, there was no bluffing. It's as though she is the commander of her soldiers. I know she is a higher ranked dragon, but it's strange to see, given that she is usually cheerful and happy.

Hildr looks from dragon to dragon and scratches her fingers through her spiky red hair. "Clearly, I have to take Drogon back to the stalls and tie him up again. This will risk exposure to Odin, anyway." She turns to Eir. "I think you should come with me. We'll try and talk our way out of this. Perhaps we can convince Odin that you were on my dragon, not Elan."

"That's going to be dangerous, Hildr," I say.

She touches her hand to the hilt of her sword. "It's a challenge that I am willing to take. I could never cower from danger. We will work this out. After all, I am returning the dragon. The most punishment I expect is a slap on the wrist. As for you, I don't know what they would do. I don't think it will be safe for you to return until things settle down. When that happens, I'll come and find you."

"Where will you go?" Eir asks me with a strange mixture of worry and contentment.

You can come with me to the wastelands.

I never thought I would hear that said in such a cheerful voice. Then again, I didn't expect anything else from Elan.

"The dragon wastelands?" I ask.

Of course. Where else would I take you?

"Will I be safe there?" I fiddle with the strap of my quiver that lies across my chest.

Elan pushes her mouth to one side, looking thoughtful. *To be honest, I have no idea. But I will protect you.*

"But you're only one dragon in how many?"

A lot. But don't worry. I'm tough. She pulls back her lips, exposes her teeth, and growls.

My mouth twitches up at the side. "For some reason, that doesn't put me at ease."

CHAPTER TWO

A knot twists deep in my stomach as I watch Hildr and Eir take off on the back of Drogon. The dragon has managed to hone his flying skills most of the time, although occasionally, he still tosses his passengers. I grit my teeth as Eir flops from one side to the other, but eventually, Drogon learns to correct himself and catches her. Eir wraps her arms around Hildr and straightens her back. A deep sadness fills her face as she glances over her shoulder at me, causing the strings to pull tighter on the knot in my stomach. I can tell she is concerned about my safety more than her own.

I don't know what my future holds. I hope that I can work my way out of this and back into the Valkyrie world, where I can prove the worth of all the wingless Valkyries. As I watch my friends disappear over the horizon, the urgency overwhelms me, but first, I have to learn how to survive in the wastelands.

I hope that Hildr and Eir are accepted back to the academy, even if it is not with open arms.

Elan dips down, and I climb on her back, encircling her neck, yanking my legs over the top of her, then hooking my heels into her sides. As I do this, the arrows knock around in their quiver, reminding me of their existence. In all the hurry and excitement, I'd forgotten that I had slung them over my back before I raced to see if I could get to Midgard. The reaction is so ingrained in me from my training that I don't need to think about it. I reach around the back of my neck with one hand. My fingers brush the hilt of my sword, and I breathe a sigh of relief. It is secured between the quiver and my back. They may not be much, but at least I'm not entirely defenseless.

I hook my arms around Elan's neck again. "Let's do this."

Elan pushes off the ground and takes to the air. The chilliness of the air stirs up my anxiety. I haven't been to the dragon wastelands since the day I rescued Elan's egg. I had run so far that day purely by coincidence, and I'm glad I did—I saved the eggs of that nest. I survived that day in the wastelands dominated by the dragons, but that was only against one dragon. Elan's mother had made it clear that she would not spare me if she found me out there again.

We fly in silence. The wind blows against my ears, blocking out the consistent beat of Elan's flapping wings. The chill of the air raises goose bumps on my skin. I didn't realize that dragons could reach such a high altitude when they fly.

I can hear your brain ticking over. What are you think and about? Elan's cheerful voice, in stark contrast to how I am feeling, pierces my head, distracting me from the thrumming in my ears.

I expel a breath. "How can you be so lighthearted? So much is weighing on my shoulders right now. I don't have a home to go to, and I have to stay among dragons who may eat me. I'm worried."

So you should be. She peers over her shoulders, and I spot humor in her eyes.

"That's not funny. It is quite serious." I glower at Elan.

I know. But you can't worry about everything. Just take it one step at a time. She remains frustratingly cheerful.

I poke her under her scales, trying to find some softer skin. I know that she is right, but it doesn't make it any less irritating. "Since when did you get so wise? You're not even a fraction of my age, and you seem to know so much."

Ah. So we're trying sarcasm now, are we? That's okay. I know I'm smart for my age. She smirks.

I roll my eyes. A deep chill encases my arms, and I shiver.

Are you cold? The smirk has left her face.

"Freezing, actually. This Valkyrie uniform is sleeveless." I look down at my leather pants. "At least my pants are long."

She tilts her head and looks at me again. *Your goose bumps are bigger than your eyes.*

"I know. I'm the one experiencing them."

She shakes her head. *You'll have to do something about that.*

"And a saddle, remember? I'm only just hanging on here. I'm surprised I'm not warm from the effort." I pull myself forward and hook my legs around her neck. "My arms are exhausted."

Elan dips, pulling us out of the clouds. On the ground below, I recognize the small spot where I had stood that day when I faced the creature who was trying to steal Elan's egg, who had scratched me in the process and left me with the large scar on my shoulder. This is the place where I had saved Elan and her siblings and stopped Elan's egg rolling off the cliff.

See anything familiar?

"Yes, I do. How close is your nest to the other dragons?"

It's not too far. I'll show you when we land. She tilts up her wings, and we drop elevation quickly. As her feet hit the earth, her body rocks with a small thud, and she kneels close to the ground. I don't see any other dragons, and I flick my legs to one side and slide down her scales off her back. It's incredible how different the ground is here in comparison to the area around the academy, even though we're not that far away. I move around Elan, searching the area and taking in the scenery. Dragon eggshells are scattered across the ground, and they crunch under my feet.

I look at Elan. "Are these your dragon eggshells? I would have thought that your eggshells would have disintegrated by now."

Oh, mine has. These are from my younger siblings.

My mouth drops open. "You have more siblings?"

Well, yeah. Dragons lay eggs at least once a year. Mother's been busy trying to repopulate our kind. She's been doing a good job too.

"Except it has captured Odin's attention, now that she is producing more than one egg a year, and that's why he's demanding that he has one of your breed every year."

He can stick it where the scales don't grow! He's not getting me or any of my siblings. There aren't many female dragons at reproducing age, and it isn't in the alliance contract. She thumps her tail against the ground. *And Mother would never approve it.*

"That's one of the things he's upset over. And because you've agreed to be with me, I'm on the firing line." I stoop down to pick up a piece of eggshell. Its gold glitters in the sun, tainted slightly by the black, creating a beautiful contrast. I run my hand over the rough surface. A memory sparks. "Does the creature still come to steal eggs?"

There have been reports that eggs are still going missing. It's increasing the dragons' intolerance to the alliance with the winged Valkyries. Between that and the missing eggs, our population isn't growing quickly enough.

"Why can't any of you keep watch and look out for the creature?"

It's a sneaky creature. The dragons eat a lot and have to go hunting regularly. And it always seems to know when to come.

"Then why don't you designate one dragon to watch over the eggs while the other dragons go out hunting?"

Elan chuckles.

"What's so funny?"

That would mean that we'd have to get along. And that just doesn't happen among the dragons at the moment.

"Is it really that bad?"

She nods.

"Then can't your mother demand it, for the sake of the safety of the dragons?"

I know it's hard to believe, but Mother doesn't like being bossy and ordering dragons around all the time. She wants peace among the tribes.

I fiddle with the eggshell in my hands. "But this particular demand would aid peace."

I still can't see it happening.

I shake my head. "It's a shame."

The ground rumbles behind me, and I drop the eggshell and spin around to come face-to-face with an angry dragon.

CHAPTER THREE

Hot dragon breath coats my face as I stare into a huge mouthful of teeth—the pointy white canines are only inches away from my face. I back off, trying not to stumble over the stony surface. The dragon snorts, and tendrils of smoke escape between the gaps in its teeth. I hold up my hands in a stopping motion, hoping that they won't become the first things that get chomped off.

"Hi. I am here in peace." I continue backing away while glancing over my shoulder, checking for the cliff's edge. The arrows in my quiver rattle, but I know they won't do me any good. The dragon's golden-brown eyes glare down at me, and the farther I step away, the narrower the eyes become.

I study the dragon from head to toe and note the two large horns protruding from the top of its wide head. Its mouth is filled with spiky teeth, and drool drips from them as it stares at me as though I might make a tasty snack. The golden glint in its scales sparkles in the sun exactly like Elan's—it's another emperor dragon. I continue to back away, hoping to hide behind her. I glance sideways, looking for her, and my face clouds with worry when she seems farther behind that I expect.

The dragon's eyes seem to dance with humor. *Oh, Elan, you brought me lunch. That's nice of you.* Elan hurriedly steps in front of me, and I breathe a sigh of relief. My heart is pounding so hard in my chest that I feel as though it is going to jump out to give the dragon an appetizer before it starts on the rest of me. Their voices rattle through my head as they speak to each other.

No, Sobek. This is not your lunch. Kara is my friend, and you should treat her with respect.

Sobek grumbles as he moves closer. *She smells of Valkyrie blood, and she's in the wastelands. She's fair game.*

Elan stands firm. *No. Kara isn't lunch. You will not touch her. She's important to us.*

Blah, blah. Whatever. Move out of the way. He attempts to shove past her.

A low rumble shakes Elan's body, and a puff of smoke escapes her teeth. *This is the Valkyrie who saved me as an egg. You are not going to touch her. Mother and I have agreed to protect her, and the only way to do this at the moment is to bring her back here despite what she said about her returning.* For the second time today, Elan's voice is surprisingly firm.

Sobek slams his tail against the dirt, and the ground vibrates. *That's not fair! She shouldn't be out here if that's the case. Any Valkyrie out here is fair game.*

Elan moves aside and exposes me to Sobek again, who surveys me with hunger as distrust taints his eyes. My feet shake in my boots. Thankfully, he's not moving toward me, and Elan remains on full alert. After a few moments, Elan backs up with one of us on either side. *Sobek, this is Kara. Kara, this is Sobek. He's my little brother.*

I swallow the lump in my throat. "Ah, nice to meet you," I say with a voice full of uncertainty. I look from Sobek to Elan then back to Sobek again, almost chuckling at her calling him "little." "I assume you mean your younger brother… because he's huge."

Elan chuckles. *Yes, younger. He was in the same clutch of eggs.*

"So one of the other two eggs in your clutch to hatch after you?" I ask. "What about the other one?"

They both hatched. My mother is very fertile. That's why she's working the hardest to increase our population. It's kind of a bummer because we all seem to be related, which makes it harder to find someone to couple with who we're not related to. She nudges Sobek on the shoulder. *And because I was born before this dragon, I'm in charge of him. He's supposed to listen to me. It's not always the case, though.*

Well, you've done some pretty stupid things, Sobek says.

I'm still learning. Everyone makes mistakes when they're learning.

Like the mistake you're making right now by bringing her to the dragon wastelands? She's definitely going to be someone's lunch before the day is over.

Hopefully, no one will find her straight away. Hopefully, it will be a slow process of introducing her, and they will listen to me and Mother, their leader.

He sits on his haunches. *You know that's not the way things work at the moment. This alliance is getting their noses out of joint. You and I are lucky that we are a rare breed.*

Yeah, about that. Odin is now searching for our kind. He captured me, except Kara found out and rescued me from his dungeons. I'm indebted to her twice now. It's getting a bit ridiculous. She tilts her head at me and gives me a strange glance. *I owe her at least two lives.*

"You don't owe me anything." I walk up to her and place a hand on her front leg. "I'm happy to have you as my friend. To me, this is enough repayment."

The looks she gives me says she's unconvinced. *The day will come, I'm sure.*

I glance at Sobek again. "What happened to the other egg from your clutch?"

I have another sister too, Elan says.

"Where is she?"

Elan saunters toward the edge of the cliff and peers over. *She's down there with the rest of the dragons.*

I walk up to the side and peer over the edge with

her. If I thought I was scared facing her brother, then I had no idea. The valley is full of different-colored dragons stomping around close to one another, some of them fighting openly and drawing blood. It looks wild and untamed, and suddenly, I'm nervous again. Elan is but one dragon. "Elan, there is no way you can protect me against them."

Don't worry. Sobek will help us, won't you, Brother? She nudges him with her butt, and he sways on his feet.

A low grumble rises in his throat.

See, I told you, she chirps at me.

I look at Elan in disbelief. "That didn't sound like an agreement."

Oh, don't worry. He sounds like that all the time.

Rocks clatter behind me, and I turn to see Elan's mother approaching. With her is a dragon who, if not for the dark streaks on her cheeks, would look exactly like her.

Her mother chastises her. *Elan. What are you thinking, bringing her here?*

She saved me again, Mother. Odin sedated me and locked me in his dungeon because Kara wouldn't hand me over. Eventually, Kara found out where I was, and she rescued me.

The mother's eyes land on me. Even her friendly face is intimidating. *Is this so?*

I nod. "I did it because Elan is my friend, not because I want to hold debts over her head. I like your daughter, and I'm happy to work with her. She helped me slay a frost giant and save the winged Valkyries and the academy, not to mention a large part of Asgard. I thought they would thank us and welcome me into the fields so I can help reap soldiers from the dying warriors for Valhalla. Instead, it turned out completely the opposite. Odin demands that he have Elan or another of your breed of dragons. He claims that you owe him because the emperor dragons are having more than one dragonette per year."

Well, he can't have one. It is not agreed upon in the alliance. Her voice rumbles with anger.

"I know, and I told him that, but then he stole Elan anyway. Now I've rescued her, and he's after me—that's why Elan brought me here. And to be honest, I'm scared. I don't want to be here, as much as I love dragons. Peering over the edge and seeing the turmoil that is down there makes me scared."

You should be scared. I cannot guarantee your safety. We will have to hide you here on this pedestal and hope that the dragons will not see you until things settle down. But it is best to try and go back home as soon as possible. Is anyone arguing on your behalf?

"My two friends were kind of dragged into this by accident. They have flown back—"

Flown back. Are they winged Valkyries? Her eyes fix on me, interrogating me.

"No. They have gone back on a dragon, one of the captured ones who has not been there for long."

The mother looks at Elan, and there's disapproval in her eyes. *What are you doing, Elan? This is not part of the deal.*

Right, Mother, it's not part of the deal that I made with you when we decided for me to go. If only you could see the joy that I have brought and feel the complete connection I have with Kara. Her friends have seen this and are keen to join in and help the alliance and stop the dragons being persecuted. They had a quick ride on me, and they are addicted. She giggles. *They're so keen to work with us that they are like little children.*

It sounds as though they are treating dragons like pets, the mother says disapprovingly.

I shake my head. "Oh, no. The dragons are making it clear who's in charge, although Naga's a bit more of a pushover because he's keen to cooperate and he's so cute."

The mother dragon grumbles deep down in her throat, and a small puff of smoke exits her mouth. I'll have to remember not to call them cute next time. Clearly, the mother doesn't like it.

CHAPTER FOUR

W*e're going to have to keep out of sight and away from all the other dragons,* the mother says.

Of course. We'll do whatever we can. Sobek stands at attention as though faced by a corporal.

I don't want any harm to come to her. Elan glances at me with worry in her eyes.

I'll have to go and sort this out so that we can get her out of here quickly. The leader of the dragons paces in front of us, her forehead crumpling into a frown between her horns. *Clearly, Odin needs reminding of our contract. It's going to be difficult. I have heard that his head is so thick that it's hard to speak to him.*

"That seems true," I say. "He seemed shocked when I let it drop that I can speak to you. He thought that was impossible, so I had to ad-lib."

It is impossible with him because he's so closed-minded.

I'll have to go and hope that Loki is there. Then he can shapeshift into dragon form so that he can translate. She paces some more. *Most of these gods are thickheaded and too hard to speak to. Thor is one of the worst.*

I find it difficult to hold back a chuckle. We are always taught to respect the gods, and it's strange hearing them talked about in this way.

Eingana.

This voice is strange to me, so I duck behind Elan.

What is it, Ness? the highest-ranking dragon asks.

Finally, I know the mother dragon's name. I have been too intimidated to ask.

Too many dragons are down there fighting, and it is getting out of hand. No one can get through to them. We need you to step in.

Hiding behind Elan's legs, I sneak a peek. A bright-red female dragon stands in front of the leader. Her eyes are framed in black, giving her a seductive, feminine appearance. I know there are red dragons in the stalls, but their look is vastly different from the other dragons, almost as though they are making a statement. Two horns on top of her head point to the sky, except unlike the emperor dragons' horns, which are straight and solid, these horns fork off like branches on a tree in Midgard. White fur lines her eyebrows, chin, and chest, with a fluffy patch on the end of her extremely long tail. Even her back is not straight like the other dragons—instead, it is humped like a camel. Coupled with the brilliant red scales, her breed of dragon looks as though it should be on display.

Ness tilts her head and nose into the air and takes in a couple of deep breaths. *It smells like Valkyrie up here.* Her eyes narrow.

I lose all feeling in my face and pull back, standing upright and hiding behind Elan's legs. My heart thumps rapidly against my ribcage, begging to escape. This will not do. If I don't quiet my heartbeat, Ness might be able to hear it. I take slow, deep breaths, making sure the air doesn't whistle in my nostrils.

Eingana discretely moves between Elan and Ness. *Oh, that's just Elan,* she says. *I've been sending her to watch over the Valkyries and try and smooth out this alliance with them so we can stop all this bickering.* The leader of the dragons flicks her tail dismissively. *She reeks of them when she comes back.*

Ness sneers, and a long deep grumble escapes her throat. *You can say that again. The smell is overbearing. Is it working?*

Some of the wingless Valkyries are on our side, but we have a long way to go. Elan's voice is level and calm. I don't know how she is doing it.

The red dragon spits. *Valkyries are disgusting. They treat us appallingly. One of my children is held there, locked up like some kind of degenerate and used as weapons practice. I want her back.*

We're working on it, Ness, Eingana says. *It is a lengthy process. And Elan is working as fast as she can. Come, let's go and sort out this fight.* She maneuvers toward Ness and coaxes her away from our spot. Thankfully, Ness moves without too much encouragement, and they fly to the dragons below.

"That was close." I move out of the shelter of Elan's belly once I see them drop below the cliff face.

This can happen a lot if you're around here. We have to find a safe place for you.

Sobek spreads a wing, indicating a spot in the cliff face. *There is a small cave on the side of that mountain just there. It might be the best spot for you to seek shelter away from the sight of the other dragons when they fly over us.*

Good thinking, Brother! Let's go check it out. Elan stomps toward the cave and holds out her wings slightly so I can walk underneath them, hidden in case any dragons fly over. She peers at me under her wing, her face amused. *You're so tiny. I don't know why they would want to eat you for lunch. There's no fat on you.*

"Somehow, that doesn't make me feel any better." I grimace at her. A loud groan escapes my stomach.

What was that? She tilts her head to the side, giving me a strange look.

"That's my stomach. I'm starving. It's just reminding me that I haven't eaten anything since breakfast."

She ushers me into the cave, her large form barely fitting underneath. I take in the rocky formation. It's certainly not comfortable, but it is cozy. The pattering of water catches my attention, and I spot water running down the side of the rocks, welling in two different holes. Thankful to have it, I run forward, scoop up a handful of water, and drink it greedily.

Elan watches me with interest. It's in times like this that I remember that we haven't spent much time together. Each of us has peculiarities that the other is not familiar with. I finish drinking then remember my manners. "Would you like some?"

She shakes her head. *No, thank you. You stay here. I'll go out and see if I can find some food.*

Before I can answer, she takes off and leaves me alone in the cave. Despite its secrecy, I still feel insecure. I am in a strange place with no real protection against any of the dragons. A sword and a quiver of arrows are not the ideal defenses against dragons, not that I want to cause any of them harm. I still have to survive.

Time ticks by slowly, and I watch Sobek standing guard outside the cave until the monotonousness of it sends me to sleep. I am woken with a thud and tiny pebbles hitting my face. I pry my eyes open and am faced with a lifeless animal that Elan has thrown in front of my face. It's probably about half my size and much too big for me to eat alone.

I pull my sword out of its sheath and set to work, removing the skin from its flesh with the tip of the blade.

What are you doing? Elan stands over me, watching

my every move. *You're cutting off one of the best parts.*

"The skin?" I pause what I'm doing and look at her in disbelief.

Yeah, the skin is delicious. Or at least the fat underneath it.

"Well, it's way too tough for us to eat, so we use it to make essential things."

Like what?

"Saddles, clothes, and weapons bags." I pause and look at her. "Do you know where to get a lot of salt?"

Sure. There is a field not too far from here that is low and hot, where salt covers the ground. We call it the death field because not a single creature lives there.

"Are you able to bring me back a fair bit?"

What for?

"So I can preserve this skin. I'm going to need it."

She huffs. *All right, but you better not be turning me into an errand dragon.*

I chuckle. "No, I won't use you as a slave. I promise. But I can't go out and get it myself."

Okay. Elan exits the cave and pushes off into the sky.

While she is gone, I finish skinning the animal then throw the skin over a boulder at the back of the cave. I wash myself off in the second puddle and take another drink from the one with the fresh water running directly into it.

A clatter of rocks sounds near the entrance of the cave, and I turn just in time to see Elan with a disgusted look on her face as she charges inside. *Where do you want it?* Her eyes look panicked, and I wonder why until I look at her mouth and see it is crusted in salt. She is holding the salt in her mouth. Yuck—no wonder she looks uncomfortable. I hadn't thought of how she would carry it.

I point to the second puddle of water, and she runs to it, spits the salt into the water, then plunges her mouth into the liquid, opening and shutting it a few times. She pulls her nose out and spits. *That was disgusting!* She indicates the first puddle with the water running into it. *Is that fresh water?*

I nod.

She dashes to the puddle and plunges her nose deep into its contents, sucking in a big mouthful. *That's better.*

I chuckle and set to work slicing off a piece of meat about double the size of my hands off the rump of the animal. I slap the piece of meat on a rock in front of Elan.

That's not going to fill me. Elan looks at the piece of meat with disappointment.

"That's not for you. It's mine. I was going to ask you to cook it for me."

She looks at me strangely. *What do you mean by cook?*

"I need you to breathe your fire over it until it is grilled enough for me to eat."

Elan screws up her nose. *Yuck! That would make it disgusting. Why would you want to burn your meat?*

"It's just the way I like it."

She shrugs then does as I asked. The smell of burnt flesh reaches my nose, and my stomach growls louder. It's nicely charred. "Stop. That's perfect."

She screws up her nose, and I shove the rest of the animal toward Elan. "The rest is yours."

Her face lights up, and she finishes the whole carcass before I finish my chunk of meat.

I wash my hands in the salty water then throw the skin into it, swishing it around a few times.

Wings flap outside the cave, and I spin around with my eyes wide.

Don't worry. It's just Sobek. He's going hunting for his meal now that I'm back to protect you.

I notice that the sun is dropping below the horizon, and darkness is engulfing its light. Elan moves farther into the cave and curls into a ball. I nestle against her body, pressing my back into her side and absorbing its heat. It's a strange, comforting feeling to be curled up with a dragon and having the heat from her body keeping away the cold of the night in the wilderness. Only a few months ago, I never would have thought it was possible that a vicious creature could turn out to be so loving and caring. Tomorrow is another day, providing I can get through the night without being eaten by a wild dragon.

I drift off to sleep only to be woken by a thump at the entrance of the cave.

CHAPTER FIVE

My eyes shoot open, pulling me rapidly from my sleep. I hope that the thump was just Sobek returning from his hunt. Quietly, I roll up to my feet then tiptoe to the edge of Elan's enormous body to peer around her at the entrance of the cave. My face is hit with an icy-cold breeze from the wastelands, pulling me further from my sleep. I can't see anything at the entrance, so I move closer to get a broader view. Despite the chilliness and potential danger, my curiosity gets the better of me.

As I peer out of the cave, I don't find any sign of movement. Sobek and Elan's sister lie together, asleep under the moonlight. Tiptoeing past them, I head to the edge of the cliff.

Another thump sounds behind me, and I spin around, my eyes wide. I can't see any movement. I know I am exposed, so I dart toward Sobek to take cover only to stop when his tail lifts then thwacks to the ground. Now it makes sense. He must be having a restless dream.

I release the pent-up breath and head back to the cliff edge to peer down at the dragons in the valley below. Most of the dragons are curled under the moonlight, though some still wander around. There doesn't appear to be as many dragons in the valley as there were earlier today. I squat and study them, taking in all the different colors and how they group among their own breeds.

A rock clatters behind me, and I twist around, startled. Charging toward me from several feet away is Sobek. A strange look is plastered on his face, and it sends shivers down my spine—I hope he's not charging at me to eat me when no one is looking. Perhaps he didn't catch anything to eat earlier and is still hungry. I want to run, but there is nowhere to run where he cannot get to me. Instead, I pull all my courage together and remind myself that he has sworn to protect me because of what I've done for Elan.

His great form halts extremely close to me, and something blocks the light of moon falling onto my body. I glance up to see that his wing is towering over the top of me.

What are you doing? Are you trying to get yourself killed? Dragons who can see in the dark are flying above.

Walking around like this is a quick way to become dragon dinner.

I move forward a couple of steps and peer past the edge of his wing. A shadow of a dragon passes in front of the moon.

They are searching for prey naive enough to be sleeping out in the open. Many animals come out at nighttime, when it is not so hot. You're so lucky you haven't been spotted. Sobek's voice booms in my head. He tucks his head underneath his wing and stares at me. The moonlight casts harsh shadows over his eyes, making them seem more intimidating.

I gulp. "Thank you. I didn't realize. The only dragons I've had anything to do with have been Elan and the ones captured in the stalls. It's impossible to learn their habits and skills when they are unable to leave the stalls to search for their prey."

He continues hovering over me with his wing spread, sheltering me like a big mother hen warming her chicks.

I gaze back over the edge of the cliff, observing the dragons in the moonlight. "There seem to be a lot of dragons here. Are there more colonies than this? If there are, then your population must be increasing."

The population is increasing, but unfortunately not fast enough, and it's only because of the alliance we have made with the Valkyries. It would increase quicker if we didn't have to hand over one youngling every year. We could breed a lot faster if we had them here and the war between the Valkyries and dragons remained finished. He peers over the edge and sighs loudly. *But at the moment, it is causing much unrest because we have to hand over these young, knowing that they are subject to the Valkyries and their unforgiving mercy. The only thing that keeps these dragons handing over their young is because the Valkyries would attack us again if we stopped this alliance.*

I search around the top of the mountain, and I see his sister still sleeping. "Where's Eingana gone?"

Mother has gone back to the academy and to the palace to spy on Odin and the other Valkyries. She needs to see what the result is from the disturbance of your freeing Elan. And to see what the outcome will be for your friends who returned with the dragon they took. Hopefully, she will be back soon. His feet shuffle a little, as though he is moving into a more comfortable position. *After she sees what's going on, she will negotiate with Odin over the new rules that he wants to enforce on the alliance.*

He shakes his body and continues standing over me. I move in closer, leaning against his scales and soaking up their warmth. Something on the ground glistens in the moonlight, and I look down, spotting several golden scales glowing dully.

I stoop down and pick one up. It is about the size of my hand. I tap on it, my nails clinking softly against the hard surface. I poke the underside, noticing that the hard surface is not budging under my pressure. Grabbing a rock, I slam it against the scale. It doesn't give. It remains as robust as it was a few moments before. I turn to Sobek and tap against his scales with the point of the rock.

He peers down at me with curiosity in his eyes. *What are you doing?*

"I'm just checking out your scales," I say as though it is an ordinary thing to do.

Ah, why?

"Because they appear to be so hard, and I notice that there are a lot of scales of your siblings lying over the ground. Is it normal for a dragon to lose scales like this?"

Like any reptile, we shed our skin now and then. The only difference is that dragons shed a scale or two at any time, not the whole surface, like reptiles. The scales get pushed out when another one pushes through—kind of like losing teeth. That way, we only have a tiny hole exposed at any time, hindering too much damage when attacked, provided we are not hit in the vital spots.

"What can your scales withstand?"

I don't think I should tell you that. If I tell you, then you may use that information against us.

I tilt my head to the side and give him a weird look. "Do you really think I'm going to use anything against you and the dragons?"

He stands in silence.

I continue, "The only time I would use it against

them is if they attacked me and I needed to defend myself. I think you guys are to be revered. I have so much respect for your kind, and I would love to see us work together, not kill each other."

He stares at me for a moment, as though trying to process the information. He nods slightly, yet his eyes don't leave me. He looks to be observing and processing information. *Very well. There is very little that our scales will not withstand. They withstand fire on the outside and trap heat when exposed to extreme cold. If we need to release some of that internal heat, we can open our scales to allow the heat to escape.*

"Do mean like how we have goose bumps?"

What are goose bumps?

"Goose bumps are when we get little bumps on our skin, and the hairs stand on end, trapping all the heat within the hairs so it holds some of our warmth."

He looks thoughtful for a moment. *I guess it is kind of like that, only opposite because we are letting the air out.*

"Clever."

It is also nearly impossible for a spear to penetrate our scales unless they manage to pierce a place that is shedding or underneath a scale and straight into the soft skin.

I pick up a scale, feel its texture, and turn it to look at the underside, feeling it there too. I notice that there is a floppy part, not as tough as the top side of the scale. This is near the connection where it would mold onto the skin.

"What about this bit?" I ask.

That is the part I am talking about. It is a little softer so it can connect.

"So this would be a perfect spot for me to sew it onto something."

He frowns. *Why would you want to do that?*

"I need protection when I am on Elan's back. Perhaps I can make something out of this, like a jacket. That way, I should be warm when we are traveling at a high altitude, and it will also act as a shield."

Then you would have the toughest jacket that anyone has ever made.

CHAPTER SIX

I gather several scales into my arms, carry them back to the cave, and toss them into a corner before cuddling back into Elan. My mind runs wild with all the things I could make with the scales. A chill runs down my spine, and I press my back against Elan, taking in her warmth, and fall asleep.

The next day, when the sun is high, it glistens off the rocks and shines straight into the cave. I force my eyes open. Elan is not lying next to me. I roll over and crawl to my feet, searching for any sign of her. A large figure stomps my way. I've found her, and she doesn't look happy.

Are you trying to get yourself killed? What are you thinking, wandering off in the middle of the night out into the open in the middle of the dragon wilderness? Her wings spread wide in frustration.

"I'm sorry. I didn't realize."

You do know that dragons have excellent hearing, don't you? You need to keep your voice down, she says through gritted teeth. She grabs something from the entrance of the cave and throws it inside. An animal carcass falls at my feet. *Here, I got you some breakfast.*

The carcass is bigger than me, and my eyes widen in delight over the size of the hide. "Thank you, Elan. It's perfect in every way."

She gives me a strange look. *Okay. Whatever you say. It's just an animal. You need to share, though.*

I gaze back at the carcass and chuckle. "Do you expect me to be able to eat all of that?"

Her shoulders rise in what looks like a shrug. *You never know. You could work up a big appetite because of all the trouble you get into.*

I grab my sword and get to work skinning the carcass, making sure I don't nick the hide. Once I finish the lengthy ordeal, I throw it into the salty solution with the other one then wash the blood off my hands and arms. I cut off a hunk of meat and place it on a flat rock in front of Elan. "Can you please cook it for me?"

She gives me a strange look. *I don't know why you insist on burning it. Just eat it raw—it tastes better that way.*

"I prefer my meat dead and without blood, thank you."

Okay. Whatever you say. She breathes fire over the piece, filling the cave with the heat until the meat turns a nice dark brown. I wash my sword in the salty solution and cut the meat into bite-size pieces.

"You know, dragon-cooked meat is quite nice. It's surprising, really." I sit at the entrance of the cave, gazing out into the sunlight as I eat.

What else did you expect? Did you think it would taste like meat breath or something? Elan says sarcastically.

"Yeah. Meat breath means bad breath, so that would mean bad tasting meat."

Elan rolls her eyes, and I chuckle.

I spot her eyeing what remains of the carcass. "Help yourself to the rest."

Her eyes light up, and she wanders over and swallows it after a few chomps.

As we eat, I stare across the wilderness, observing Bifrost crossing the sky in a beautiful aurora of lights shining like rainbow beams from the sun. The colors break and gather then straighten again.

"There must be another reaping happening," I say, watching as it repeats this sequence. I'm tempted to jump on Elan's back and ask her to charge for Heimdall's Tower, but there is no point trying, especially right now. I would only be sent back to Asgard or imprisoned. Even so, I can't help wondering about Harut, the unusual angel of death I met briefly on Midgard, and whether he would be there, fighting the winged Valkyries for the souls of the dying warriors so he could take them to the underworld. Our brief encounter had been a strange one, and the angels of death should be my enemy. Instead, he had shown support for my cause because I was different from the other Valkyries he had met.

I push him from my mind and focus on life in front of me. "Is your mother back?" I ask, not seeing her among the siblings.

I haven't seen her. She must be checking everything out and discovering all the information she can.

A large cloud of worry crowds my mind. "You don't think she would have been caught, do you?"

Elan casts me a disbelieving look. *Um, seriously? Have you met my mother? Like she's going to let herself get caught. It's not like she's going to lie there and forget to make herself invisible and get caught, like someone else I know.* She rolls her eyes and shakes her head, and I know these gestures are aimed at herself. *Especially with the warning you've given her.*

"Well, you never know. Someone else was silly enough to do it." I lay a hand on her front leg, and she puffs out a stream of smoke. Her eyes dart my way, and I flinch from the sharpness. "You know I'm kidding, right? It wasn't your fault that you got kidnapped. Odin didn't give us any warning."

Yeah. I know. But it doesn't make it any less embarrassing. That's twice you've saved my life now.

"I'm sure you'd do the same for me." I say, shoving another lump of meat in my mouth. The Bifrost splits then straightens again, undoubtedly with another group of Valkyries taking off to Midgard.

I let out a deep sigh before swallowing the lump of meat. *How do I get myself out of this predicament?*

A FEW DAYS PASS, and there is still no sign of Eingana. A deep churning knot worries my stomach. I hope she's okay. I know she's a big, bad dragon and all, but Odin is tricky.

To fill the time and occupy my mind, I set to work on the hides of the animals that Elan has been bringing me. At least twice a day, she supplies me with another animal—each one, I skin then soak their hides in the salty solution. If I stay out here any longer, I will have enough hides to make the things I need. I finish the tanning process, following the steps I learned at the Valkyrie academy.

We are responsible for making and fixing our own leather uniforms and other protection for our skin. Alongside this, we learned how to make more quivers for when others become worn out. I found that kind of work relaxing, a welcome break from all the bickering with the winged Valkyries and menial tasks set for the wingless Valkyries. I lack the tools that were available to us at the academy, but I will improvise. My sword proves useful for cutting the material, and I source a sharp, pointed rock to jab holes into the leather so I can thread the pieces together. Thankfully, Elan hasn't been tearing the hide too much with her teeth. They would be ruined if she had been biting them across the middle.

First, I cut the leather into long, thin pieces and plait them to make them stronger and thicker. The first thing I need to make is a bridle. Each time Elan enters the cave, I measure and fashion the ties around her head, shoulders, and waist. When complete, I set to work on the medium pieces of leather, fashioning a saddle.

Each day Elan brings me more hides, I am thankful. It will take a lot to fashion a sturdy saddle and enough straps to reach around her large waist.

When I'm satisfied with my progress on the saddle, I set to work making myself a leather cape. I cut and measure the sleeve to reach to my wrists and fall slightly over my hands. I make sure the leather of the cloak falls to my ankles, and I fashion a hood to pull over my head. I am determined to keep out the cold from the altitudes. Then I sew the golden scales from the hem of the cloak to the edge of the hood and sleeves. There is a large collection of scales available circling the emperor dragons' precipice—I have plenty. As I sew, I smile to myself. In this cloak, I will blend in with Elan when I am riding on her back. Once finished, I try it on and stroll in front of Elan.

Well, look at you. You almost look like a miniature dragon but without the nasty teeth and fire.

Pride fills my chest, and I can't help but parade in front of her a few more times.

I don't know if she picks up on my pride or if she means it: *What you've made is completely awesome.*

"Do you think that it will hold against a sword?" I spread it out wide, looking it over as I pose in front of Elan.

I don't know. Let's see.

I take the jacket off and hang it over a rock, spreading it out with the scales facing out. Pulling my sword from its sheath, I swing it directly at the scaled area. A loud clatter sounds, and the sword bounces away, letting the full force hit my sword. I drop the sword when the vibrations rattle up my arm. I dash to the cloak and have a look at the scales that I hit. Not one of them is dented.

"Look at that, Elan!" I can't contain my excitement. "This may even be stronger than a shield. What's even better, it protects more of my body."

And that is worth its gold! It even looks like me.

I weave my arm back through the sleeves of the cloak right as a heavy thump sounds outside.

I glance out into the sunlight and see a brilliant-red dragon standing not far from the entrance of the cave.

I still smell Valkyrie blood. This cannot be from Elan several days ago. Ness lifts her nose to the air and breathes in deeply. *In fact, the Valkyrie blood reeks stronger than before. Where is she?*

CHAPTER SEVEN

The red eyes scan the area and stare straight into the cave. *I can smell her. Let her out! Let me get to her! I'll rip off her limbs one at a time.*

Sobek moves discreetly into the space between Ness and the cave. *Isn't that a bit drastic?*

After what they've done to our younglings, that's what they deserve. They have enslaved my youngling for over a year, and she is treated terribly.

I'm sorry to hear that. Despite the threat, Sobek sounds sympathetic. Still, he does not move from standing between us.

I tuck myself behind a rock and pull my scale cloak over me. A crack between two rocks leaves just enough space to peer through and see what is going on.

The red dragon prances in front of the cave, her long red tail whipping behind her. *Where is she?*

Her footsteps become more impatient, and she stomps back and forth in front of the entrance, her nose twitching as she sniffs the air. *The Valkyrie reek is strong. Let her out. I need to get my claws on her.*

Elan casts me a glance, noticing that I'm squatting under cover of the scales and rocks. She strolls out of the cave and chuckles. *Oh, Ness. I don't know what you're talking about. It's just me.* She pauses at the entrance, blocking it from the red dragon with Sobek. *I know I've been hanging around the Valkyries way too much. Here, I can prove it.* She moves closer and tilts her wing, shoving the spot where she had been cradling me earlier in Ness's face.

The red dragon gives her a strange look.

Here, smell this. It reeks, doesn't it?

Ness screws up her nose.

See? It's just me. I've been spending way too much time in the Valkyrie area, trying to sort out this alliance and stop what is happening to the younglings. I'm so sorry to hear about your daughter. She shoves her wing in the red dragon's face some more. *But this smell is just me. It happens every time I go. I've just come back again, and I been sitting inside that cave, which makes it impossible for the fresh air to push away the smell of the Valkyries.*

The red dragon's nose screws up tighter. She pulls her snout away from Elan's underwing and snorts a puff of smoke followed by a blast of fire as she sneezes. *That's an awful stench. Have a bath, for dragon breath's sake!*

Or do you love the smell of Valkyries so much that you can't stand to wash it off? She exposes her teeth in a sneer.

What? Do you think I bathe myself in Valkyrie smell? I'd rather roll in dragon manure—and I have tried to wash it off. It doesn't go away. The oils from their skin stick to me.

Even though Elan sounds convincing, Ness's suspicions don't leave her face. *You're just a Valkyrie lover. You and your family worship the ground they stand on.*

Elan sits upright, looking put out. *I beg your pardon? I'm not a Valkyrie lover. Even so, certain Valkyries aren't as bad. I've met a few. They are the ones without the wings. They don't fight against us to hurt our dragons.*

Liar! Ness sneers. *You're just a liar. You have been smooching up to these Valkyries and looking after your own family. You don't have to hand over any of your younglings. That's not fair!*

Elan puffs up her chest and pulls her shoulders back. *Do you realize who you're talking to? You should be showing me respect. I am second in charge of all these dragons, and you should be bowing down to me and doing as I say.*

Ness sneers, and she prances in front of Elan and Sobek. *Right! That's not going to happen. Just because you are born with golden blood does not make you a leader. You have to earn your right by fighting for it.* She spins on a heel, her eyes challenging. *If you think you're so high and mighty, then fight me to prove it.*

Sobek stands tall, his massive frame towering over both the female dragons. *Hang on. Those aren't the rules.*

Elan is second in charge and the one to be obeyed when Mother is away. You can't fight her. You have to do as you're told.

Make me! Ness pulls back her top lip, revealing her pointy teeth.

Sobek moves toward her, and she lashes out, striking him across the face with her claws. Crimson blood runs from his face and tarnishes his golden scales. She had run her talons through the underside of his scales. *There. That proves it. You bleed just like the rest of us. There is nothing special about you or your blood.*

Elan rises from her haunches and stands defiantly. *You will not treat my family this way.* Anger radiates from her every scale, showing off her impersonation of her mother, which I have witnessed a few times now. Each time is just as intimidating as the last. During moments like these, I can see why Elan is the next in line to rule the dragons. She may be born of the blood, but she has every bit a leader lying deep within her despite her talkative and friendly nature.

I don't want her to fight. I don't want her to get hurt. I don't want any of them to get hurt, but there is nothing that I can do right now to stop the inevitable. I feel like a coward hunkered down behind boulders, peering out between the cracks and remaining cloaked inside my scaled gown. *Please don't let this happen,* I say to myself over and over, wishing it to go away. But as I do, Elan lashes forward and scratches Ness the same way that the red dragon had scratched Sobek.

Ness throws her head forward, letting out a deep growl accompanied by a large plume of fire aiming straight for Elan. Elan turns and shelters herself with her scales while spreading her wings high, spinning around until she hooks Ness, slashing her face with the claws on the edge of her wings.

Ness pulls her head back, and Elan takes the opportunity, tilting her head down and charging at the red dragon with her horns pointing forward. Ness darts to the side and lashes out with her claws as Elan runs past. The talons fail to dig past the scales, leaving Elan unscathed.

Elan spins around with bared teeth and charges for Ness's wing. The red dragon darts to the side, using her wings as leverage, and Elan's teeth connect near her shoulder.

Elan bites down, clasping and piercing the membrane of the wing. She shakes her head and rips holes into the upper wing as well as gashes in the shoulder of the other dragon.

Ness bellows, and it echoes down the valley and across the wastelands. I can't see the dragons down there, but I can imagine every head turning toward the cliff face. It's not the kind of attention I want up here.

Ness's teeth remain exposed, and she lashes her head

around and sinks them into the side of Elan's neck. The sharp, pointy tips of Elan's scales shoot into Ness's mouth and pierce the inside of her mouth. It doesn't stop her from clamping her teeth down deeper into Elan's side.

The combined blood of two dragons pours down and splashes onto the ground, leaving crimson puddles. I want to call out and tell them to stop, but that would just put Elan in more danger because it would prove her a liar and show that she is sheltering a Valkyrie. I don't want any more harm to come to any dragons. I want peace in the land, not a dragon fight.

Elan twists her body and scratches her claws into Ness's underbelly. At the same time, she swings her tail around and hits the red dragon on the head, knocking it enough to make her let go. Ness bellows in agony, unclamping her jaws at the same time, setting Elan's neck free.

Oh, Vanir! I am so worried. What happens if Elan loses? My mind ticks over all the possibilities.

Sobek moves to step in, and Elan screams, *Don't you dare! This is my fight!* The brother halts and watches, his face contorted with anguish that deepens as Ness pounces and digs her teeth deep into Elan's neck.

CHAPTER EIGHT

The ground rumbles, and a menacing roar thunders through the cave and down the valley, more profound than either dragon has managed to expel thus far.

I cringe, hoping it's not a dragon from the valley, an older dragon who knows how to fight better than the dragons in front of me. The urge is strong to dart around and see who it is, but I can't afford to expose myself. These dragons scare me at the best of times, and the last thing I need is to be a small meat sandwich between ten or more dragons several sizes bigger than me.

The two fighting dragons halt then stagger to stand straight. They pull their eyes from each other as they search for the invading dragon.

The ground bumps and rattles as a big dragon

stomps its way toward the two fighters. *What is the meaning of this?*

I breathe a sigh of relief. It's Eingana, the leader of the dragons—she has finally returned. A sense of safety fills me as she stomps toward the two dragons, her teeth showing in a full nasty growl.

Sobek approaches her. *Ness flew down and demanded to know where the Valkyrie smell was coming from.* His voice is humble and hesitant, and his eyes flick toward the cave. *Elan proved that the scent is from her because the stench has clung to her scales from spending so much time with the Valkyries.*

He glances at the dragons one by one, finishing with Ness, then he continues. *Ness did not believe her, despite the awful stench clinging to Elan's body. Elan even shoved her underwing in Ness's face.*

His mouth tilts up slightly into a quirky smile for a moment, but it quickly disappears. Eingana watches him intently, and I am sure that she noticed.

Sobek continues, *Ness did not believe Elan and challenged her position as second in charge of the dragons in the area. Elan did not strike first, Ness did.* He indicates the gash on the side of his face. *This is proof.* He raises his chin high. *It is after this that Elan jumped in to prove her honor, as you were absent, Mother.*

Eingana stares at the red dragon, back to Elan, then back to the challenger. *Ness, is this true?*

Ness stares at the ground and doesn't answer.

I take this as a yes. I hear that you have a substantial nest. You have five eggs about to be hatched.

A look of dread crosses Ness's face, and her eyes flick up to Eingana, the redness in them spreading to her whites. It is like the spread of a contagious disease taking over her.

Because of your actions, you will be handing over your firstborn from the hatch. You will have to give from your babies to take another red dragon's place this year.

She appears to be in shock. *No. Please, no. I sacrificed one of my babies only last year. They have been mistreating my baby. There must be another dragon ready to give away one of their babies.*

You have no one but yourself to blame for this. Eingana pulls her shoulders back, and her voice remains strong. *You have not obeyed our rules, and this is your punishment. I have the final decision over any of the other tribes if a particular dragon disobeys my ruling, and this you have done. The decision is final.*

No. Please, no! Ness falls to her knees and begs.

Let this be your lesson. Eingana turns her back to the red dragon. *Now leave.*

The terrified look does not leave Ness's face even as she bends her knees and pushes off into the sky. Her flight is lopsided from the injury caused to her wing. The damage was not so significant that she can't fly, but it stops the wing catching the air completely. Although it will heal in time, she will never be a fully functioning dragon again. Ness has learned the hard way. Even though it is my blood she was after, I still feel pity for her because I understand her plight.

Sobek runs up to Elan. *Are you all right?*

Eingana stomps up, observing Elan's injuries. *She shall live. She'll be sore for a bit, but she will heal. It is part of being the leader of the dragons.*

I don't hear much sympathy in her voice, but I guess that is what she has become, a tough leader in any circumstance, cutting away the emotion of what happens to make level decisions. *Is the Valkyrie okay?*

Elan and Sobek both nod. *Yes,* Elan says. *She hides in the cave.* She tilts her head toward the cave, and Eingana turns around to look inside.

I don't see her.

She is hiding, and she's hiding in an extraordinary way. A quirky pride fills Elan's voice. *You can come out now, Kara. Show Mother what you've made.*

Leaving my hood over my head, I emerge in my scale cape. Eingana tilts her head to the side as she watches me step out into the sun. The golden scales on my cape glitter in the sunlight.

Interesting. What is it? she asks.

"It's a cape. It has a leather lining that will protect me from the cold when I'm on Elan's back and when she takes me into the clouds. That altitude makes it chilly for me." I open the cape to show off the inner leather lining then close it to show off the neatly attached scales.

"It is also a shield. I won't have to carry that big bulky thing I used back at the academy when I need protection in a fight or if they ever let me help protect them during the reaping. I can just keep this with me. As you know, your scales are tough, and it is hard for anything to penetrate their protection."

Ingenious. Eingana nods in approval.

Silence hangs in the air, and I wait for her to say something, but she doesn't. My impatience grows. "Is there any news? Has anything changed at the academy? Are my friends okay? We were so worried about you. You took so long that we had thought you had been captured or something."

She snorts out some smoke. *That's not going to happen!*

"You know Odin can be quite persuasive and aggressive."

He will achieve nothing if he tries to harm me. He may be a god, but that doesn't stop me making him my lunch. Eingana lifts her chin.

So what happened, Mother? Elan's brow creases. *Did you manage to fix anything?*

A look of pride passes across her face, and she nods. *As a matter of fact, I did.* The mother glances at me. *Kara's friends were impounded under Odin's Palace. He did not forgive them despite their innocence and the fact that they were only taking the dragon for a quick ride before bringing him back. It took me several days, but I managed to track down Loki and demand an audience with Odin.* She frowns. *I wouldn't be surprised if Loki has been up to mischief. Over the last few years, he has been using his shapeshifting forms too many times. But for once, I demanded he use it for good and change into a dragon to help communicate with Odin. It was a meeting that Odin couldn't understand.*

Her mouth works up at the sides. *Loki has some interesting facts and theories. He has an amazing mind with what he thinks about and plans. He is a schemer, that's for sure. We will have to watch him.* She paces in front of me. *After a long talk with Loki, he transformed into god form to talk to Odin then back into dragon form so Odin would think that Loki's dragon form was the only way he could understand us. Through this discussion, I managed to get Kara's friends released. It was part of the bargaining. I don't think they have been received back into the academy very well yet, but that will come with time. Your friends are tough, especially the redheaded one, Hildr.*

"Oh, yes. She is." I nod.

What about the dragon alliance, Mother? Elan asks. *Did you manage to sort Odin out and put him in his place over demanding one of ours?*

It took some threatening, but yes, I did manage to get this sorted. He cannot have one of ours. We are still low in numbers. He is not happy about it, and I do not trust him, but he has no right to an emperor dragon. Unfortunately, the alliance remains the same. We must still give up one dragon of each breed every year.

What about Kara? Sobek asks. He had been standing so still that I had almost forgotten he was with us. *Can she go back yet? She won't be safe here. It's too hard to protect her in this little area. The dragons are way too wild to accept her being here. Being a Valkyrie is an extra reason for them to eat her for lunch.*

Eingana stares at me for a long moment. Something is lingering in her eyes that I am unable to decipher. She looks at Sobek. *The discussion of Kara was brought up, yes. I have proven that she was only doing what was right by sticking to the alliance. I mentioned that Elan's capture by Odin would have made me angry, and Kara was releasing Elan so that my wrath would not be brought down on the Valkyries or Asgard. Odin knows he is in the wrong, but he doesn't want to accept that Kara was right. He has agreed to let Kara come back.* Her eyes drop to the ground, and she looks troubled.

What is it, Mother? Elan spreads her wing, touching her mother's back.

She releases an agitated sigh. *I cannot guarantee Kara's safety or that she won't feel Odin's wrath if she returns to the academy. I'm afraid, not only because she is wingless but also because she is allied with the dragons, that it will cause her much grief among the Valkyries of the academy.* She turns to look at me. *It is up to you, Kara, if you want to risk it.*

I glance at Elan, Eingana, and then back at Elan before gazing at Sobek. They have done much for me in the last few days. The blood pouring off of Elan's wings catches my attention. I meet Eingana's eyes. "Is there anything here to help Elan heal better? I can only imagine those dragon bites will become infected over time if not treated properly."

Eingana shakes her head. *We do not have healers. We have to let our bodies heal on their own. That is part of living in the wilderness.*

"Then the decision is made for me. I must take Elan back and take her to the healer to get some proper treatment."

But what about your safety, Kara? Elan's scales wrinkle between her horns. *I can't go into the academy and protect you.*

"I know. I'm willing to take that risk. I will have my weapons with me at all times, and I will hang out with my two friends. I know that they will look out for me too." I look up into her golden-brown eyes and see worry flooding through them. I stand in front of her and stroke her snout. "Don't worry, my friend. For you, it's worth it."

CHAPTER NINE

I dash into the cave and pull out the completed saddle. It took me hours to complete, but I had plenty of time while I was waiting in the dragon wastelands. I thread the leather around Elan's front legs, loop it around her torso, and pull it tight before adding the strap for around her neck.

I stop, though. "I think I will leave your neck free for the moment. It needs time to heal. I don't want the straps digging into your injuries. The straps around your front legs and torso should hold the saddle steady enough for now."

Elan is a fantastic guinea pig. She stands still, letting me thread the straps around her body without showing any signs of a dragon's arrogance. It's hard to believe that she challenged another dragon not that long ago.

The only telltale sign is her silence and lack of chattiness. She is more sedate while holding the responsibility for my safety within her talons. She watches me as I work, peering over her shoulder and wincing every time the lead squashes one of her wounds.

When I finish securing the saddle, I stand in front of her and hold her snout gently in my hands. Her eyes look tired, and her shoulders sag. "Are you going to have enough strength to fly back?"

She yawns, and her hot breath surrounds me. *I'll be fine. I've just lost a little bit of blood. But don't worry—dragons are tough. It's not that big of a flight anyway.*

I study her a bit more. "If you say so. But I want you to stop anytime you are struggling." I climb up to the saddle, hook my feet in the stirrups, then pull the reins tight. "Do you promise to do that? I don't want you passing out on me or anything. The last thing I need is to crash to the ground because my dragon has passed out."

Oh, thanks for your concern. It just reeks from your voice. She chuckles, glancing over her shoulder.

"You know I mean it." I give her a stern look.

She chuckles harder. *Ow! That hurts.* She stops chuckling. *Of course I know you mean it. I was just messing with you.*

Sobek shakes his head at her. *That's Elan—always joking around. You would never know that she is next in line to be in charge of the dragons.*

And a good leader she shall be after much education… if she keeps her mouth shut, Eingana says, and I almost think I see a glint of mischief in her eyes.

I tap Elan's back. "Did your mom just joke?"

Oh, under there somewhere, she has a sense of humor, Elan says lightheartedly. *Occasionally, it comes through.*

"Where is your sister?" I ask.

She has gone down to the dragons to make sure there are no more disruptions over what has happened here, Eingana says. *She must also train to become the leader in case something happens to Elan, for she is the next in line.* She raises her chin proudly, and her voice returns to the usual seriousness that I know.

"Say goodbye to her for me." I pull tightly on the reins and check the stability of the saddle.

Eingana nods once.

I wrap the cloak around me to maintain the perfect temperature under the scorching sun. It surprises me how it is blocking out the intense heat yet still traps the correct amount of warm air within. With my feet tucked securely in the footholds, I lightly click my feet against Elan's sides.

I do a last check on the reins again and move my backside around in the saddle. The molded leather is comfortable. "Right. I think we're good to go, Elan."

She jumps to her feet, and I hang on tight. The leather rubs against my hands, but it is nothing in comparison to the pointy ends of the scales that were my only security before.

Right, let's do it, Elan says, uncoiling her wings and pushing off into the sky, heading in the opposite direction of the valley filled with dragons. Her strokes are labored until we rise above the clouds.

The flight home isn't long, but it seems to drag. I don't know what I'm going to face when I get there. I don't know if they're going to send me to Odin to be imprisoned. The fact that Odin won't guarantee my safety proves that he will not help or stand up for me. But thinking it over, I know it's asking too much to expect a god to admit that he was wrong. It would be a massive blow to his pride if the god of wisdom were to be publicly proven incorrect. I have no sympathy for him.

Elan flies higher, and the icy winds push up against my face, numbing my skin, yet my arms and body are warm. Despite my worries, I am elated that the cloak is working against the icy chill.

Elan descends below the cloud cover, and her body disappears from underneath me, leaving me sitting in the air on a saddle, holding the reins as I float closer to the ground.

When I spot the academy in the distance, my stomach churns wildly inside of me. Physically, my ride home was easy, but emotionally, not so much.

Elan lands firmly, and she stomps forward a few steps before halting. I dip as I feel her front legs bend so she's lower to the ground, allowing me to slide off. I swing my feet over her neck and slide to the earth below.

"Can you turn visible for a moment? It will be easier to get the saddle off you without aggravating your wounds."

Her golden scales form in front of me as she turns visible, and I unhook the saddle and tuck it under my arm. I stroke her side. "Wait here. I'm going to find the healer to get you some ointment."

Elan nods then turns invisible before I run inside with my saddle. I dash to my room.

Hildr sits on her bed. Her face is pale and filled with uneasiness, and her hair is exceptionally spikey, as though she has been rubbing it enough that it stands completely on end. Eir sits not far from her. Her usually peaceful face is also worried. I remove my golden cloak and throw it on my bed with the saddle. I'm surprised they haven't seen me yet.

"Who died?"

Both of them spring up to look at me. Eir squeals with excitement, and Hildr embraces me into a rough hug, her sword hilt hitting me in the process. "You're whole," Hildr whispers in my ear.

I reach down and move her sword to the side then

return the hug. “What’s going on here? Have you gone soft on me all of a sudden?” I laugh and pull myself away.

Hildr’s eyes look at me in disapproval. “When do I go soft? I can’t help it if I get upset because you’ve disappeared. I thought you might have been eaten by a dragon, for goodness sake.”

“Nearly. Elan did protect me. Which reminds me, I have to go and get some ointment off Anita.” I turn to leave the room.

“We’re coming, of course.” Eir charges after me, followed by Hildr.

“I didn’t expect anything else,” I call back to them. “On the way there, you can tell me everything that has gone on since I’ve been gone.”

“Oh.” Eir sounds stressed. “Mistress Sigrun really has it in for you.”

I roll my eyes and shake my head. “Oh, please. When doesn’t she have it in for me?”

“She’s pretty peeved,” Hildr agrees.

“Like that’s something new! I’ll deal with her in a bit.”

We reach the healer’s room, and it takes no time for us to convince the academy’s healer, Anita, to give us some ointment. As we leave, she calls, “Kara, be careful! Mistress Sigrun is pretty peeved off.”

“Not you too,” I say. “Don’t worry. I’ll deal with her soon.”

We run out to Elan, and I smother her wounds in the salve then kiss her on the nose.

The moment I set foot inside the academy walls, I hear the screech of mistress's voice, "Valkyrie! My office, this instant!"

CHAPTER TEN

I stop and look at my friends. "I'll see you guys later, okay? Only I can deal with this one."

"Good luck," Hildr says.

I follow the stomping mistress down the corridors and into her office. Medals and trophies line every wall, accompanied by statues of winged Valkyries—it's almost like a shrine for them. Candles burn in little circles in front of the figurines. I roll my eyes and enter the room, closing the door behind me. "Yes, Mistress." I use the most bored voice I can muster.

Mistress Sigrun yanks her tan leather jacket closed over her white T-shirt then dusts off her medium-blue-leather pants. She is wearing the winged Valkyrie uniform, causing me to think that she must have just finished leading one of their training sessions. Her stunning pale face is set in a frown, as it so often is when she looks at the wingless Valkyries. She lifts her chin and shakes her head, tossing her perfect golden locks over her shoulder. Her majestic white wings pull in close to her body before she plunks her bottom down in the chair and glares at me from across her stone desktop. "You have caused too much mischief in the academy."

"That's what you keep telling me, Mistress." I study my fingernails, noticing the dirt underneath them.

"You have stolen something from under Odin's nose, and he is peeved." Her tone rises as she observes my actions.

I pick out some of the dirt and let it fall to the floor. "Actually Mistress, I didn't steal the dragon. Odin stole her, and I rescued her." I sit back in the chair and cross my legs. "And Odin knows this." I know I am being much more defiant than normal. I can't help it. It is hard to respect someone who rules with discrimination.

"Young Valkyrie, you will be respectful with me and when you are discussing a god. Your lack of respect for authority is appalling."

"No, Mistress. I don't lack respect for authority. I lack respect for stupidity." I know I've done it this time, but they have taken it too far.

"Is that right? You're calling Odin and me stupid?" She stares at me, waiting for an answer that doesn't come. "That's it. You're on cleaning duty."

"Oh, the change." I roll my eyes. "What is it this time? Dragon cell cleaning again?"

"No." She rises to her feet and stomps around the other side the table, towering aggressively over me. "It's worse. You're on toilet cleaning duty."

My shoulders sag. She's right—it is worse. I would much rather clean up after dragons than clean up after Valkyries. "Really, Mistress? Can't it be dragon stalls again?"

"You deserve the worst punishment." She shoves a key across the desktop then turns and dusts off a statue. "You will find the cleaning cupboard just down the hall. Go! You are to start now."

"But Mistress, I have only just come back from an extremely tiring ordeal. Can't it wait till tomorrow?"

"No. It can't. You have a lot of work to do to make up for your stupidity and defiance."

I exhale loudly, grab the key, and turn to leave. "Whatever!"

I trudge down the hallway and find the cupboard and all the bathroom cleaning equipment. I collect the cleaning items labeled "bathrooms" and close the door. Searing pain shoots through my shoulder, so strongly that I almost drop the equipment. I pull back my sleeve. The pain is in precisely the same spot as the scar that the creature gave me a couple of years ago. I haven't seen the creature in days. Surely, it can't be lurking around the academy—it wouldn't fit within its walls. I cover the scar and rub it through the material. I'll have to ask Anita if there is a cure. The old woman I ran into in the wilderness comes to mind. *What did she say about the scar again? It was really strange.* I frown when it doesn't come back to memory. With a shake of my head, I trudge down to the first bathroom I find.

Slowly, I push the door open and peer inside. It looks like it hasn't been cleaned for a while. The room stinks.

Cautiously, I enter, and the urge to tiptoe is strong. I push back the door of the first stall and screw up my nose. I can't believe that this is an all-girls academy—the stench is lethal. It's even worse than cleaning the dragon stalls. Something dark lies on the ground. I don't even want to know what that is. *This is disgusting!*

I block my nose and hold my breath. I don't want to smell this. After slipping on the rubber gloves, it takes a while to gather the courage to begin the cleaning process. I bend my knees, ready to stoop to pick up whatever it is when I hear something behind me. I straighten and exit the stall only to come to face-to-face with Rota, Prima, and Mist. *Great! My arch-nemesis and her buddies. They have hassled me since my first year.* I have not missed their faces while stuck in the dragon wilderness. I roll my eyes. "What do you guys want?"

"I heard you were coming back today," Prima says with a sneer. "So we made sure that this was a suitable job for you. We may have nominated you for this job to Mistress Sigrun then set to work making sure you had a little extra to clean up." She indicates the several suspect dark patches in the room. "I hope you like our decorating."

Studying the dark patches and taking in the stench, I am sure that it is not chocolate. My mouth straightens into a thin line as I look at Prima. "If that's yours, you can pick it up."

"Oh, wingless! That is not going to happen." Rota moves closer. "That's what you second-class Valkyries are for. In fact, you should be cleaning that with your face, not a rubber glove."

She approaches me, and my arms move up instinctively, ready to fight. She looks at them and sneers. "You forget who we are."

Mist moves forward, and I reach out and slap her with a gloved hand.

"Eww!" She groans. "That's disgusting!"

As Mist distracts me from the front, Prima scoots forward and grabs my arms from behind. "It's swirly time."

Mist's pretty face screws up in disgust. "Getting your head flushed is gross."

Rota grabs one side of me and helps Prima drag me to the toilet. I twist and lash out with my feet, kicking them in the thighs. They cringe yet somehow manage to secure their grasp.

Mist cheers them on, "Let's make her ugly black hair wet and sloppy." She giggles.

With bared teeth, I stretch my neck to try and bite

Rota's shoulder. She notices what I am doing before I can make contact. I try to do the same to Prima until someone clears their throat. It sounds too old to be Mist. Rota glances behind us then stops. Confusion flickers over her face.

I twist around, still in their grasp, and my jaw drops with disbelief. The old woman from the wilderness stands at the entrance of the bathroom. "Young Valkyries! What do you think you are doing?"

Prima and Rota drop my arms at the same time, and I shake free.

When no one answers her, the old woman approaches us. "This is not the way to treat each other. I know this young Valkyrie. I have met her before, and I consider her a friend."

I should be grateful that she has stopped my archenemies from dunking my head, but I am too caught up in confusion. "What are you doing here?" My scar starts to ache again, and out of habit, I rub the spot.

The old woman raises an eyebrow. "Ah, it is giving you trouble again, I see. Here, let me have a look." Her old feet move surprisingly quickly across the floor, and she yanks my uniform down from my shoulder, revealing my scar. She runs her hand over it, and a strange tingling sensation runs the entire length of the scar and down my arm. My body convulses briefly.

"What did you do?" I ask.

"Time will tell." She smirks. Her faded eyes land on

the three winged Valkyries, one at a time. "Now, Valkyries. I would be leaving Kara alone if I were you." Without waiting for a response, she spins on a heel and leaves.

My mouth drops open. *What just happened?*

"Crazy old bat!" Prima spits then grabs my arms again, assisted by Rota.

"She is one crazy old lady. I hope I'm never like that," Mist says with a tone that is so vague that it can't be taken seriously. She twirls a strand of her blond hair in her fingers while staring at the empty entrance.

My attention is yanked away as they start to drag me in the direction of the toilet. No matter what I do, I can't break free. After all, they're both warriors with much more training than what we have been given. Strange sensations stir in my scarred arm. It doesn't stop, and it feels different than it did when the creature was around. *What did the old lady do?*

Rota yanks my scarred arm forward, and the toilet bowl seems to leer up at me. Twisting my arm in a final attempt, I manage to grasp hold of her, with my hand bracing myself from being shoved farther. Something wells within the scar tissue then shoots down my arm, out my hand, and into Rota.

My eyes widen. *What was that?*

Rota squeals and drops to the ground.

Prima drops my other arm, and her wide eyes stare

at the unconscious Rota. "What did you do?" Her voice is barely a whisper.

For a moment, my feet feel glued to the spot. I glance at Prima, then at Mist, then finally down at Rota's still form. My jaw drops, and I bolt out the door.

THE END

Did you enjoy this book?
You can make a big difference.

HONEST REVIEWS of my books help bring them to the attention of other readers.

IF YOU'VE ENJOYED this book, I'd be grateful if you could spend a few minutes leaving a review (it can be as short as you like).

The review can be left on Amazon and Goodreads.

Thank you very much.

KATRINA COPE

INFLICTED

VALKYRIE ACADEMY
DRAGON ALLIANCE

BOOK 4

EDITORIAL REVIEW

Cosy Burrow Books

Valkyrie Academy Dragon Alliance
Book Four

INFLICTED

"*Inflicted* is filled with quick-witted dragons, plenty of action, and commanding heroines." - Stefanie B., Red Adept Editing Line Editor

Inflicted
Ebook first published in USA in September 2019 by Cosy Burrow Books
Ebook first published in Great Britain in September 2019 by Cosy Burrow Books

www.katrinacopebooks.com

Published by Cosy Burrow Books

ISBN: 978-0-6486613-3-7
ASIN: B07VV7K1S6

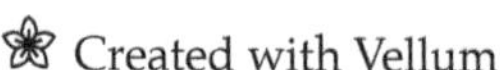

Colin & Glenys ~ Thank you for the peace you supplied (with a view) while writing this book

CHAPTER ONE

The pounding of my shoes on the floor reverberates off the walls of the corridor. My feet won't run fast enough. I must move quicker. By the time I reach the main door of the academy, my lungs are screaming for air. I glance at my left hand. The strange current that ran down my arm and out my hand before firing into Rota is a mystery to me. No reasoning in my mind can explain what happened—not even the old woman who touched me only moments before. It was my second encounter with her, and although both meetings were brief, every fiber of my being makes me think she may be a witch. She was too old to be a Valkyrie and too weird to be normal. Although I'm not an expert in this field since I haven't met a witch before.

I burst out of the front door of the academy and spin

around to check if anybody is following me. Coming up empty, I keep going. Despite my panic, I can't help thinking about how strange it is that the elderly lady entered the academy. Making things weirder was the briefness of our meeting. It was almost as though she'd sought me out and followed me here.

My eyes flick, searching relentlessly. Perhaps the old lady is following me. I can't see her, but that doesn't mean she's not. I'm not even sure how she knows my mother, whom I haven't seen since starting at the academy. As a rule, all students who join the academy must break contact with their families. Academy students must become hardened warriors and learn how to cope and deal with problems by fighting their way through them.

I'll have to consult the library to see what it says about witches. Perhaps it holds more books like *The Tales of How Brynhildr Got Her Wings*. I know it's just a myth, but I have never given up hope that one day I can become like the winged Valkyries and help reap souls for Valhalla—even if I can't grow wings.

My left arm tingles with the strange sensation that continues to run through its veins, and I rub my hand up and down it. Surely it couldn't have been magic that passed through my arm. Could it? And why would it be this arm? My fingers tickle the scar, and a thought runs through my head. It is the arm that the beast marked when I scared it away from stealing Elan's egg.

I shake my head. No. I must be imagining things. I didn't do anything to Rota back in the bathroom. She must've had a medical seizure or something. I couldn't possibly have harmed her. For a start, I am wingless. That means I have no extraordinary power, and I only work for the winged Valkyries as a slave. On top of that, Valkyries can't have magic, as far as I know.

As I stare out into the open lands, I think about running to my room and talking it over with Hildr and Eir, but I'm not sure they will understand. Even if they do, I doubt they could do anything to help me. During all the time we've spent together in the last couple of years we have lived together, we have never talked about magic.

I shake my head and remind myself this isn't magic. It's just a figment of my imagination. Rota had some kind of medical seizure or something. That's got to be all.

I stop in my tracks—there is no need for me to be running. This isn't my fault. I change direction and decide to speak with Elan. After all, she has been through a lot today because of me. Her mind must be in a flurry with events from the past day, as well as trying to cope with the injury she received while defending me against the other dragon. She has only been in my life for such a short time, but I am growing more fond of her every day. These dragons are not the vicious creatures that others have led us to believe—well, at least not the dragons like Elan and her clan, who have shown us kindness. As for the other dragons, I should fear the ones in the wild and the ones the winged Valkyries have treated poorly. I do not hold their bitterness against them. If I were treated as badly as they are, I'm pretty sure I would also become vicious.

I stroll to the place where I left Elan. I instructed her to stay invisible. We don't want Odin or anyone else capturing her again. She is meant to be free.

I don't see her, but as I wander closer to the area, a rumbling noise catches my attention. I shake my head. Her snoring would alert the deaf—it's that loud. So much for staying in hiding. The snoring crescendos as I get closer, and I follow it until I collide with her side. A strange pride fills me as I run my hands along her body against the direction of her scales. Pain shoots up my leg as something snares it. That will definitely be a bruise later. As I work my way down and grasp the object within my hands, I feel its shape. I realize it's one of her horns.

"Elan." I shake the horn. "Elan…"

A short burst of snorts interrupts the monotone rhythm of snores, followed by a clicking of the tongue, as though she is savoring the flavor of something. This pauses, then her slow and lingering snores break the silence again.

I stare at the vacant spot in disbelief then reach down to grab her horn and shake it again. "Elan!"

Slowly, her golden scales form before me, and she raises a weary eyebrow, staring at me vacantly with her golden-brown eyes. I already feel better.

Kara? Her tongue clicks against the roof of her mouth again, then she yawns, exposing her enormous mouth filled with sharp, jagged teeth. *Kara, is that you?*

"Who else would it be?"

She suddenly sits up on her haunches and gazes around. *What's wrong? Why are you here? Do you need to go somewhere?*

I chuckle. "Relax, Elan. I'm fine. I'm visiting you to see how you are."

But we only just got here. There must be something wrong, or you wouldn't be out here already. I had just fallen asleep. That salve had a real kick to it, and I think it messed with my brain.

"Yes, I heard you sleeping. You snore like a trouper, by the way."

I do not! I sleep like a baby—not a single sound.

"You keep telling yourself that." I pet her patronizingly on the leg. "But I know what I heard." I smile. "Relax. I'm just here for a visit."

She stares at me, the disbelief prominent in her eyes. *Something must have happened. What was it?*

"What? I can't visit an old friend?"

You can. But I know you have Valkyrie friends, as well. They're ones you trust. So why would you come to see me instead of Hildr and Eir? Not that I'm complaining. She adds quickly, *I love your company.*

Exhaling loudly, I stare out into the distance. "Have you ever seen a weird old lady?"

Aren't you old?

I glare at her. "I'm not old."

You are compared to me. I'm like, what... two? And you're like... She screws up her face. *Almost eighteen?*

"Almost. But that is still not old, especially for a Valkyrie. You must be feeling better. You're starting to get cheeky again."

Just saying! You know how it is.

I roll my eyes. "When I say old, I mean as in wrinkles everywhere and gnarly hands. Have you seen anyone around here that looks like that?"

No. I haven't. Why are you asking?

"Because something strange happened inside." I look out over the rugged landscape, studying the valley below. The wind catches my hair, blowing its long dark-brown locks across my face. I hook it behind my ear.

Like what? Elan's gaze turns intense as her protective nature surfaces.

"An old woman touched my scarred arm, and a tingling sensation ran down it." I pull my gaze from the valley and rub my arm, staring at my pale, unchanged skin. "It's still tingling."

Maybe you just knocked your funny bone before she

touched it, or perhaps you knocked it when you were flying home.

I shake my head. "No. It only happened when we arrived back here, and after the older lady stroked it. She came out of nowhere and touched me right in the middle of Rota, Prima, and Mist attacking me in the bathroom when I was doing my duties. And the worst thing is that my left palm connected with Rota when she was trying to do something mean to me." I stare out into the distance again, trying to let the view take away some of the painful, confusing memory. "The next thing I know, Rota has fallen on the floor, unconscious. It was scary. I didn't even try to do anything." I pause while rubbing my arm absentmindedly. My forehead pushes into a frown. "Do you think there is magic in Asgard?"

Do you think there are gods in Asgard? Sarcasm fills her voice.

I glare at her with disapproval.

Her face holds innocence. *What? You ask me a question I give you an answer in a query. Is there such a thing as gods in Asgard?* She repeats. *Is there such a thing as dragons talking to Valkyries? My point being that anything is possible. There are many supernatural forces at play.*

The thought tosses through my mind. She's right. By pointing out those two small facts, anything is possible.

But then again, perhaps she just fell and had a seizure. I don't know. She shrugs. *Why don't you touch me with that hand and see if anything happens to me?*

Worry clouds my vision. "I don't want to hurt you."

Tsk, tsk. Oh, please. I'm huge. I'd be surprised if you can do anything to me.

I shrug. "Okay. You asked for it." I place my left hand against her flank and concentrate.

Elan throws her head forward and roars.

CHAPTER TWO

Yanking my hand away, I look at her with horror. "Oh, no! I didn't mean to hurt you."

The scales on her forehead pull together in agony. Hearing a noise behind me, I spin around. Her roar must have attracted attention. This is bad. Someone might be coming to capture Elan, and she can't defend herself because I hurt her.

Panic engulfs me when several winged Valkyries take to the sky. From that height, they will find her in no time—she is no longer invisible. I'm torn between telling her to turn invisible and seeing if she's all right.

"I'm so sorry, Elan. Are you all right?" I turn and see that she's invisible, and a wave of relief and confusion sweeps over me.

I'm fine. I was just having you on. She chuckles.

"Elan," I grumble, failing to see the funny side. "That's not funny. I was extremely worried."

I know. It was worth doing it, just to see your expression.

I lightly slap the back of my hand against her invisible form, aiming for her leg. "You're so in trouble. Way to play the guilt trip." I shoot daggers at her with my eyes. "Did you feel anything at all?"

When her chuckling subsides, she says, *I didn't feel a thing. You couldn't have hurt that Valkyrie—nothing came out of your hand. It's got to be your imagination.*

"Then how do you explain her collapsing to the ground and the tingling in my arm?" I ask.

It must've been a coincidence. Rota must've had a seizure or something right after you touched her. It serves her right, really. She shouldn't be treating you like that.

"Yeah. Like you dragons get along so well?" I cross my arms, still annoyed that she faked being hurt and made me worry. I watch as the winged Valkyries fly off in the opposite direction, probably just stretching their wings while checking the grounds and making sure there are no threats in the area.

Strong hues of orange, yellow, and dark blue line the horizon as the sun exits the realm for the night. A deep sadness fills me as I realize that I have to return to the academy. "Elan, what am I going to do?"

What do you mean? Slowly, she turns visible, and I lean against her side.

"The way Rota, Prima, and Mist treated me was

horrible. What happens if all the winged Valkyries want to treat me like that?"

You will probably find it is just a rotten few that are going to be mean like that. What you need to do is show how tough you are and how you can stand up to them. She rocks sideways, swaying me slightly. *And I know you've got it in you. That's why we chose you. You have a lot to prove yet. I'm not going to give up that easily.*

Standing in silence, I think about what she said. "You're right, Elan. I need to stand against them like I always have. I need to rise and prove that they are wrong. Just because they've had more combat training than me doesn't make the winged Valkyries better than me." A strange combination of determination and peace fills me. "How are your injuries healing?"

They are still sore, but I can feel the ointment working. Thank you. I should be a lot better by morning and after a good feed. She prods me lightly with her wing. *Enough about me, you should go inside so I can hunt. I'm starving!*

I push off from her side. "You're right. See you later. Remember to keep invisible so Odin can't find you."

She disappears from view as I stroke her on the leg in parting.

I return to the academy, keeping my eyes peeled for any Valkyries who might be pursuing me, including Mistress Sigrun. None come. I walk down the corridor, gaining confidence with each step. Walking toward the dining hall, I pass several winged Valkyries doing nothing more than the usual sneer. The smell of the food wafts my way, and my stomach growls, screaming its protest at having no food since breakfast. I grab a plate and load it up with a charred steak and a side of fries. It's not my healthiest choice, but after being stuck in the wilderness for so long, I feel like some comfort food. I spot Hildr and Eir in the far corner, and I make my way over then sit opposite them.

"Hey, you. Where have you been?" Eir's gentle eyes search me as if looking for problems.

"Have you finished all the chores given to you?" Hildr's green eyes sharpen on me, and she plays with her left ear, which is loaded with piercings.

I swallow the unchewed mouthful, and it struggles to slide down my throat. "I've forgotten about them."

"What?" Hildr cries. "How can you forget? You were just given them."

"I know, but Rota, Prima, and Mist attacked me in the bathroom."

"Pfft. Typical!" Hildr exclaims. "I gather you taught them a lesson, because you look unscathed."

Clenching my teeth together, I grimace. "I don't know what happened. I touched Rota, and she dropped to the floor, unconscious. I panicked and took off the second they released me. I know they are going to blame me."

A chair pushes back, its legs grinding on the marble floor, and a wingless Valkyrie unceremoniously plunks herself down at the head of our table with her plate full of food. The three of us stare at her. She doesn't look familiar, and judging by Hildr's and Eir's reactions, they think the same thing. She tosses her long brown locks over her shoulder and picks a fry off her plate. She crunches on it without looking up.

"Hello." Eir smiles, and her light-brown eyes shine their welcome. "I'm Eir. This is Hildr, and that's Kara." She indicates us with her hand. "Who are you?"

"I'm the new girl." Without gazing up, she shoves another fry in her mouth.

Hildr's auburn eyebrow rises, and a hint of impatience flashes through her green eyes. "Yes. We gathered that because we haven't seen you before. Are you in your first year at the academy?"

"I guess so." She looks up at Hildr and smiles broadly. I think I see amusement flash through her eyes.

Hildr frowns, looking perplexed over the lack of information she is receiving. "Well, you look rather old for a first year in the academy. Are you older than fifteen?"

"No. I'm fifteen." The Valkyrie's head twitches to the side before she shoves another fry in her mouth.

I have never seen a Valkyrie twitch before, and I frown in confusion. She doesn't seem like an ordinary Valkyrie.

"Well, welcome." Eir is the only one of us who smiles broadly.

"Thanks." She pulls a book from her lap, places it on the table, then flicks through the pages.

Hildr casts me a bewildered look. "Look. It's not unlike Kara. She reads everywhere she goes."

"I'm not that bad," I say. "I haven't had a chance to pick up a book in a while. After all, I've been stuck in the wilderness. I'm getting withdrawals."

The new girl ignores us as she munches on some more fries and turns a page. It's weird behavior for a dining hall, but I'm not one to judge constant reading. I've lost count how many times I didn't want to put down a book.

I slide my plate along and scoot closer. "What are you reading?"

She shrugs and continues picking at her food. "Just a book from the restricted section."

"Do you mind if I have a look?" I try to sneak a peek past her hand.

"Yeah. Kara loves books," Eir says.

The girl shrugs, so I shuffle a bit closer and look at the book from the odd angle. The strange tingling sensation runs up my left arm. I don't know what happened back there in the bathrooms, but my arm hasn't been the same since.

As I gaze down at the book, she flicks the page, and my hand freezes its rubbing, pausing over my upper arm. My mouth drops open.

The newest page shows a picture of the creature that

has been flying around Asgard for the last three years—the one that marked my arm and gave me the scar. I point at it in disbelief. "I have seen that creature."

The girl keeps her nose buried in the book and shoves another fry into her mouth. She shrugs and says with her mouth full, "That's a zmey."

"Does it say how many there are? Are they rare?" I edge forward, trying to get a better look.

"I believe this is the only one."

"Does it say anything else?" I search the page from the odd angle, trying to work out the upside-down writing.

"Only that they live for a very long time," she answers, sounding bored.

"Are they normally vicious?" I ask. "I was attacked by one while I was chasing it away from something it was trying to steal."

"They are vicious if they really want something and something stops them from getting it."

I remember how it attacked Heimdall at his gate when I escaped to Midgard. If the creature would only have attacked because it couldn't get to something it was after, it didn't make sense why the creature would attack Heimdall. *Unless…* I stop my thoughts on their tracks.

There is no way the zmey would have done what I thought a second ago. I shake my head. It's a fantasy to think that the creature was purposely distracting him so

I could escape from Asgard. "How do you know so much about these creatures?"

The girl shoves another fry in her mouth and gives me a bland look. "Because I read."

I frown then glance at my neglected plate before taking another mouthful of steak and chew it slowly. As much as I love reading and the knowledge it brings, that wasn't a believable explanation. I'm starting to think this girl is hiding something.

CHAPTER THREE

Getting the feeling that I'm invading her space, I scoot a seat away from the strange Valkyrie and watch her flick through her book. I am dying to rip the book out of her hands, but that would be an unforgivable crime to a bookworm. She casually turns more pages that reveal all kinds of creatures, some in the shape of humans. I can't quite see the pictures correctly from where I am sitting, but I can't imagine that any of the images would spark my interest like the creature did.

Trying my best to ignore the Valkyrie, I face Hildr and Eir, focusing on my meal.

"Oh. Look who it is." The spite in Hildr's voice carries over the din of the dining hall, and I search over my shoulders, looking for the person drawing her interest.

I spot Rota, with Prima aiding her into the room. Mist follows not far behind, twirling her beautiful blond locks. I swallow my food with difficulty, and the lump sits just under my esophagus. Rota's perfect face is pale under her blond locks, and her eyes are haunted as though she has been pretty shaken up. Prima's eyes narrow as she glances around the room. It is uncanny how all the winged Valkyries look almost the same, with only slight variances that distinguish them. Although their mannerisms often help tell the difference between their perfect faces, blond hair that falls to their shoulders, and majestic white wings protruding from their shoulder blades. The wingless Valkyries lack these things, along with their esteemed uniform of the tan leather jacket and the long, tight medium-blue leather pants.

Seeing Prima assist Rota is a strange sight. Valkyries are supposed to be tough and rarely in need of assistance. Because of this, they are trying to hide the fact that Prima's arm is hooked around Rota as she aids her through the food hall.

"What's wrong with her?" Eir asks. "She almost looks like she's ill."

My tongue lies frozen in my mouth. I don't know what to say. Explaining what happened will be hard.

The new girl looks up from her book. "I hear she was struck by magic today."

The three of us stare at her.

"Magic?" Hildr scoffs. "There is no such thing here, unless you are talking about her pride getting handed to her. That's what I would call magic."

The girl shrugs, her hand still holding the pages. She looks nonchalantly back at the book then at Rota then at me. "You'd be surprised what could be floating around. A single scratch or touch—they could be life-changing."

Her dark-brown eyes bore into me, and a shiver travels up my spine.

"What are you talking about?" Eir asks. "You almost sound as crazy as me."

Hildr scoffs. "Yeah. She's a peacemaker that's living in a Valkyrie academy. Go figure! That is one crazy idea."

The peculiar Valkyrie's eyes do not leave my face, and her hands still clasp the pages of the book. A strange knowing look passes across her face. "It is just as I said. I will let you work that out."

She closes the book and tucks it under her arm with the back cover facing out. Still keen to know the title of the book, I search the cover. Nothing is written on the back cover or the spine. She stands and walks away without saying a word.

I study every feature of the book as she walks past. I'll have to go search for that one in the library—it has me intrigued. I want to find out more about that creature and if it resides anywhere else or is mentioned anywhere else in the library books. She said it was a zmey. I've never heard of it.

When she is gone, I search for Rota again. Whatever happened to her certainly knocked her about. Valkyries heal quickly, yet she still needs to be aided by Prima.

Eir stares at Rota with concerned eyes. "What did happen to her?"

I weigh my options, wondering how much I should tell them. I can't explain it myself, but these two have been through a lot with me. They have been there supporting my theory on the dragon alliance and befriending dragons. They have even taken it further and have been locked up because of me. I think they deserve an answer, and because of this, I will give them the best I can.

"When I met with Mistress Sigrun, she sent me to clean the bathrooms as one of my penalty chores. Knowing that this chore would be allocated to me, Rota, Prima, and Mist made a disgusting mess throughout the bathrooms. They wanted to watch me clean it up, so they came and, as usual, started fighting me. They even secured me so that they could give me a swirly."

Eir screws up her nose.

Hildr slams her fist on the table, making me jump. "How dare they!"

I nod. "But not just that. While they grabbed me, the old woman that I met in the wilderness walked in and touched me. She said something weird and nicely told them off, and then she walked back out again."

"That is weird." Eir pulls back, looking at me strangely. "You would have thought she could've stepped in and helped, or at least told someone."

I shake my head. "She just walked in and touched me on my arm. The scar the creature gave me a couple of years ago went berserk with tingling, but it plays up now and then, so I didn't think anything of it." I stabbed a fork into my food. "The weird thing is, not long after the old woman left, I touched Rota, trying to defend myself, and she fell to the ground unconscious. None of us know what happened." I throw down the fork, and it clatters against the plate. "Prima dropped her hold on me, and I took one look at Rota. Then I ran. Mist was only worried about looking at herself in the mirror. I guess she thought the other two had it covered." I shrug.

"Where did you go?" Eir asks.

"I ran straight out the door to Elan. I wondered if Rota was hit by magic, but after running it through with Elan, it sounded crazy. So to help me ease my worries, Elan told me to touch her with the same arm and see what happened."

"And what did happen?" Eir takes a sip of water from her glass.

"What do you think happened?" I asked her.

"We don't know." Hildr's freckly face screws up

with impatience. "It was only a few days ago that we thought talking to a dragon was impossible."

"Nothing happened. She didn't feel a single thing. So it had to just be the timing. There's obviously something wrong with Rota, and she passed out right when I touched her."

We watch Prima as she sits Rota down and helps with her food. When she finishes looking after her, she sits next to her to eat. Her eyes search the room then land on us. They narrow.

"Now what?" Hildr huffs. "That girl hasn't left us alone since we came back from our flight."

"I don't know." I lean over my plate, no longer interested in my food. Prima doesn't take her eyes off us as she shovels food into her mouth and chomps down hard. I wish she would leave us alone. One day without them annoying us would be a godsend.

My eyes wander over the dining hall. From what I can see, nearly all the Valkyries are in the room, getting their meal. Valkyries are few, and the academy caters only for the younger generation. Because Valkyries are immortal, to stop the population from expanding too much, they are rarely able to bear young.

"How many Valkyries do you think are in the academy?" I ask.

"About forty," Eir says. "There's about ten for each grade."

"Why's that?" Hildr asks.

"Just curious. How many wingless Valkyries are there out of all those?"

Eir counts them on her fingers. "About ten."

"So we're completely outnumbered," I say. "It's like they're the blessed ones and we're the ones that are disabled by the curse of a weird mutation—we lack wings."

"Yeah. That's been obvious from the start. What's your point?" Hildr asks.

"My point is that it is easy to pick on the ones that are fewer in numbers," I say.

"And if your headmistress is constantly putting you down and encouraging the majority…" Hildr's eyes travel to the far corner of the room, and her face screws up with annoyance.

I spin around to see what caught her attention. Mistress Sigrun stands at the entrance of the dining hall. She claps her hands together three times in a loud staccato.

"Attention, Valkyries." She repeats the staccato clap. "I have an announcement to make." Her eyes land directly on me and tighten.

CHAPTER FOUR

It takes all my effort to look at her. "What have we done now?" I ask.

"I haven't done anything. Perhaps it's the ones who didn't finish their chores." Hildr nudges me lightly and smirks.

"It wouldn't be the first time." Eir grins with her.

"This is because she gives us so many stupid chores." I slam my back against the chair and cross my arms. "And I'm always in the firing line."

"You're always the one racing off and causing trouble." Eir beams.

"I second that." Hildr grins like a Cheshire cat. "But I have had a taste of it now, and I like it."

"Valkyries! Attention!" Mistress Sigrun calls out again. "I have demanded your silence."

A loud clatter pierces the room as the cutlery hits the

plates, and the hall falls into an eerie silence, waiting for Mistress Sigrun to begin.

The mistress tilts her chin to the group, acknowledging the silence. "It has come to my attention that a few wingless Valkyries here think they're more important than the winged Valkyries. So much so that they don't finish their chores." Her eyes circle the room and land on me. "This is not tolerable, and my patience has run thin." She crosses her arms and paces a few steps in front of the doorway. Her tight leather pants creak with every movement, and the clack of her shoes on the hard floor echoes through the silence. "And no matter how much I try, these Valkyries will not pull into line. And it is appalling." She paces more, then stops abruptly, spinning around to face the Valkyries in the room.

"So today I have come up with a plan. Tomorrow at first light, we are going to set a challenge. For these three wingless Valkyries that think they are better than the winged—and I'm sure you all know who they are, so I'm not going to hide it." Her eyes land on me again. "They will have to prove themselves in a competition." She holds up a finger. "But, to make this fair, even though they don't deserve it, I'm going to choose three winged Valkyries from within the same grade level as their opponents."

The hairs on the back my neck prickle. Mistress Sigrun being fair to wingless Valkyries—that's something I've never seen.

She starts pacing again. "This challenge will have no particular rules. And this challenge will be until the Valkyrie's opponent is wiped out. If it ends in death, then there will be no consequences for the Valkyrie responsible." She smirks, and her wings twitch, making her seem more pompous. "Because we all know which side that will be." She loops her hands behind her back and paces more. "There is one catch. This fight will take place at the top of one of our mountains, and there is only one way down from the top—and that is flying, unless you are a rock climber experienced in free climbing. The only way down besides the path up will be sharp, jagged cliffs. That way, there will be no escaping." Her smirk grows broader, and she lifts her chin. "Well… not for the wingless Valkyries."

"That doesn't seem fair," one of the wingless Valkyries calls out.

Mistress Sigrun glares at her, and the Valkyrie cringes on the spot.

Despite her cowering away, I thought she was quite brave calling out like that. I thought it was only me and my little group who challenged the winged Valkyries. Perhaps there are more of us who would like to prove to the winged Valkyries that they are not superior. This thought alone gives me hope. I know I definitely agree with her. It doesn't seem fair. If we fall, we have no means to save ourselves from our fall. The winged Valkyries, of course, have their wings.

After staring intently at the other Valkyrie, Mistress Sigrun walks over to Rota's table. She squats and chats quietly to Rota. After a while, Rota nods, and Mistress Sigrun rises to her feet and walks back to the entrance of the hall.

"Right. As we all know who the wingless Valkyries are..." All eyes fall on my group. "Kara, Hildr, and Eir, you are the wingless Valkyries."

"And what happens if we win?" I ask Mistress Sigrun, tilting my chin in the air. If I am putting my life at risk, I am doing it with pride and something to fight for.

She glares at me, then her eyes soften with amusement as she dismissively flicks her hand in the air. "Pfft. I guess you'll get some sort of prize."

"What about being able to go to Midgard to help with the reaping of souls for Valhalla?" I call out before she has a chance to offer something insignificant.

She stops in her tracks and turns to me, her face a mixture of shock and displeasure before it morphs into laughter. "Sure. Let's make that your reward." She couldn't have been more condescending. "I know you have no chance of winning anyway. So sure." She holds her stomach and looses a hearty, belly-jerking laugh.

Despite her reaction, I feel elated. There's a chance that I get to go to Midgard without being kicked out.

Mistress Sigrun interrupts my thoughts. "Now these three imbeciles will be going up against the best in their level. If they want to prove that they are the best, then they must go up against the best. They will be going up against Prima, Rota, and Mist. And they cannot whine that they have been hard-done-by because they are even getting an advantage—Rota hasn't been well today and possibly won't be better tomorrow. As much as Valkyries can heal quickly, Rota has been hit with a virus that will take longer than a few hours to disappear." She dusts off the front of her shirt and pulls her tan leather jacket closed. "There, my kindness is done. I have given you inconsiderate wingless Valkyries leeway. And even though Rota is putting her life at risk because she is not in the best of health, she has still agreed to fight. She believes in our cause and the dominance of the winged Valkyries and putting the wingless Valkyries in their place." The mistress walks in a slow, purposeful pace with her chin held high, peering down at all the wingless Valkyries. "Her passion alone will win the fight and ride over any of her illness."

"Oh, what hogwash!" Hildr says only loudly enough for us to hear while thumping her fist on the table. Her face turns a contrasting red to her spikey ginger hair.

"I can't agree with you more." A knot of anxiety and hope twists deep in my stomach.

"Why me?" Eir asks. "I haven't done anything. I just want peace. Sure, I'm friends with you guys and agree with your cause, but I haven't done anything."

"You have. You were born wingless," Hildr says. "To make things worse, you've stuck with us."

Eir sighs. "And you're the best friends, so I wouldn't have it any other way."

Mistress Sigrun claps her hands a few times to silence the room again. "Now remember—first light, people. Anyone who's late is immediately disqualified. And losers... don't be late!" She sneers at us before smiling at Rota, Prima, and Mist then exiting the door.

CHAPTER FIVE

When Mistress Sigrun leaves, the room fills with the clatter of cutlery and excited chatter. Distrusting sneers and side glances cut our way.

Eir stabs her food with her fork, but it never makes it into her mouth. After a while, she plonks her fork down. "I'm going to go visit Naga. I haven't had a chance to ride him after we talked. That's something I want to do before I die."

"You're being a bit melodramatic." Hildr plays with the clump of earrings on her left ear. "Our fighting skills are just as good as theirs."

"Yeah, yours and Kara's fighting skills are almost as good as theirs. I can fight, but I hate disrupting the peace. I prefer to talk it through rather than fight."

I place my hand on her back. "We'll work something out. Don't worry." As I say this, I feel like a hypocrite, and my stomach churns. There are no rules. They can force us off the edge of the cliff, and we could fall to our deaths. If we do the same to them, they can fly and return, along with their combat training being much more advanced than ours. The academy has never given the wingless Valkyries the same training poured into the winged students.

I put on a brave face and rub Eir's back. "Then let's go. I like Naga. He's a cheerful fellow. Maybe he can cheer you up."

We push back our chairs and stand before making our way out of the dining hall and to the dragon stalls. As we near the exit of the academy building, someone calls out. "Hey, wait up."

I spin around to find the wingless Valkyrie who had challenged Mistress Sigrun about the unfairness of the challenge. She jogged up to us and stopped. "I want to say that I'm proud of you guys. You do a great job. More of us should stand together and stand up against them. This is my last year at the academy, and no one else would help me stand up against them. It was just me. That's great that you guys are coming through."

"Thanks," I say a bit hesitantly, confused over the sudden attention.

"No problem." She turns to leave before I can ask her name, then pauses. "Oh, by the way, if you're fighting Rota, remember when she goes to do a spinning knockout kick, she leaves herself wide open for a hit. Take stock of that and use it to your advantage."

"Thanks," I say with more enthusiasm. "Any help is great."

"There are no rules. They can play dirty, so you play just as dirty. You need as much advantage as you can, using whatever surprise elements you can muster."

"Thanks. What's your name again?" I ask.

"Britta."

"I am—"

"Kara. You're Hildr and"—she points to Eir—"you're Eir. Yeah, I know who you are. You're starting to be legends amongst the wingless."

My mouth drops open. "Oh. We had no idea. We are just trying to change the attitude of the winged Valkyries."

"I wish you luck. Even if you're not winning against the winged Valkyries, you're starting to get through to the wingless. If they don't watch it, the academy will have an uprising." She slaps Hildr on the shoulders before turning to leave.

We step out into the open air, and the moon paves a path along the valleys of Asgard.

"That was strange," Eir says.

Hildr falls into step with me. "Look what you've done, Kara."

"It's not just me. You're part of this too."

"Please. I've hardly done anything in comparison to

you. We got ourselves locked up for a while, that's about it. You did the rest." Her tone is not accusing, merely a voice of encouragement.

"The support you have given me is priceless. And comments like what Britta gave us show there is hope for us all. We need to win this battle tomorrow."

We cross through and follow the path toward the dragon stalls. We reach Naga's stall and roll the stone door aside. Together, we stick our heads through. Naga sits in the corner with his back straight, sitting at attention. His flat head turns, and his eyes land on us. His tail wags.

"Aww! You really are cute, Naga," Eir says as she charges through.

Naga sits still, and his eyes widen as he watches her approach. He seems shocked yet pleased that Eir is charging over to greet him.

He sits still, patiently waiting. His eyes are wide. *Hellos. What… what's happening?*

"We've come to visit you, Naga," I say, and my heart sings as his tail wags some more.

Naga likes visits. Naga wants more.

"And you will get some more." I smile. His inability to speak English correctly makes him more adorable. "Am guessing you don't know, Naga, but Eir wants to connect with you. She wants you to take her for flights and to be her dragon friend."

Naga's eyes widen as his eyes bounce from me to Eir several times before landing on Eir. *Is this truth?*

Eir looks adoringly at the dragon. "Yes, Naga. This is very true. I think you're delightful." She rushes forward and hugs him around the neck. He tilts his flat head, nuzzling into her with his hornless head.

Even when I's got cold and when I's sneeze fire?

Eir smiles. "Yes, Naga. Even when you sneeze fire, only please try to aim them away from me."

I wills try. He jumps to all four feet and jigs in front of her, stretching out his wings and showing off the white dots that look like stars against his blue membrane wings. She giggles, and he charges up to her, slinging his blue body to sit next to her, and accidentally knocks into her. She stumbles and lands on her backside. She jumps to her feet, still giggling, and throws her arms around him, embracing him around the neck and trying to remain on her feet as he laps up her affection. There doesn't seem to be a nasty bone in his body.

After watching them for a few minutes, I interrupt their reunion. "Now, Naga, do you promise to stay in your stall, as per the Dragon Alliance agreement, if I take these cuffs off you?"

Naga nods enthusiastically. *Yes. Yes, I promise I stay.*

"I mean it, Naga." I tilt my head and look at him under a raised eyebrow. "You have to stay here, or else we can get into a lot of trouble because you have run away. Odin becomes very angry when the dragons disappear. He doesn't even like it when they disappear for a little bit and come back. But I would like to free you to see you roam a little bit."

I be good, Naga says quickly. *I promise.*

Gazing deep into Naga's eyes, I can see he is telling the truth. He has such an innocence about him that makes him adorable. I run my hand over his flat head then circle to his back leg secured with the chain. I fish for my skeleton key, stick it into the lock, and move it around until the lock clicks and the chain pops open.

Why you doing this? Naga asks.

"Because tomorrow, we have to face our enemies in the Valkyrie Academy."

Eir goes in and cuddles him around his neck to mother him some more. She lets him go then looks at us. "I am so worried about tomorrow. My stomach is doing little flips."

"The Valkyrie back at the academy is right. There are no rules. We can do whatever we want to them." Hildr stands with her legs in a fighting stance as if preparing for tomorrow.

"But they can do whatever they want to us too, and that includes pushing us over the side." Eir strokes Naga down his blue neck, and his eyes look at her adoringly. "We cannot fly. It's not fair. Tomorrow could be our last day to live."

Naga's eyes widen. He nudges into her, and she

obliges by hooking her arm around his neck, cuddling him close.

"At least I got to come and be with you, little guy." Eir presses her face into his neck. "That made my day. It is one of the things I wanted to do before I died."

Naga pulls back and looks at Eir with wide blue eyes. *My English no good. But Naga think that you sad. I thinks you say you die.*

Eir returns his gaze with serious eyes. "That is possible, Naga. Tomorrow morning, at first light, we have to fight the winged Valkyries." She sits on a rock and cups her hands in her lap, playing with her fingers. "And I'm scared."

Then don't fight, he says.

"We have to, Naga. We don't have a choice. Really, this is a competition that they're making us do because they want to kill the three of us. It all started because of what we did with the dragons—because Hildr took a dragon for a ride and Kara saved Elan from Odin's captivity. Now they want to make us pay."

CHAPTER SIX

The next morning, a horn blasts me from my sleep. My eyelids fling open, and my first impression is that it's a call to Midgard for another war. The room is dark, and the sun has not yet risen. The horn sounds again, and I realize that the sound is different from the usual Midgard call. It must be a call for the fight this morning. As I stare across the room, the realization hits me—we are running out of time. I reach over my bed for my bedside table and rub the glow rock, and it illuminates. The light shines on the pale faces of Hildr and Eir. It has been a restless night's sleep for all of us, tossing and turning, in anticipation of what is going to happen. I swing my legs over the side of the bed, and my feet fall to the floor. I rub the sleep from my eyes and stretch my arms to the ceiling.

"I'm not ready for this." Eir's mouth is downturned, and she almost looks depressed.

"Eir, you have to stop being so negative," Hildr snaps. "I know you're a peacekeeper and all, but you can do it. We've seen you fight. When you're on a roll, you're an excellent fighter. It's only your mental attitude toward peace that stops you from winning sometimes. You need to remember that there are no rules and that they may kill us."

Eir's shoulders sag in defeat. "I know. I have to put on my tough face."

The horn blows again, and Hildr complains, "What, we don't even get breakfast?"

I rise to my feet. "Clearly not. Although I don't know if I could keep anything down right now." I start pulling on the black fighting leathers of the wingless Valkyries. I grab my favorite quiver of arrows and shove my sword between the quiver and my back. I hook my sling on the back of my pants. I've always loved that sling, ever since it helped defend me in the wastelands against the creature I now know is called a zmey. I run an apprecia-tive hand over the rough texture of the sling's material. That day holds so many memories, and it was the start of my involvement with Elan.

I slide on my boots and run my fingers through my long dark-brown hair. "I'm going to grab a roll on my way past the kitchen anyway."

"I'm coming too," Hildr says.

We pass by the kitchen, grabbing a roll, and I grab one for Eir and hand it to her.

"Gee, thanks," she says half-heartedly. She tucks it inside the pocket of her black jacket. "I'll eat it later. Right now, my stomach is a mess of knots. I think I'll get through by adrenaline alone."

We step outside of the academy walls, and someone grabs me from behind. I spin to see the strange girl from the dining room with the curious book. The girl's hand grasps my left arm, and a strange look is plastered over her face. Yanking backward, I try to release her grip, but it doesn't give. Tingling, stronger than it was before, shoots down my arm. She must have stirred up the injury. I tug again, and this time, her grasp releases. Without saying a word, she spins and leaves.

"That's odd." Eir's expression is confused as she watches the girl leave.

"You're telling me!" I shake my head and rub my arm.

We turn away from her and walk a few feet around the corner of the academy, where we meet Mistress Sigrun and a couple of winged Valkyries.

"It's about time you arrived." She plants her fists against her hips. "I was about to charge into your room and drag you out myself. We thought you were trying to skip it."

"Good morning to you too, mistress." I smile cheerfully, hiding my nerves. "Where are we heading?"

She glares at me then spins around, aiming her finger at the highest peak. The flat surface at the top of the mountain is barely visible.

"How are we going to get there, mistress?" Eir asks as all the remaining color drains from her face. "It even looks impossible to free climb that mountain."

The leader of the academy looks down her nose at Eir. "I was going to make you climb up the rocks, but that would make us wait too long for a wingless. Instead, the winged Valkyries are going to be doing all the work for you again. Not just one, but two winged Valkyries will have to be put out. Unfortunately, we need one for each side to carry you up there."

"How considerate of you, mistress." Hildr's fist opens and closes at her side.

Mistress gives Hildr a sharp look, noting the sarcasm in Hildr's voice. "Yes, it is. Yet you wingless still don't treat us with respect," she says. "The winged Valkyries do so much for your kind."

Suddenly, strong hands grab both my arms and hook underneath them. Before I know it, I'm rising off the ground and into the air. My stomach lurches over the harsh treatment without warning.

I'm flanked by winged Valkyries with beautiful blond hair flicking behind their shoulders as they fly. Their majestic wings beat powerfully, pulling me into the air. Their pale, beautiful faces focus on the top of the mountain. It is a vast rise to the top. If we fall, it will definitely be to our deaths.

Neither of them says a word as they fly toward the top—my only comfort is the monotonous beat of their wings. I try hard not to glance down. Riding a dragon would be safer than being carried by two winged Valkyries. There is just so much more security on the back of a dragon, feeling that vast size and power underneath my body.

My stomach reels over the lack of security, churning so much that it takes all my mental effort not to throw up. To pull my thoughts away from the possibility, I search for Eir and Hildr. I hear the flapping wings behind us, and I assume that it's winged Valkyries carrying the other two behind me, but they are out of my sight.

The rugged terrain sinks beneath us, and the journey seems endless. Even with their powerful strokes, it takes quite some time to rise to the top of the mountain. Finally, we reached the edge of the top of the mountain, and my feet fold underneath me when the winged Valkyries drop me to the ground. They aren't even gentle when they set me down.

The sun peeks over the horizon, bathing the land of Asgard in a golden glow. Opposite me across the other side of the flat top, Rota, Prima, and Mist stand ready, their faces screwed up in their usual scowls. My eyes travel farther, and I notice that winged Valkyries from the academy surround the plain. They hover in a circle formation around the edges. The sun's beautiful light casts eerie shadows on their faces. Because of the location of the fight, there is not one wingless Valkyrie among the spectators. They will not be able to watch the fight and see if it is fair. Again, they are excluded. Here we are, fighting for their rights, and they can't even watch and support us.

A thump sounds on my left, and I turn to find Hildr's Valkyrie escorts have unceremoniously dumped her, as well. Then they push up into the sky and join the other winged Valkyries circling the plain. Another thump catches my attention, and I look to my right to see Eir being given the same treatment before her escorts also join the other spectators.

Hildr's hand hovers over the hilt of her sword as she eyes each spectating Valkyrie. "What's stopping them from joining in, as well?" She nods, indicating the live circle. "There is nobody to witness that they have cheated, and it wasn't an even match of three against three. Naturally, the winged Valkyries are going to stick up for their own if this fight turns sour for them."

My cheeks turn clammy as I stare up into the glaring blue eyes. There is a significant element of truth to Hildr's words. There is no one to witness any unfairness, and there is nowhere that we can go to escape it. I don't see even one friendly face.

"I want this to be over with already," Eir says. "If we win this—"

"*When* we win this," Hildr interrupts.

Eir rolls her eyes. "Okay. When we win, we need to teach this bunch of hypocrites a lesson."

"Well, they sound like fighting words." One side of Hildr's mouth lifts in a smirk. "As far as I'm concerned, I'm ready to start now." She positions her legs, planting her feet shoulder width apart, with one foot in front of the other, and sliding metal rings as she draws out her sword. She holds it above her head.

As I mimic her with my sword, the sound of sliding metal resonates, followed by an echo to my right as Eir does the same.

"Bring it on!" Hildr says through gritted teeth.

CHAPTER SEVEN

A sharp whistle blows, and all eyes focus on the newly arrived mistress of the academy.

"Get ready… Go!" Her voice carries over the distance before she blows the whistle and it screams through the air.

At first, my feet remain fixed as I study the circling Valkyries to see what they will do. When I am confident they are not about to interfere, I loose a pent-up breath. This may be a fair fight after all—at least for now. Rota, Prima, and Mist edge toward us. We imitate them from our side—all three of us together approach at the same speed. Our arms remain ready, with our swords drawn.

My arm tingles, and I try to shake it out. The tingling is frustrating, always doing this at the most inconvenient times. Despite the burning urge to rub away the tingling, I can't spare the hand holding the sword. I just have to let the sensation run its course.

A gust of wind blows the dark strands of hair over my face, and I hook it back behind my ear. In the excitement to leave the room, I forgot to tie it out of the way. I curse my absentmindedness. There is nothing worse than fighting with hair obscuring the view.

I shake my head. I can't believe I just thought that. The last thing I need to do is think about hair when I'm about to go into battle. *Way to go, Valkyrie! You're showing the true signs of a warrior,* I chastise myself sardonically.

My attention careens to Eir. Her hair is pulled back into a ponytail that falls down her back. Beads of sweat pearl on her face, and it glistens in the early-morning sun.

"You'll do good, Eir." I try to offer words of encouragement.

She nods in a jerky, unsure movement as her eyes remain focused on the three approaching Valkyries. Mist stands directly opposite her. This is a stroke of luck. I think they will be a better match. Mist is usually too worried about her looks to focus on fighting properly.

In the middle, directly opposite me, is Rota. Her face is paler than usual, giving her the appearance of a porcelain doll. The crisp morning air brings a slight rose to her cheeks, making her look healthier than she did the night before. Her eyes hold a subtle wariness as she moves closer to me. I find this strange. She seriously can't be regarding me as though I hit her with magic yesterday. No Valkyrie has magic.

My arm tingles again, and I try to shake it out. Rota's eyes flick to my arm and widen with fear. I shake my head, trying to clear my vision. I can't be seeing what I think I am. Rota is a fantastic fighter and a formidable opponent. If I beat her, I would be doing well. Fear churns in my stomach, and I pull extra motivation from the reminder of the prize. If we win today, Mistress Sigrun will have to let the three of us go to the fields in Midgard when they are reaping souls. I'm going to hold her to that. After all, she said it in front of the whole academy.

On my side, Prima is eyeing Hildr. These two are a good match. Hildr is a strong fighter, but Prima has had more training. Usually, what Hildr lacks in skills, she makes up for in determination. Hopefully, today will prove to be the same.

A soft whistle pierces the air, and it pulls my attention back to the fight. I turn just in time to see an arrow heading in Eir's direction. She swings her sword while dodging to the side and cuts the shaft in half. It falls to the ground, broken in two. She spins back to the three approaching, and her eyes land on Mist, who has another arrow nocked in her bow, taut and ready to be shot toward Eir. Mist doesn't even wait until we approach and reach each other before starting to fight. I find this rather unbecoming and rude. But then,

Mistress Sigrun did say that there are no rules in this fight.

Another arrow flies Eir's way. Without a moment's hesitation, she darts to the side and swings the sword, timing the slice perfectly to slash it in half. Mist reaches her arm over her head and pulls another arrow from her quiver. She starts to nock it in her bow, aiming directly at Eir. Quickly, I search the ground and find the perfect-sized stone, and I scoop it up while unhitching my sling at the same time. I slide the stone in the rough material and fling it around my head. I let the rock fly, hitting Mist on the head. Her hand shoots to her head as she cries out in pain and drops her bow and arrow. Her eyes narrow when they land on me and spot the sling in my hand.

Technically, she's not my opponent at the moment, but I wasn't going to let that stop me. She's not playing fair. She rubs her head and shakes it. When she pulls her hand away, there's a nasty welt not far from her temple. My heart dances between beats. My aim has improved during my last couple of years at the academy. I chuckle inwardly. Mist won't be happy that there is a mark on her beautiful face. She will scowl every time she looks in the mirror until that bruise heals.

Mist pulls her sword out of its sheath, charging toward me. Eir darts in front of me and blocks her path, clashing her sword against Mist's. That was a gutsy and aggressive move for Eir, and my heart swells with pride that she would do that to stop Mist from attacking me. She may be a peacekeeper, but she is loyal to the end. That is one of the things that attracted me to be her friend—plus the fact that she puts up with me.

After seeing Eir dart in and start a sword fight before any of us, Hildr charges forward, aiming straight for Prima and stopping her from helping Mist against Eir. Clanging metal rings out as swords clash as the receiving Valkyries block each attack. Several blows are delivered at the other, slicing and chopping, trying to be the first one to succeed with a hit. Hildr swings her sword, knocking Prima's aside. She retreats in time to swing it in a different direction for another attack. Prima pulls her stomach in, and the sword skims lightly across her torso, the tip slicing open her white T-shirt. I hold back a cry of delight. Hildr was so close to connecting. As intrigued as I am by Hildr's fighting skills, I must pull my focus away and concentrate on my own opponent.

My eyes connect with Rota's, and that strange tingling runs down my arm again, reminding me what happened yesterday. This incident is frustrating me. Despite being impossible, it's like my brain refuses to believe that Rota's collapse was just a coincidence. It wants to think that something did charge out of my hand. After all, I did feel a funny tingling sensation charge down my arm right as it happened yesterday. *Didn't I?*

I shake my head and flail my arm, hooking my sling back onto my pants and grasping the hilt of my sword firmly. Slowly, I maneuver forward, each step sliding and cautious. Rota watches me intensely, her eyes flashing down to my shaking arm, and her eyes widen. Perhaps it is something the old lady did when she spoke to her yesterday. Maybe it was the old lady's actions that made Rota believe something happened to my arm. It was a strange coincidence. It has me baffled, but I have to push this aside for now.

Rota pulls her eyes away from my arm and focuses on my face. From training, I know that she is also skimming my posture with her peripheral vision, watching for my first move. Concentrating on my eyes is also the perfect way for her to steel her emotions and make herself focus, ready for the fight. Her training and practice are starting to manifest. Her other hand creeps up to the hilt of the sword, and she embraces it with two hands. Her eyes are flat and determined—all emotions cleared from her focus.

Oh, Vanir! It is about to start. She is definitely ready to attack. I try to mimic what she is doing. It's difficult. I am not a seasoned warrior. Even though I've had several training sessions, it is nothing compared to what Rota has done, including practice on the fields. Nothing teaches more than a life-and-death fight. Rota and the winged Valkyries have had much practice against the angels of death and any other creatures that decide to attack them while they are out in the fields.

The sound of metal clanging against metal rings out on both sides of me. It takes all my strength to ignore the urge to see if Hildr and Eir are okay. I must focus completely on Rota. I blink, only to open my eyes and see Rota swinging her sword directly at me.

CHAPTER EIGHT

My vision tunnels, and the high-pitched sound of clanging swords pierces my eardrums. I move just in time to block Rota's sword from slicing me. My heart thumps rapidly. She pulls back and swings again, the sword careening down, aiming for my head. Thankfully, my training kicks in, and I swing my sword, blocking it just in time. I have to pull my thoughts together. Britta's words enter my thoughts. I blink and notice Rota's underarms are wide open as our swords are locked.

I twist and land a side kick to her ribs. She lurches forward with a groan, pulling her sword down and narrowly missing my leg. As she pulls herself together, her thoughts play out on her face. Then she lunges forward, swiping at me with her sword. I block it, and she retreats then instantly attacks from the other side. I twist and block it with my sword again. These maneuvers repeat as if we are playing a fencing game, swords clashing every time and no one getting through. Weariness swamps my muscles, and my arms ache, making each block or strike a more difficult feat. She pulls her sword away after another of our clashes and swings it horizontally in my direction. My exhausted muscles react too slowly, and the sword slides past my defense. The pain soars through my body, screaming from my torso where the blade connected. My eyes widen, but my vision narrows into a tighter tunnel. Clenching my teeth together, I do my best to pull it together and ignore the pain. I can't let this get to me. Otherwise, it'll distract me from my fight, and things will get worse.

Fear surges through me as I worry about the depth of the injury and the pain it causes me. I grit my teeth and push it aside. Gripping my sword, I swing again. She blocks it, and I spin quickly, striking up from the other direction, knocking her sword aside and nicking up her arm. The sleeve of her tan leather jacket splits open. Her crimson blood runs down her sleeve and stains her medium-blue leather pants. She stumbles back, glancing at her arm, and the icy confidence in her eyes wavers when she looks back at me.

Darting forward, I slice again, but her sword blocks my strike just in time before she stumbles backward a few steps. Seeing her hesitation fuels me forward. I lurch, chopping the sword down at her, and she darts out of the way.

Clanking rings out on either side of me, like music to my ears. Both Eir and Hildr are still fighting, although I am not game to see if they are injured.

The Valkyries around the edge start clapping and cheering, calling out the names of the winged Valkyries. They continue framing our circle, flapping in unison like a grand parade. I wonder how such beautiful creatures can be so mean, then I remind myself that Valkyries are bred to be ruthless and aggressive. We are meant to be warriors first, trained to choose who should live for Valhalla and who should die. Sympathy will only muddy the decision. That is the training of a winged Valkyrie, anyway, and this is what we have to contend with.

Hearing the Valkyries cheer on the winged Valkyries spurs my determination. I slash and swing with so much ferocity and force that Rota backs away. Before I realize, I have pressed her to the other side of the plain. A gasp travels from the bottom of the mountain. I can't imagine it being possible because it is so far below—unless the wind is carrying the voice. But there is no way that they could know what is happening up here. They can't see what is going on. But one thing is for sure—hearing the wingless Valkyries is inspirational enough. They are waiting for us to win so that they, too, may prove that we are worth more than they give us credit for.

I dart forward with my sword tip pointing at Rota, and she backs off. Then her feet slip. She uncoils her wings and flaps, stopping herself from falling—exercising the unfair advantage that we do not have. She hovers in the air for a moment then dives down toward me. I strike out again. She swerves at the last second, narrowly missing the edge of my sword.

Eir gasps to my right, and I want to see what is happening, but it is too risky to check. I hope she's okay. Rota swoops down, and I spin out of the way, swiping my sword at her. I feel it connect with her skin and drag down her side. Her cry of pain reaches my ears. Her first injury is already mostly healed, just like mine. Healing is the gift of being a Valkyrie, especially for simple wounds like sword wounds.

With blood tarnishing her torso, she dives at me again, and I spin, managing to dodge the strike and catch sight of Hildr. From my glance, I think she is okay. I spin farther, catching sight of Eir to see her balancing just on the edge of the cliff face. Mist has backed her into a corner, attacking her from flying positions just as Rota has attacked me. Eir swings her sword, managing to scratch Mist along her face. Mist's eyes cloud over with anger. Again, she has been injured where it can wound her vanity.

Instantly, her posture changes, overtaken by aggression. She spins around, flicking her wings forcefully before she charges at Eir, spooking her backward. Eir's heel clips a boulder, and she stumbles over the edge of the cliff. A scream crescendos as Eir struggles to find something to grasp. But there is nothing. Her body falls over the edge, and her hands fail to find purchase. Her loud scream pierces the valley, echoing up to the mountaintop.

I scream, "Nooo!"

At the same time, Rota has another go at me. I spot her coming and feel the anger welling up inside. I let the emotion soar through me, pouring into every part of my body. It sparks the tingling down my left arm. The sensation grows stronger each second, making my arm feel as though it is about to explode. Raising my left arm, I hold my hand out to fend off Rota, and it connects with her body as she collides with me. I deflect her sword with mine, and an explosion shoots through my left palm and into her body. Rota's body is flung back, and I watch in amazement and horror as her eyes turn lifeless. She crashes to the ground, her wings crumpling beneath her.

My mouth drops open, and I look at my left hand. Confusion roars through my head as I try to figure out what is going on. I wish I could talk to someone about this. I wish someone could tell me what is going on. The shock consumes me, and I look blankly down at Rota's body on the ground. I don't want to become a killer, but

I don't know if I have already crossed that line. I'm not sure what this hand is doing. This time there was a definite surge of power. I throw my hands on my head. Emotion overcomes me. Eir has just fallen to her death, and I may have just become a killer.

A thud sounds beside me, followed by another thud. The fog clouding my mind refuses to clear. Another thud hits the ground not far away, then several more. Removing my hands from my head, I manage to clear enough of the emotional fog to look around. My jaw drops, and my eyes widen. Arrows are embedded deep in the ground surrounding me and have somehow narrowly missed me. Other arrows lie uselessly on their sides. I spin, searching for the culprit. Catching sight of another flying arrow, I am appalled but not completely shocked when I see the flying arrow coming directly from the Valkyrie circle above the plain. Every second Valkyrie has an arrow pointed directly at me, nocked and ready to be set free. More arrows hit the ground around me, and I'm completely encircled with embedded arrows.

A scream disrupts my shock, and I gaze over to see an arrow implanted in Hildr's shoulder. She stumbles backward, nearing the edge of the cliff. I cry out and run toward her, hoping to catch her before she topples over the side, but I'm too far away. Hildr doesn't seem to notice me, and her feet continue their dangerous retreat.

I dig in my toes and sprint, ignoring the arrows slamming into the ground around me.

I don't understand how I haven't been hit. Perhaps I am moving too fast. I can hear footsteps behind me, but all my energy is focused on rescuing Hildr. She is reaching the edge way too fast. A fresh round of arrows surround Hildr, and she stumbles.

I cry out—tears already filling my eyes, making it hard to see. "Nooo!"

I can't lose another friend. My hands reach out, trying to grasp her… but I fear it is too late.

CHAPTER NINE

My feet won't stop as I continue dashing forward, trying to grasp Hildr. I'm too late. She's already over the edge before I get there. Eventually, somehow, I manage to tell my feet to stop only a few feet away from the edge, before I tumble down after her. Despair hits me as I realize I have arrived just in time to see her topple out of my sight. Her freckled face is white, and her green eyes are wide with horror. My heart breaks. I can't do anything. I can't fly. I can't run down and save her.

We are surrounded by Valkyries that fly, but not one of them dives down to grab her. Not one of them grabbed Eir, either. Eir's as well as Hildr's deaths are too much to bear. Tears blur my vision, and my shoulders slump. I am crushed. There is no will to go on.

Britta's and Elan's faces fill my thoughts, giving me the will to continue, just as I hear the sound of a sword being drawn. It slices the air, and I spin around, my automatic defenses kicking in. I block Prima's attack with the clash of our swords. With my right hand busy with the sword, I spin around backward and land my left palm straight on her stomach. A burst shoots out of my palm straight into her torso, just as it did to Rota. All the pent-up aggression and emotion rebounds from the top of my arm and out my hand. Barely seeing through my tear-filled eyes, I watch Prima's eyes widen then drain of life. She crumples to the ground, her head slamming against a rock, and her wings fall over the top of her as she lands face first. Arrows thud into the ground around me, surrounding me again, yet not one hits me. I can't for the life of me understand why. These are expert marksmen.

With the shock of recent events catching up to me, I blink a few times and look around. The arrows are definitely flying down. A large double-edged circle of arrow shafts sticking out of the ground surrounds me. I blink a few more times, thinking that this may register where I have been hit—for surely I have been hit by now, but I'm just too numb to realize it. Except I don't feel any pain. Several more arrows are locked in position, ready to be set loose in my direction.

A cloud pulls out from in front of the sun, releasing

its light and bathing the ground. Yet a shadow surrounds me. I frown and look up. Nothing is above me.

A movement catches my eye in my peripheral vision. Mist is approaching quickly, another arrow nocked. As I watch her, I am almost ready to give up. Everything I have worked for has failed. All my efforts to prove wingless Valkyries are worth as much as winged are futile. To make things worse, my best friends in the entire academy have just fallen off the edge to their deaths. This is not a fair fight. It was supposed to be three against three, not thirty against three.

I blink the tears from my eyes again, letting the warmth run freely down my face, and look at all the faces of the winged Valkyries hovering above me with their arrows nocked. My eyes land on Mistress Sigrun. She doesn't have a bow in her hand. This is surprising, but on her face is a large smirk of victory. She lifts her chin and looks down her nose at me. The arrows continue to fall, and I still don't understand why they are missing me. I spread my arms and gaze up at the sun. It is uncovered by the cloud, and still, a strange shadow covers the top of me.

Mist takes a few more steps toward me, and slowly, a glimmer of gold grows around me and towers over the top of me like a massive building with four golden pillars holding it up. I glance up and realize that I'm staring at Elan's belly. She is so big that I can fit underneath her chest, and she hovers protectively over me, sheltering me from the arrows. Her head shoots forward, and she roars in Mist's direction. Mist freezes on the spot, her eyes opening wide with terror.

She moves to back up until a thud sounds behind her. Drogon has landed, blocking her escape. He is not as big as Elan, but he is still intimidating, with a head full of horns, especially when he bares his teeth like that. He roars at Mist, shooting fire in her direction, then faces the Valkyries hovering above and does the same. When they shoot another round of arrows, he traces the circle with his plume of fire. The fire does not reach them, but the message is loud and clear.

As I watch him, my heart melts. He will be heartbroken when he finds out about Hildr. He was too late.

A strange slapping sound reaches my ears from behind me. I walk underneath Elan, ducking under her tummy, and peer over the edge from underneath her protection. A blue flash darts through the sky, going from Valkyrie to Valkyrie, knocking them from the hovering circle. As it continues passing through the Valkyries, I focus on the blue flash. I almost squeal with delight when I realize that it is Naga, purposely flying headfirst into each Valkyrie. He is walloping them as if they were balls, and they are having trouble righting themselves. If they try to avoid him, he darts in from a different direction, knocking them in different spots. His face fills with glee, and he is so joyful that for the first time all day, I feel the urge to laugh. My joy is short-lived when I remember that my friends were knocked over the edge to their deaths. It is going to break my heart to tell him. In fact, both dragons will be heart-broken in just moments.

Naga continues his game, and I can hear the Valkyries' bones cracking. Mistress Sigrun sees him coming and darts out of the way, a look of superiority filling her face.

She calls out, "You have not won, wingless. There is still one standing."

I gawk at her in disbelief—I cannot believe she is saying this. This has been such an unfair fight until now. Knowing I can't let her win, I steel myself, ready to head back and fight. I have come so far. I have to pull myself together and end this—otherwise Hildr and Eir will have lost their lives for no reason.

Grabbing my sword from the ground, I head in Mist's direction. I stop when a dragon's tail flings out and knocks Mist off her feet. Her legs fly up in the air, and she topples, hitting her head hard against a rock, knocking her unconscious.

Lifting his chin to the sky, Drogon's big brown face focuses on the mistress and snarls. *The last one standing is Kara. I dare you to challenge it.*

Mistress Sigrun glares down at us, and she looks as

though she is about to disagree, but Drogon stands on all fours and flings his head forward, breathing out a large plume of fire right in the direction of the mistress. *That is my last warning,* Drogon roars.

Mistress Sigrun's gaze travels from Drogon to Mist then to me before finishing with Elan. She flaps her wings and takes to the sky, followed by the rest of the conscious winged Valkyries, leaving Mist, Prima, and Rota lying unconscious on the ground. They don't even care for their prized Valkyries enough to pick them up and take them back to the healer.

Elan moves to my side and sits down. *Are you all right?*

I nod then shake my head. "No. Both my friends have died." Tears cloud my vision and plow warm paths down my cheeks, and I drop to my backside. "I have to tell Drogon and Naga." Cloaked in depression, I search for the dragons, but I can't see them anywhere. "Where did they go?"

Elan doesn't answer me, and I turn to ask her again. I spot a small smile creeping onto her face, exposing a couple of her pointiest teeth.

I frown. "Why are you smiling?"

I think you'll find things are not as bad as they seem.

"No, they are worse. I have lost my two best Valkyrie friends and have a treacherous, lying, and conniving nasty leader."

That you have. But your friends—

A thud cuts her off, and I turn to see brown legs standing next to me. My eyes travel up to a face that is full of joy, and I can't for the life of me understand why, especially when my heart is broken by the sad news that I have to tell him.

I can't let it wait any longer. "Drogon, I—" My shoulders sag.

"Oh, Vanir! That was awesome!"

I glance up and see Hildr climbing off Drogon's back. My mouth drops open in disbelief. "Hildr?"

"In the flesh, baby." Her freckles have faded as her face is flushed with excitement.

"But you fell off the side..."

She winces and holds her shoulder. "I did. But Drogon caught me. I'm just dropping by to see if you're all right. Then I'm heading straight to Anita. This arm is killing me."

My heart flutters, and I smile at Drogon before dashing forward to hug Hildr. "I'm sure it is. You have no idea how glad I am to see you alive."

A lighter thump sounds next to me, and I turn to spot Naga. His tail is swinging happily as though he is ready to play.

I crossed my fingers behind my back before I let my eyes travel up to Naga's back. I squeal in delight. Sitting on Naga's back, Eir looks pale, yet she is smiling. I run forward, and she slides down to the ground.

I throw my arms around her. "Oh Vanir! I was certain you two were dead. I'm so happy."

"Not only that, we kicked their butts, girl." Hildr barges in from the outside, hugging us around the shoulders.

CHAPTER TEN

My heart swells with joy. "I'm so glad you guys are here." Turning to Elan, I say, "Thank you for protecting me from all those arrows. I couldn't understand why they were missing me."

Of course. I will always protect you. She drops her head down to my level and nudges me with her nose. Her sharp scales catch on my clothes.

I unhook the leather from her scales and lean into her snout, caressing her briefly. "How did you guys know about this and when to come?"

She raises her head and gazes at Naga. *You did have a full conversation in front of Naga. His English may not be so good, and he may not be the brightest dragon, but he certainly understood that you were in danger.* She shows off her full display of teeth in her vicious smile. *The moment you left him last night, he flew out of his cell and warned me, then I visited Drogon. We got together at first light to see what would happen. We didn't know if there were any rules involving dragons or not. But after seeing how the winged Valkyries on the sides attacked, as well, we gathered there were no rules.* She pauses, and the scales between her horns clump together. *It is utterly unfair for all those winged Valkyries to fire upon you when it should be three against three. They already had an advantage. They didn't need to cheat.*

"Technically, it isn't cheating when there are no rules." Hildr's face screws up with contempt. "Now we need to see if Mistress Sigrun carries through with her promise to let you go to Midgard, Kara. After the way they cheated here today, I wouldn't be surprised if she reneges on that too."

Eir scowls. "She better not. That was an agreement made in front of the whole academy. Surely she must have to stick to that. It was even made in front of the other wingless Valkyries."

"Only time will tell." The knife of the traitor twists deeper in my stomach, yet determination pushes me onward. I look at the three dragons. "I'm glad you're here, not only because you saved us, but also because we need a lift down this massive mountain. Can we get a ride, please?"

Of course. We'd love to help, Elan says, her voice back to its normal cheerful tone.

"What about them?" Eir points to Rota, Prima, and

Mist. "We can't just leave them here unconscious, even though the winged Valkyries have."

I'll flick them off the side. Drogon stomps toward Prima. *It would be my pleasure.* He takes a few more steps.

Drogon! Elan calls. *You can't do that!*

Yeah, I can. They didn't fight fair, so we shouldn't play fair with them. Besides, they have wings.

But they're unconscious, Drogon. Elan scowls. *If we do something like that, we will never get this alliance sorted. The Valkyries will want to be our enemies forever.*

Drogon huffs, and smoke billows out of his nostrils. He tosses his head aside. *Oh. All right.* He stops in his tracks.

Good choice, Drogon, Elan chirps. *Now, let's get these three down and get them healed.* She gives me a sideways glance. *And you and I are going to discuss what's going on with that arm.*

"I wish I knew." I climb onto Elan's back and hook my legs around her neck.

I'm sorry I didn't have time to grab the saddle. And besides, it is a bit hard for me to be invisible when it is on my back, Elan calls over her shoulder.

"After everything you've done for me today, this is the last thing I'm worried about." I slide my hand gently under her scales and touch the soft skin underneath. "Thank you, Elan."

Always my pleasure. Now I've paid you back once.

I roll my eyes. "I never expected you to pay me back for anything, Elan, but thank you." She pushes off the ground, and Drogon and Naga follow with Eir and Hildr on their backs. When we land, I escort them to see Anita.

The dragons push off and into the sky to collect the winged Valkyries still at the top of the mountain. Despite everything they've been through and seen, they're still doing the right thing, and my heart fills with pride. I don't know how I've ended up being so lucky—just because I saved her egg a couple of years ago.

I escort Hildr and Eir to Anita and assist them onto the gurney table, and they wait for Anita, who is busy in the other room.

"Will you guys be all right if I take off for a bit?"

"I think we will be all right in the healer's hands." Hildr screws up her nose.

"I don't know, Hildr. She could be after us, just like the winged ones," Eir says with a smirk.

I rub Eir's shoulder. "I'm pretty sure you will be safe here."

"I know," she says without the slightest hint of apprehension.

Leaving the healer's quarters, I head to the library. I'm determined to find out if I can find anything about that zmey creature and what's going on with my arm.

I press through the double stone doors into the library. It is several stories high, with books lining every wall up to the ceiling. Surprisingly, ladders are supplied for anyone who doesn't have wings, which is a nice change and a strange sight for the Valkyrie academy. But it all makes sense when I turn to the counter and spot the wingless Valkyrie in charge of the library. A librarian is undoubtedly a better job than a cleaner. It may not be as esteemed as a healer, but in my eyes, it's a valuable position.

Instead of searching on the shelves, I go straight to the librarian. Her thin frame is curved over the bench, and a veil of chin-length black hair hides her face as she leans over a book. I reach the counter, and she turns the page and hooks a strand of hair behind her ear. She looks up, and I can't help but notice her eyes wander over my shoulder in search of reassurance that I don't have wings. I suspect it is an old habit from her days at Valkyrie Academy. She smiles broadly, accentuating her Valkyrie beauty.

"Morning, Jannika."

"Kara, I haven't seen you for a couple of weeks. How can I help?" She even sounds keen to help—a nice change from the day I've had so far.

"I'm looking for a book that has weird creatures in it."

"Are you talking about Asgard or any of the other realms? That's a lot of books to cover. Can you be more specific?"

"I'm looking for one creature in particular. I have

only seen it in Asgard a few times. Someone said it is called a zmey."

Creases form on her brow as she frowns in thought, and her lips push to the side. "I can't say that I've heard of it. Can you describe it?"

"It has big membrane-like wings, with beady eyes, and its body is round and short… as in not as tall as me. And it's chubby." I pause for a moment, thinking. "And its face is ugly, and it has claws big enough to hold dragon eggs."

One of her eyebrows arches. "How many times have you seen this creature?"

"It's only been a few times, but I believe there's only one, and it's living in Asgard."

She rests a finger across her lips, and the loose ends of her pale-pink sleeve flops to her elbow. Her brow furrows into a frown. After a moment, she raises her finger. "Ah! I think I might know the one. Come, follow me." The material of her navy culottes swishes as she walks to the far wall at the back of the library. Jannika grabs the ladder and drags it to the far end of the library.

"Wait here. I shall bring it back down." She climbs and climbs, and I wonder if she is ever going to stop. Balancing on the top rung, she reaches into the shelves and pulls out a large book. Briefly, she studies the cover before tucking it under her arm and climbing down the ladder.

Her black heels land softly on the carpet, and she dusts off the cover. "It's strange, you know. It was only yesterday that someone else borrowed this for the day." She hands it to me with the cover facing up.

With both hands, I take it from her and stare at the cover. "Is this for real?"

She looks at the book and looks back at me. "Why yes, of course. Have a good look through and see if you can find the creature."

I turn to leave. "Thank you," I say at the last second, remembering my manners. She has always been kind to me. I take it to the nearest desk and start turning the pages. An artist's illustrations of strange creatures of all shapes and sizes cover the pages. After several pages, my eyes land on the exact image of the creature that marked my arm. I stare at it in disbelief and blink, trying to decide if I'm imagining things. I know I briefly saw it when the other Valkyrie had the book in the dining hall, but it is still hard to comprehend. I shove my hand in the page's position and close the book to stare at the cover. I reopen the book to the page and stare at the creature. My brain is having a hard time processing the information. Every picture in the book is hand drawn, but the likeness is still staggering.

I flick through a few more pages and find a picture of the old woman I met in the wilderness then encountered in the bathroom that day. And then I close the book again, with my arm marking my place, staring at the cover in disbelief. I open the book back to the same position then browse through a few more pages. My jaw drops. Before me, perfectly captured by the artist, is the young Valkyrie who sat at our table in the dining hall, reading this very book. To be certain, I flick back to the cover and reread it. The book is titled *Known Shapes of the Shapeshifter Loki.*

~

The End

Did you enjoy this book?
You can make a big difference.

Honest reviews of my books help bring them to the attention of other readers.

If you've enjoyed this book, I'd be grateful if you could spend a few minutes leaving a review (it can be as short as you like).

The review can be left on Amazon and Goodreads.

Thank you very much.

KATRINA COPE

EMPOWERED

VALKYRIE ACADEMY
DRAGON ALLIANCE

BOOK 5

EDITORIAL REVIEW

Cosy Burrow Books

Valkyrie Academy Dragon Alliance
Book Five

EMPOWERED

"Kara the wingless Valkyrie's journey continues, and in this installment of the story, she sets out discover why the trickster god, Loki, would steal dragon eggs, and she finds a mysterious mentor to teach her how to control and use her magic to prove her worth and help Asgard." Susie D., Line Editor, Red Adept Editing

Empowered
Ebook first published in USA in October 2019 by Cosy Burrow Books
Ebook first published in Great Britain in October 2019 by Cosy Burrow Books

www.katrinacopebooks.com

Published by Cosy Burrow Books

ISBN: 978-0-6486613-4-4
ASIN: B07W57HJND

❀ Created with Vellum

Midgard ~ for your endless beauty and inspiration

CHAPTER ONE

The pages rustle as I flick through the book, my fingers stiff and uncertain. *This can't be right.* My mind wants to reject what I'm seeing. The need to slap myself across the face is strong. I have to prove that I'm not dreaming. After closing the cover, I stare at the front. It is a picture of Loki in his god form. The artist has portrayed him well—the pale skin contrasting with his long black leather pants and vest, and the cape that flows to his ankles. His dark hair is greased back and falling to his shoulders, accentuating his pointy nose and narrow, spirited eyes.

My eyes refuse to move away from this picture. Rarely have I seen Loki, but maybe he travels around Asgard in other forms or doesn't stay on Asgard for long. I'm not sure. He doesn't usually associate with the Valkyries, although the dragons seem to hold him in some kind of regard. Unlike the other gods of Asgard, he is able to change into dragon form and communicate with them. The dragons have trouble communicating with the other gods because of the gods' thick-headedness.

But Loki's changing into a dragon to understand them is purely an act. From what the dragons tell me, Loki is intelligent and can understand them in all forms, but they don't want the other gods, like Odin, to know that the dragons can speak to most beings directly.

I open the book to the page that holds the creature then turn to the page with the old woman, followed by the page with the girl who looks slightly younger than me and could disguise herself as a Valkyrie. They are all images of Loki. Each well-crafted image by the artist of this book is a reflection of what Loki has shifted into.

I flick back to the creature that they call a zmey and stare at it, taking in the pointy snout, the sharp teeth, the ears like a bat's, and the talons that are large yet shaped like a bird's. The short round fluffy body is a sharp contrast to the dragon-like membranous wings that protrude from the zmey's back. The zmey has given me much grief over the last few years.

As I stare at the picture of the creature, my mind swirls, trying to process the information and work things out. More recently, I have spotted the creature flying around Asgard. It attacked Heimdall the day that I broke the rules, distracting him, and I used the opportunity to enter Midgard, yet I have also run into it on several occasions. I now understand why this creature was in the area when the old woman pulled me aside to talk to me—the same woman illustrated in this book as a shape Loki shifts into. They are the same. The creature wasn't after the old woman, as I initially thought. The scar on my shoulder, which the creature gave me, tingled when I met her and the young girl. It even prickles when the creature flies over me.

I study the page with the creature, and underneath the image is a bulleted list of symptoms from the creature's scratches. My finger traces the words.

Beware of this creature.

- *It has long, sharp claws.*
- *It is shrewd like Loki.*
- *It can attack, and just because it is Loki doesn't mean it won't attack you.*
- *Beware of its scratch. If it scratches you, you have been marked with the curse of magic.*

Symptoms:

- *A sharp pain that pierces deep into the scar when you get within a certain range of this creature or other forms of Loki.*
- *Tingling combined with a strange numbing*

sensation running through the area of the scar and any limb attached to it.

Be warned:

If a form of Loki touches the scar, it will increase the chances of the magic manifesting. With each contact, the magic will grow until eventually, it will explode. At first, this magic will not show. It will only manifest when emotions require it to or desperation occurs. Eventually, though, you will soon be able to demonstrate this magic at will.

Beware of this creature, as with anything to do with Loki. One must always be on guard. He is the god of mischievous intentions that do not change with whichever form he takes.

I STARE at the page in disbelief. So this creature has marked me with magic, just like the old woman warned, the one that I now know is a form of Loki. He must've been seeking me out so he could touch the scar and make the magic rise to the surface. Precisely as the book describes, with each visit from one of these forms, the tingling manifested. No wonder the old woman was so keen to touch my arm.

I'm a wingless Valkyrie with no unique talents, so I don't understand why he would choose me. He could have flown away that day that I chased him off the dragon's nest and left me alone without marking me.

A tingle in my arm erupts, and I rub it absentmindedly. Perhaps the sensation has surfaced because my head is in this book and I'm thinking so hard over it that it's making me remember the scar. But then I remember what happened in the bathroom and before the fight on the top of the mountain. I gaze at my body. I still have blood and scratches from the battle all over me, and my wound is still aching and weeping. It wasn't a dream. I had used my magic—magic I didn't know I possessed and don't know how to use.

I look at my left hand—the culprit of the damage—and can see nothing special. Somehow this hand made Rota and Prima unconscious. It wasn't a dream at all. I take in all the creases and lines within the hand's shape, then hold my right hand next to it. It looks the same. Nothing has happened to the right hand, only my left. The one attached to the shoulder tarnished with the scar that was marked by the zmey. The hands are still the same color, and the lines appear the same. Yet somehow, the left hand managed to cause damage and knock some Valkyries unconscious. I have never heard of this happening before. Perhaps the elves or the fairies have this magic or have heard of a Valkyrie having it before.

Staring at my hands, I try to let it sink in, and I wonder who can help me with this. I will need training and help to discover the answers. I don't know any fairies or elves, let alone any that can help me. We are taught that they are dangerous and untrustworthy, yet I don't know anyone else to ask.

Observing the image of the creature a little longer, I curl my fingers into a fist before closing the book. Loki stares at me from the cover. He's probably the best one to ask, if I can track him down.

My chair grates across the stone floor as I push it back and stand. With the book hooked under my arm, I approach the library desk. The librarian is hunched over another book and glances up when I approach.

"Jannika, where would be the best place to find Loki?" With the cover facing up, I place the book on the bench, and it scrapes as I push it forward.

She takes in the cover of the book then eyes me with a serious expression. "If you are after Loki to discuss the contents of this book, then you're going to have a hard time. The author wrote this book because Loki is hard to track down." She grabs the book, and it scratches the surface as she spins it to face her. The front cover thuds on the bench, and the pages rustle as she flicks through them. "These are only a few of the shapes that the author knows Loki has represented. Loki will only be found when he wants to be found." Her mouth tweaks at the corner. "He will often take on one of these forms. However, he has many other shapes, making it almost impossible to find him. Especially if he thinks you know of this book."

"Would he be around the palace?" I watch as she flicks through the pages.

She glances up and smiles, her eyes full of understanding. "If Loki was there in god form, don't you think you would have seen him while you were lurking around the palace?"

"Oh, I don't lurk around the palace."

She peers at me, arching an eyebrow.

"I only visited there briefly to rescue my dragon." The words tumble out of my mouth.

The eyebrow drops. "Yes, I know. That was my point. I know that you have upset Odin and he wishes you harm, or to have you locked up in the dungeons."

"Is that all anybody knows?" I let out a frustrated sigh, and my shoulders slump. "Doesn't anybody know about the good things I've done?" I push back from the bench and take a deep breath. "Besides, the things I did —like stealing my dragon back—was to follow the agreement of the alliance. Odin is not supposed to hold her."

She closes the cover of the book with a soft thud. "Yes. But what Odin is supposed to do and what Odin wants can often be two very different things. Just be careful. And I doubt you will find Loki there, so don't go putting yourself at risk to find him."

"Thank you."

"Go get this cleaned up." She indicates the bloody and torn patches of leather on my body.

CHAPTER TWO

I reach for my side and look down at my clothes. The librarian is right. I need to see the healer and get cleaned up. My wound is healing slowly, but it is best to check that it's not infected. After the unfairness they displayed in the battle, it wouldn't surprise me if the winged Valkyries contaminated their blades. I should also check on Hildr and Eir to see if they're okay.

My leather pants squeak as I wander down the hallway, and my mind is overloaded with all the information I have learned from the book. It is hard to process it all, especially when mixed with what the dark elf has told me. It is shocking to learn Loki is involved, and I can't imagine why a god would mark me then pursue me afterward.

I want to run to the palace and demand to speak with Loki, but as Jannika said, he's probably not there, and I'm not convinced that Odin won't arrest me. He told Eingana, the leader of the dragons, that he wouldn't touch me, but he often changes his mind. I'm eager to find Loki and see if he will fill me in on what is going on.

As I glance at one of the flickering sconces on the wall, it hits me—Loki is the one stealing eggs. Apparently, the zmey is still taking the eggs from the dragon wastelands. If the book is correct, then the dragons mustn't know the creature is Loki, or else their trust would shatter. The dragons are using Loki as a translator for Odin. *Is he betraying them to Odin?* If he is taking their eggs, he must be betraying them.

The knowledge torments me. I don't know if I should tell the dragons that it was Loki who tried to steal the dragon's eggs. If they find out it is Loki, then this may make them distrust the Asgardians more. It may also ruin my relationship with them. But then again, it might ruin my relationship with them if they find out that I know and didn't tell them. A whirlwind builds in my stomach, and I clutch at it, not sure what to do. I ponder over the decision until finally, I decide I will have to find out for sure before I tell the dragons. Otherwise, if it isn't him, then their relationship with him would be ruined for no reason. By the time I stumble into the healer's section, my head is pounding.

Anita darts toward me. "Kara, you look terrible." She grabs me by the arm to stop me from falling. "Come sit down over here." Gently, she leads me to a corner, bypassing the unconscious Rota and Prima, and sits me down on the chair.

I search every part of the room, and I can't seem to find my friends. "Where are Eir and Hildr?" I ask as the healer investigates my wounds.

"I've patched them up already. They are healing nicely. What happened to you?" A curly auburn strand of hair falls forward, hiding some of the concern in her green eyes. "I hope you weren't like this straight after the fight, or else you shouldn't have left."

"I… I… I don't know." Rubbing my head, I try to think. "I'm a little confused."

"Well, I'm not surprised. I hear that something weird happened up at that site."

"What did you hear?" My mind is filled with confusion as a piercing headache shoots through my frontal lobe.

"These two"—she indicates Rota and Prima—"have been touched by magic."

"How do you know?" I stare at them, but they are unmoving.

She gives me a strange look from the corner of her eye, and I get the feeling that she doesn't buy my innocence. "I've been healing long enough to see the signs of magic. I have been around much longer than you have." She joins me in staring at the two unconscious Valkyries. "The last time I saw something like this was back when dark elves attacked some Valkyries. They, too, were knocked unconscious. What I saw in Rota last night was the same but not to the same extent. The outcome manifesting today is much more intense than what she felt yesterday." She pauses, and I feel her eyes on me again. "I hear that it was you who touched Rota in the bathroom yesterday. And it was you who fought against them today, touching them and rendering them unconscious."

I rub my temples. "What is happening to me? How did I get magic? Valkyries don't have magic, do they? And if they do, what kind of magic do they have?" My questions come thick and fast, and I watch the healer's face, but it remains calm and collected while she processes each query.

"This is a strange world. Anything can happen in this realm. The nine realms have a mixture of gods, fairies, giants, and all sorts of odd creatures. I'm starting to think anything is possible." A drawer squeaks as she slides it open to retrieve a bandage, which she places beside me. "At times, all these things stretch my healing abilities to the limit, but it makes my job so interesting and rewarding when I manage to heal unusual wounds and illnesses."

"But I've never had magic before, and I haven't heard of other Valkyries having magic. How is this possible?"

Anita pulls back my sleeve, revealing my scar. "I

think you know already." She rubs her thumb along the thick part of the scar then pushes my sleeve back down. "I think I remember you mentioning that a woman warned you about this mark earlier, and about the beast that caused it. Anybody who's been marked by this beast manifests magic eventually." She picks up a small flashlight and clicks it on before directing the light at one of my eyes then the other.

"But I don't know how to use magic." I glance at the two winged Valkyries that I had rendered unconscious. "I don't know how I could even hurt anybody with magic."

"Look back at the light." She directs the flashlight across my eyes a couple more times and places it down on the bench. "Sometimes, desperate situations require desperate measures and force us to bring out what is hidden—even without us intending it to manifest. From what I heard from Eir and Hildr, today's fight on the mountain wasn't fair. All the winged Valkyries stood against you, and you had no choice but to call forth whatever you could from within your body."

She pulls out some solution and cleans some of my smaller wounds. "If you ask me, I think they all deserved it. I also heard that your dragons came along to save the day." Smiling, she dabs some more ointment on my wounds. "I can't think of a better ending. Perhaps there is more to what you have been doing with these dragons. The bond is helping the wingless

Valkyries to become more prominent. For centuries, winged Valkyries have been belittling the wingless Valkyries. It is about time someone strong enough stands up to them with the aid of a formidable partner that is strong enough to bring the winged Valkyries to their knees and realize how unjust they are. Then perhaps they will realize that the wingless Valkyries should be at the same level as them, not be looked down upon. Maybe then they can understand things can be better."

I flinch as she dabs at the wound on my torso that was created by the sword. "But why is this work allocated to me? I was only trying to get myself into Midgard to help serve Asgard and protect us from Ragnarök by reaping the souls of the warriors. I never intended any more than that. I don't understand how I managed to get caught up in this, causing the majority to gang up on my friends and me."

She stops dabbing ointment and begins to bandage my wounds. "That's what bullies do. And that's exactly how the winged Valkyries often treat the wingless Valkyries. They make things worse than what they originally were by trying to stop the person proving their value is more than what the bullies give them credit for. And in this case, because other, big factors are becoming involved, they may well be in for the shock of their lives. You make me excited just thinking about it."

Anita pulls the bandage tight and secures it with a

clip. "As I said before, I am too old to be going into the fighting scene now, to try to reap souls for Valhalla, but I will certainly be here to mend your wounds and offer encouragement whenever I can. Come and use me as a counselor at any time." She smiles, and her face shines with kindness. "I will always be a friend you can talk to."

"Thank you, Anita. It's nice to hear that. To be honest, talking about it has lifted the cloud that was fogging my mind. Everything is a bit clearer now."

She finishes bandaging my wounds. "Now, I think you're fine. You should have these wounds healed in a few hours. You are not that knocked up, considering what you have just been through."

I huff a laugh. "You should see the other guy."

At first, she seems confused, and she gives me a sorrowful smile. "I think what you really need is rest. The lack of it is messing with your mind, and you need rest so your body can recuperate from using magic."

"Which reminds me." I frown. "Do you know where I can find Loki?"

She shakes her head. "He floats around a lot and is often hard to find. He even travels between the realms. Why?"

"No real reason. I just want to ask him a few things."

"Well, in the meantime, I have someone that I know can help you with training that magic," she says.

"You do?" I ask, shocked.

"Yes. He is rather strange, but I know he will help. He revels in magic's power and loves to share his ability and train people to use it. Here. I'll write the name down for you."

A piece of parchment crackles under her touch as she scribbles something on it and hands it to me. "Don't lose it."

After I take the note from Anita, I fold it then stuff it into the pocket of my pants. "Thank you. I'm going to get some rest."

I walk down the hallway after the promise of rest, and my curiosity gets the better of me. I pull the note out of my back pocket and study the name and the scribbled map to the address: Gilroma. *What an unusual name for an Asgardian.* I fold the parchment then place it back in my pocket and head out the door of the academy. I'm not going to rest before checking this out.

CHAPTER THREE

Shivers run up my spine as I follow an ominous tunnel. The wind whistles through the enclosed space, and goose bumps cover my skin. I pull the folded parchment from my pants pocket to check my progress. Dog-eared creases mark the corners, and it crackles its protest as I work in vain to return it to its original condition. Deep inside of me, I hope that I'm going in the wrong direction. This tunnel is giving me the creeps. My stomach feels queasy when the map confirms that I am going in the right direction. It takes all of my strength to remind myself why I am here, and curiosity finally wins. With my nerves barely intact, I push on, my feet stumbling on the jagged rocks. The tension from the eeriness stirs the magic in my arm.

Eventually, a small light glimmers, growing brighter as I slink closer. This tunnel is directly opposite the mountain where the fight was held earlier. Perhaps whoever was down here saw the fight. Rechecking the map, I confirm that this is the right direction. *Where has Anita sent me?* If I didn't trust Anita completely, I would be bolting out of here. The wind howls through the tunnel again. *This is so unnerving.*

Stopping, I straighten my shoulders and take a deep breath. I should've told someone I was coming here. But once again, my tendency to dive into something adventurous overtook me. I should have brought Hildr and Eir. But they're probably just as confused as I am over the magic. No, this is best done alone. I am the one that has the magic, not them, and I shouldn't put them at risk over something that is my problem.

I flick my fingers, trying to release the tension, and progress forward. The tunnel narrows, and the dull light flickering ahead is too dim to see clearly. I wish I'd brought a lamp.

After traveling several more feet, the tunnel encloses more, and I'm starting to doubt whether I'm in the right spot or have taken a wrong turn—except I didn't pass any turns. I pull out the scribbled map for what seems like the millionth time and take a look. Nope. It definitely says it is here.

For a moment, the light ahead glows brighter. I stop, trying to hear any sounds. "Hello?"

Silence is my answer. My arm starts to tingle, and the sensation pushes me forward despite my fear. The tingling spreads to my fingers, and I shake them out, but it continues. I begin to wonder if I'm in danger, because this is often what it does when I seem to be close to things of the dangerous kind.

I slowly press forward some more and call again, "Hello?"

Nothing. And despite my gut churning its disagreement, I continue to move forward. I'm determined to find out what to do with this magic. I am tired of it playing up regularly and twitching, like it needs my attention, and doing strange things when I don't expect it to. It acts as though I should automatically know what to do with it.

With each step forward, I try to avoid stumbling over the protruding rocks and reduce the amount of noise I am making. I cringe as a rock clatters after I kick it. My ears are on full alert as I try to listen for anything that may be ahead of me. I'm not sure if it is best that I arrive quietly, in case I run into something hostile, or if I should let Gilroma know I'm approaching.

Something rattles, and it sounds like a rock falling off other rocks. I pause and listen, but the sound has fallen silent. Perhaps it is an echo from the rock I knocked, or maybe it is the natural erosion of the mountain. This thought doesn't bring me comfort, but I continue anyway. More clattering sounds come from ahead.

"Hello? Is anybody there?"

Again, silence greets me. I'm getting tired of the unknown. I can't wait to reach the end of this tunnel. My body instinctively moves into defensive mode, hands ready, knees slightly bent with each step. I'm prepared to spring in any direction, eyes peeled for the slightest movement. It's drilled into us in battle training, causing it to become an automatic response anytime we feel insecure or threatened.

The tunnel turns a corner, and the top of the cave skims my head. I have to bend over slightly as I follow the light, which is brighter now.

Rounding another corner, I come upon a little room. Several candles are burning in different locations on the walls. All kinds of weird symbols and ornaments lie around the room, and a small pot has something simmering in the corner.

When I started this search for the reasoning behind the magic, I didn't know what to expect. I wasn't sure if I was going to find potions and herbs, but I don't see any sign of them lying within this room, and I wonder what kind of magic this person deals with and why they are so deep within this mountain.

I tuck my hair behind my ear, and the dark-brown locks fall over my shoulder. Dizziness overcomes me, and I press against the wall, holding my hand on my forehead. I wish I'd listened to Anita and had some rest instead of rushing into this.

Weird ornaments of different creatures line the room,

their faces illuminated by several candles. My anxiety settles when I realize that no one is in this cave, ready to attack me, and I consciously work on catching my breath. I slide my back down the wall in the far corner and land on a flat rock.

My head is not clearing, and the prickling in my arm has intensified, reminding me of the sensation before I knocked a Valkyrie unconscious. I rest my head against the rock wall and take in the room. Nothing here makes me think of who might reside here. It's certainly no one I know. After I have taken everything in, I rest my elbows on my knees and hold my head between my hands as I gaze at the rocky floor. I have found myself in some strange situations over the last week or so, and I would never have thought my desire to help reap warriors for Valhalla and prove the worth of wingless Valkyries would turn my life this way.

After a while, my dizziness fades, and I study the room again. Over in the far corner, behind a pile of rocks, are the edges of a stack of books. I gather my strength and stand to have a look.

The top book has been left open, and it has images with intricate details of different weird things. After picking it up, I sit on the rocks and set the book on my lap. I mark the open page with my hand and close the book, unable to resist running my fingers over the design on the cover. A lot of work has gone into this weird embossed design, although it is strange. The spine is held together with straps of leather pinned to the front and back covers. On the top third, a strange-looking skull that looks as though it has been cut from a tree sends shivers up my arm as my fingers trail over the details.

I pull the front cover open and gaze at the title page. The words are in a language that I can't understand, but something about them pulls at something in my memory. The probing is unsuccessful in bringing it to the surface, so I run my fingers over the title page then slowly start to turn the thick parchment pages. The crackling of the pages sends excited anticipation running through my body. Unusual pictures cover each page, and strange writings hold my intrigue as I scan through the pages.

Something in the corner of a page catches my eye. It almost looks like an underlined eye with slashes through it. As I stare at it, it dawns on me that this image is a symbol of the dark elves. It means "I am one with the darkness."

My face loses feeling, and my mind races. I can't help wondering if I'm in danger right now. Surely not. Anita wouldn't have sent me somewhere that would put me in danger. She offered to heal my wounds and support me with my cause. The more I think about it, the harder I find it to believe that she would send me somewhere dangerous on purpose.

I focus my thoughts and study the book some more.

The language in this book must belong to the dark elves. They hold magic, but I have only heard of evil dark elves—ones who want to destroy the Valkyries or anybody in Asgard. *Is the occupier of this cave a dark elf wanting to destroy Asgard and its occupants? Or is it a hobby of theirs to collect items belonging to the dark elves and learn their language? Maybe they are obsessed with their magic.*

Resting my head against the rock wall for a while, I ponder everything that has happened. It has been a very eventful day, and perhaps I am reading too much into this. Or maybe I'm not, and I should escape this cave before it is too late. This might not be the best place for me to be.

Images run through my head of what Odin and Mistress Sigrun would do if they found out where I am. Despite their certain disapproval, I can't squash my burning curiosity, and I flick through a few more pages before setting the book aside. I reach for another book, curious to see what lies within its pages. Each page I turn is filled with the language of the dark elves. Some of the images are disturbing, with someone's flesh melting away from the bone. A sick feeling rises in my stomach, and I close the book and stack it neatly in the corner with the others.

The itch to leave grows strong. Magic or no magic, I don't think this is a place for me. I rise and make my way toward the door, observing the strange figurines as

I pass. Perhaps I should research these in the Valkyrie library. As I reach the entrance of the room, a noise sounds around the corner. Pausing, I listen, and it sounds again. This time, I am sure I hear footsteps crunching the rocks on the floor of the cave. I back into the room and press my back against the stone wall on the same side as the door. There is no way out. Whatever is coming, I have no choice but to deal with it.

CHAPTER FOUR

My nails scratch the wall as my fingers hunt for security by trying to dig into its surface. With each approaching footstep, my shallow breaths rasp, and I steer my focus to calm them, keeping them deep and quiet, but I struggle, and my heartbeat quickens. I'm trapped in this cave, forced to wait for whatever is around the corner. Some more rocks clatter. I don't know if it is a dark elf or something else. Whoever it is, they are almost here. I push even farther back against the cold stones, and the footfalls pause just around the corner.

"I can smell you, my dear. I can smell your fear." The voice is raspy and tainted with intrigue.

His words don't make me feel better.

"Oh, stop it! You just got worse. It was meant to calm you, my dear." Amusement mixes with curiosity in his voice. "I'm coming in, so don't attack. I'm not going to hurt you."

True to his word, he enters the room, and I gasp. He is a dark elf but nothing like I expected. The dark elves that I have seen in pictures often have long, luscious hair that falls past their shoulders, and their physique is usually thin. This dark elf is stockier, his head bald and his cheeks scarred. His eyes are sunken, and deep gashes line his cheeks in vertical stripes. I stare at the tattoos that run along his cheekbones from his eyes to his mouth like jagged tear streaks pointing to his jaw, which is lined with warrior tattoos. A symbol resembling the head of a trident with spiky prongs decorates his forehead, with a hollow directly over his "third eye."

As impressive and intimidating as these tattoos are, they can't hold my attention like his glowing yellow eyes. They narrow, and he enters slowly, his eyes never straying from mine. Despite his promise to not harm me, each step he takes doesn't allay my fear. Something about the glowing yellow eyes and warrior tattoos makes me feel uncomfortable. A long crimson gown flaps quietly with each movement and covers his long, flowing charcoal pants and matching long-sleeved top, which is open to the waist, showing off his muscular chest and two dangling silver chains. He tugs at the two black hoop earrings hanging from his pointy left ear.

"Gilroma?"

"In the flesh." He gives a mocking bow, his eyes never leaving me.

I steel my courage and take a deep breath. "You know, staring at me like that is not making me feel any more relaxed." My voice sounds calmer than I feel, showing my expertise in bluffing my confidence.

His eyes soften at the edges, and he waves a hand at me. "Oh, relax! I'm not going to hurt you." This time he sounds more upbeat and sincere and, somehow, less creepy.

Refusing to let my stare drop, I make sure to read all of his body language to see if he is telling the truth. Something is familiar about him, but I don't know what. Surely I would remember someone with glowing yellow eyes. "Have I seen you before?" I ask.

"I doubt it," the dark elf says. "I tend to keep a low profile. The likes of me are not necessarily welcome in Asgard, which is why I have adopted such a secluded and secure place to reside in." He lifts his palms, indicating the room. "It keeps me safe from the menacing Valkyries and gods who think they know better."

"I can't imagine why you're not welcome." Sarcasm oozes from my voice.

His hairless eyebrows lift with intrigue as he enters the room farther, leaving the entry open and giving me the option of escape. "Although I enjoy a visit from a friendly face, there must be a reason why you have come here."

I lift my chin slightly. "I was told this is where I could find some answers."

He clasps his hands behind his back and stands in the middle of the room, blocking my view of the books. "About what?"

Even though I am here to learn, my tongue remains idle, and my eyes betray me, darting to where I know the books lie behind him.

"It's all right, my dear. I will not harm you. I can sense the question raging within your mind. In fact, I think I can answer it for you without you having to voice it." He lifts his large nose and sniffs deeply. "I can smell the magic on you."

I frown. "What? How can you smell it on me? What kind of nose do you have?"

"They should teach you more in Valkyrie school. You Valkyries tend to be so focused on just one thing that you forget that there is more to life than reaping souls for Valhalla." He flicks his cape over his shoulder, revealing more of his clothes.

"Well, they don't. You mustn't be worth much to the Valkyries, or else they would teach us about you." The words come out harsher than I meant. I don't know why I'm being so snarky. He hasn't made any indication that he wants to hurt me. Perhaps it is a replacement for my fear.

The dark elf sits in the far corner of the room, his eyes never leaving me, then holds his hands out toward my left side. "Why don't you step forward and show me that hand of yours?"

Stunned, I ask, "How do you know it is that hand?"

"I have a way of sensing things."

Eyeing him suspiciously, I decide to step forward and hold out my hand. He clasps my wrist and flips it over to turn the palm face up then uses his other hand to trace a circle in the center. A tingling feeling surges up my arm, bounces within the confines of my skull, and shoots back down my arm and into my hand. My body lurches slightly backward as white light fires out of my palm and into the air, narrowly missing the dark elf's face when he pulls to the side just in time.

I gawk at my palm in shock. "It's never done that before."

"And it shouldn't. You must get control over this magic. You could harm yourself and many others you care about if you don't learn how to use it properly. Whoever sent you here is right to do so. They had your best interests in mind." His wide eyes don't leave me.

"What?" I ask. "Why are you looking at me like that?"

His hairless eyebrows rise. "I have a good idea of who might've sent you. You don't need to tell me the name. I know of a wingless Valkyrie within your academy who is fond of anyone pushing the boundaries against the winged Valkyries and their rules."

I raise an eyebrow right back at him. "And who do you think that might be?"

"Someone I have helped with addressing magic abilities before. Your healer is quite resourceful. Use her wisely. She makes a great ally."

"I'll keep that in mind. Although I'm already starting to get that impression." I have no reason to deny what this dark elf already knows.

"Good. Let's have a look and see what you can do."

I observe my hand. A swelling mark in the shape of a whirl lies in the middle of my palm. "Did you do that?"

The dark elf almost looks hurt. "I merely traced a mark so your magic has a portal to come out. You've been marked before." His hand slides up my arm, and I flinch. He stops and looks at me. "It's okay. I won't hurt you."

I grit my teeth, and eventually, I nod.

His hand travels farther up my arm, revealing my scar. "This is where you've been marked before. I have merely made a spot on your palm so your existing magic has a place to escape more directly rather than only through emotion. Once you have learned to use this wisely, we shall look at other avenues."

I flip my palm over and rub my thumb slowly over the new mark. "Why didn't I see the white light come out before when I used my magic?"

"Because it didn't have a clear release. There were

small barriers in play that caused some of the magic to bounce back within you."

"Then wouldn't I have knocked myself unconscious?"

"No, because it is already a part of you, and you are filled with this magic. What you hit your enemies with was only a diluted solution of your pure magic. So you need to control this. Control the strength that you allow to exit your body, and also what you can do with it and how you direct it."

I gulp. "Do you mean I could have done worse to Rota and Prima? I didn't mean to harm them any more than to get them to leave me alone. I didn't want to hurt them that much."

He nods. "I know. You're lucky that you've been directed here."

"Do you know this creature that marked me?"

"Yes." He studies me again. "Why?"

"Why would it mark me?"

"The creature only marks someone they think is worthy."

"But I was fighting the creature. It was going to steal one of the emperor dragon's eggs. Why would it see me as someone to mark? I thought it was attacking me, not marking me."

A strange smirk that makes me uncomfortable crosses the dark elf's face, but I ignore it. "Clearly, the creature saw something of value in you, something that not even you see, and it decided that you were worth marking."

I struggle to understand this, and I frown.

Ignoring me, he continues as though nothing is unusual. "I want to concentrate on the magic welling in your arm. Now that you have this mark in your hand, I want you to concentrate on the magic in your arm and that tingling sensation you're feeling." He runs a finger up and down my arm. The tingling feeling ignites farther to the top of my shoulder. "I want you to gather it and hang on to it."

I focus on the sensation, imagining walls enclosing around it, feeling the power swell.

"How are you doing with that?" he asks.

"I think I'm gathering it, but I'm not sure. I've never done this before."

"Okay. After you think you've gathered it into a concentrated ball and feel that the power is ready to burst through the edges, concentrate on that far wall. Then aim your palm at the wall before shooting your magic out of your palm and onto that spot."

I squint at the spot on the wall, picturing it in my head, and follow his instructions precisely, shooting a bolt of white light out of my hands and into the wall. A large chunk of the wall crumbles and falls to the hard floor.

"Oh, Vanir!" My mouth drops open.

CHAPTER FIVE

By the time I leave the cave, I'm elated with power and a dangerous sense of invincibility. I have learned to control a small amount of my magic with the dark elf's help, and I can't wait to share my experience with Hildr, Eir, and Elan. So much has happened that it almost seems as though I have left them behind without meaning to. I stumble along the rocky tunnel as I rush to see them, remembering that my curiosity was so piqued that I didn't even call in on them after they were discharged from the healing ward.

Finally, I stumble out of the long, dingy tunnel into the sunlight, welcoming the warmth that hits me fully in the chest and fills me with more cheer. I feel across my torso where the sunlight hits my bare skin. The wounds I had before I ran into the elf have disappeared, not only aided by my Valkyrie blood but also accelerated by

Gilroma's magic. Turning my face toward the sun, I close my eyes and smile. I can feel the magic, no longer an object of fear, surging through me.

Heading toward my room in the Valkyrie Academy, I pass several winged Valkyries who stare at me with disdain as I walk down the corridors. I lift my chin. It's not my fault that they cheated, causing me to unleash my magic before the dragons decided to join in and help us.

As one of them stares at me, I return her gaze. "What's wrong? Didn't the dragons beat you up enough the first time? Would you like me to bring them around so you can receive a second beating?"

Her mouth drops open, and I smile, thinking I must be succeeding in annoying them and putting a stop to how they treat us. I smirk. *Good. It's about time.* I've come a long way since Rota, Prima, and Mist tried to give me a swirly the other day.

My shoes clop as I charge into our bedroom, and I spot Hildr and Eir sitting on their beds with bandages covering different parts of their bodies. For a moment, I am taken aback and halt at the door, staring at them. The bandages give the impression that they were hurt worse than I thought. "Are you guys healing okay?"

Hildr's pale, freckly face flushes as she notices that I am staring at the bandages. She glances down then looks back up with a guilty look on her face. "Oh, yeah. We're healing just fine. We just haven't taken them off yet." She unwraps a bandage and shows me the spot underneath. It has healed perfectly.

"Then why are you still in our room?" I ask.

Eir's long, wavy locks of light-brown hair fall over her face as she feels along her bandages, checking for any residual wounds on her skin. "Because we are physically tired and weary of them making jeering comments as we walk down in the corridor." Her face screws up in disappointment. "You know, because we were beaten in battle—especially me."

"You shouldn't be bummed at all. Both you and Hildr did well." I place a hand on her shoulder.

"No, you nailed it." Hildr's green eyes fill with shame as she shakes her head and looks down at her blankets.

It kills me to see them this way. There is no trace of Hildr's fighting spirit. I'm determined to lift their dispositions. "Only with help from you guys, and with the dragons. If it weren't for a united effort, I wouldn't have nailed it."

Hildr scoffs. "It has nothing to do with you being a magic holder as well."

I twist to look at her directly, dumbfounded.

"Yeah, we have heard about that," Eir says sadly. "Everyone is telling us about how you used magic to wipe out Rota and Prima."

Holding my palm up, I gaze down at the new whirl drawn on it. "You're kind of right. Something weird is going on with my hand—some sort of magic. But I still wouldn't have nailed it without help from you guys and the dragons." I pull my gaze from my palm and take turns looking at them. "You should be proud of that. You helped heaps. It was only three of us against all of them, not a fair fight at all."

My heart drops when I noticed that they still don't believe me. I try to think of anything that will cheer them up. "One thing you two did miss out on was how the dragons helped. Naga was especially entertaining. He flew around the circle of the winged Valkyries and head-butted each one out of their positions." I chuckle. "If only you could have seen them flying sideways. It made it easier to defend against our true challengers."

The horn rings out across the land, and my heart skips a beat. I can't believe it. It is the horn for Midgard, and we were promised a clean entry if we defeated the winged Valkyries.

I turn to the other two expectantly. "Who's coming?"

They shake their heads in unison.

"We don't get to come," Eir says.

"Yes, we do." I place my hands on my hips. "We defeated them even though it was an unfair fight."

"No, *you* defeated them." Hildr's freckled face sets with disappointment, and I struggle with this image. It is a strange sight when her spiky red hair is usually matched with determination. "You get to go. We'll go visit our dragons, I guess."

They stand to leave, and my heart caves with sadness for them. "One day, we will get you there. You deserve to go just as much as me and any winged Valkyries."

"We'll see. At least we have our dragons to go to." Hildr straps on her sword sheath, probably more out of habit than anything, before leaving with Eir.

After replacing my damaged leather clothes with new ones, I race to my bed and grab my dragon-scale cloak, my bow and quiver, and my sword and throw them over my back. I attach my sling to my back pants pocket, and I charge down the hall while throwing my scale cape on. This time, the hallway is empty of all the winged Valkyries, leaving me to run down the corridor without their torments and glares.

I bolt straight for the place where Elan usually sunbathes. It seems to be her favorite spot. I don't see her, but knowing she could be invisible, I call, "Elan!"

It doesn't take long until her scales start to shift into view. *What is it?* Her voice sounds in my head.

"We need to get to Heimdall's post right away."

Why?

"We need to ride Bifrost to get to Midgard and help reap warrior souls for Valhalla." I strap on the saddle then climb up and throw my leg over her back, hooking my feet into the stirrups. "I want to make the most of my newfound access."

She pushes off the ground and climbs into the air,

heading straight for Heimdall's post. For only a moment, the wind thrums noisily against my ear, and I pull my hood over my head, restricting its effect. Even though I shouldn't be surprised, I am amazed at how little time flying takes compared to my usual task of climbing up the cliff face and running across the plains. It seems like only seconds before the ride ends and Elan is landing in front of Asgard's sentinel.

I remain on Elan's back as Heimdall's hands rest on the hilt of his sword, which balances point first on the ground. His dark-brown eyes stare at me from under his horned helmet, then he looks at Elan and back at me. "Young Valkyrie. What is the meaning of this?"

"Heimdall. I defeated the winged Valkyries in competition, and Mistress Sigrun agreed that if I did so, I would be able to go to Midgard to help with the battle and to reap the souls of Valhalla."

Confusion flicks across his face.

"I intend to start today and to make sure she honors this agreement."

Heimdall's body freezes briefly as he ponders this information. His eyes take on a darker shade as he stares at me then back at my dragon. The moments that pass seem like an eternity. "I do not believe that you are telling me another fib, young Valkyrie. I find it hard to believe that you are so dumb as to do this if you didn't have the right of passage. I will grant you the right this time. If I hear differently, there will be consequences to pay."

"I understand," I say. "Thank you, Heimdall. You are making the right decision."

The gatekeeper opens the entrance to Bifrost, and Elan struggles to squeeze through the portal. Instantly, we are sucked down a massive slide, and after a few seconds, we land hard on Midgard's strangely green surface lined with trees that obscure any view to the battlefield. I scan the surface and take a deep breath before letting out a contented sigh. The air has a fresh, light smell to it. "This planet is vastly different from Asgard and utterly beautiful."

Oh, I like it! Elan's eyes are wide as she scans the horizon.

When I notice that she is visible, I chuckle. "I think you might scare the residents, Elan."

Then maybe I should disappear. She turns invisible.

"Yes, I think that's the best option for now. Let's find the battlefield."

Elan's body moves to face the bushes. *What kind of stuff is that?* She huffs, and before I can stop her, fire shoots out of her mouth, setting the bush on fire.

"Elan!" I cry, sliding off her back, then I remove my scaled cloak and hit the flames with it.

Whoops! That was very flammable.

"Yes, Midgard is extremely flammable." I hit the bushes a few more times, managing to put out the last of the flames. "You can't do that. It is such a beautiful place."

I didn't mean to wreck it.

"I know." Watching the spots where the fire used to be, I slide the cloak back on. "It's out now." I climb onto her back and spread the cloak out around me. Noticing how it covers the saddle and some of the straps, I smile, proud of my handiwork. The scale cape completely covers everything vital. "Let's go and fight."

You betcha! Elan says.

I kick my heels lightly against her flank, and she pushes off into the air.

CHAPTER SIX

As Elan flies into the air in her invisible form, I pull the hood of my cape over my head and keep my ears tuned, listening for the cries of war. Eventually, I hear them not too far away from where we landed in Midgard. We follow the screams to find a primal scene of people fighting with swords and archers lining the outskirts, shooting people with arrows.

Valkyries and angels of death are flying above the fighting field and landing in different places. There are many warriors to choose from, but each time a Valkyrie and an angel of death land next to the same soldier, a fight erupts.

A Valkyrie lands next to a soldier she wants and begins to reap his soul, but she is interrupted by an angel of death, and they clash swords over the warrior, who is approaching his final breaths. Pain shoots in my stomach. This warrior's pain can be taken from him in an instant, except he has to wait for the battle for his soul to be finalized, if he can hold out that long. It is a scene that is being replayed many times over the field, sometimes with the angel of death being the first to arrive at the soldier's side.

I see no sign of Rota, Prima, or Mist. A small twinge of guilt pulls at my heart when I realize that Rota and Prima are probably still in the healing ward, recovering from my magic.

A puff of steam erupts in front of me. *This is barbaric,* Elan says. *And I thought dragons were terrible. Do you really want to be part of this?*

"Being barbaric is not what I have in mind. My goal is to prove wingless Valkyries are just as valuable to the cause of saving us from Ragnarök."

There must be a better way to do it.

I shake my head then realize that she probably isn't looking at me. "No. This is all Valkyries are bred for—to reap the souls of the brave warriors so they can fight and defend Asgard in the final battle."

Okay. If that's what you need to do, then let's do it.

Elan flies in, grabs an angel of death by the shoulders, and flings him aside. His body pivots, and his eyes widen as he is tossed, back first, toward a tree.

"What are you doing?" I watch the angel as he spreads his wings to soften the blow and searches for the cause of his sudden change of direction.

I'm helping. She swoops down, aiming straight for the next angel of death in line, and picks him up by the shoulders and flings him beside the last one.

It surprises me that they don't see me in the saddle before being snatched from their duty. The last one looked directly at me but still didn't flinch when my body dived at him. He continued as if I didn't exist.

After flinging that angel of death aside, Elan flaps her mighty wings, and we lift into the sky and circle the battlefield before aiming for another angel.

Can't I just breathe fire over them? That would be fun.

"No, don't do that. I don't want to kill the angels of death. I only want them to get away from the souls that we are trying to reap."

You take all the fun out of it, Elan says with light-hearted disappointment.

"I guess. If that's what you call fun."

My stomach lurches as she dives to the next angel of death, and he looks up, a puzzled expression on his face.

As we near him, it occurs to me that I know this one. "Elan! Stop!"

She is only seconds away from gabbing him by his shoulders. His face remains turned up with a strange expression, but he doesn't recognize me, even though I am sure it is him. Elan swoops up at the last second, narrowly avoiding his shoulders.

A Valkyrie darts at him with a sword in her hand, and I call, "Harut! Look out!"

The puzzled look remains on his face as he searches around him and spots the Valkyrie a few feet away. She swings at him with her sword, and he retrieves his in time to block the blow. The sound of clanging metal echoes across the valley.

"Can you break that up, please, Elan?" The tingling surges in my left palm. I can feel the magic stirring inside me.

What? That is a strange request.

"I want to get closer to stop this fight. This angel of death has done a favor for me before, and I would like to return it."

Okay. She circles around and lands on a patch where no one is fighting, not far from Harut. *Since when have you known an angel of death?*

"It's a long story. I'll tell you later." I swing my leg over her back and slide down. My feet hit the ground with a soft thud, and the grass crunches under my boots as I head toward him. I clench fists as I watch the Valkyrie swinging at him with full force. He stops the blow in time and fights back. His fighting skills are impressive, but I still don't like seeing him put in danger. I know from experience that these Valkyries will fight to the death.

My left arm is burning with magic, and I'm dying to throw some magic at the Valkyrie. Thanks to the dark elf, I have perfected my aim. I tug at the hood of my cloak, securing its protection of my head and neck. A surge of confidence rises with each rub of the cloak against my legs. "Stop!" I call.

The battle is too intense at this point, and neither of them stops their attack. I rush forward, darting between them and dodging the blade of the sword. Harut's sword swipes along the dragon scales of my coat. "Stop!" I call again.

The Valkyrie's retaliation swings toward me, and her blade stops in midair.

Her eyes narrow when they focus on me. "Step away, wingless. You shouldn't be here."

"You know I have permission to be here." I remain between them and cross my arms. "That was the agreement if I beat Rota, Prima, and Mist. Not only did we beat them, but we also proved that we can still succeed with all of you winged Valkyries going against us in an unfair fight."

When I approach her, she backs away with her sword held high. "Don't you dare touch me with those hands." She glares at them with a look of disgust.

"What's the matter? Are you afraid that you'll end up like Prima or Rota?" I tilt my head to the side.

"I don't know how you came across such power, but you shouldn't have it. Your side wasn't fair either. You brought magic to the ring, like some witch or dark elf."

"So you're afraid of a wingless Valkyrie with a little

bit of power. Now there's a change." I have no desire to use my magic on her, especially if she leaves Harut or me alone, but a small part of me is happy to see her cringe after how they have treated the wingless Valkyries in general.

"You still shouldn't be here," she snaps before pushing into the air and flying in retreat.

Behind me, Harut looks confused as he observes me with a raised eyebrow and his sword still hanging by his side. When I remove the hood from my head, letting it fall to my shoulders, he smiles, his pale cheeks puffing out, and his dark eyes dance with amusement. "It's nice to see a friendly face in this battle," he says while tucking his black wings closer to his back.

Elan is visible behind him, and her upper lip screws up into what looks like a snarl, except her eyes don't hold viciousness. She looks at me and says, *There's a rotten smell coming from that direction,* then turns invisible again.

I chuckle. That was such an odd thing to do.

Harut's black eyes search my body as he observes me and my cloak. Heat rises to my cheeks. "What are you wearing?"

Welcoming a distraction, I look at the sleeves of my cloak. "This is just something I've made."

"It's an odd choice, but I like it."

I laugh nervously. It would seem like an odd choice to him because he hasn't seen Elan. "I've made friends with a dragon, and I made a cape from their scales. It acts as a shield, except it is lighter in weight, and it protects more of my body."

"What a brilliant idea." He circles me, taking in the details, then stops in front of me. "How did you get here?"

"On the back of my dragon."

His face drops. "There's a dragon here?"

I nod. "Yes."

He searches the field and the sky. "Where?"

"She's invisible."

"Invisible? She has that ability?"

"Yes. She was staring at you before."

His face somehow turns paler. "Before when?"

"You were looking up into the sky, and we were coming straight at you, just before the Valkyrie attacked you.

His forehead crinkles into a frown. "I didn't see you, but I did see some strange strap things floating through the sky."

I point behind him, and he turns. "Like those straps?"

"Yes. It was like those but without the saddle." His voice is hesitant, as though he thinks he is seeing things.

I chuckle, as the saddle sitting in midair does look strange. "Elan, can you show yourself?"

For a moment, Elan's golden scales shimmer in the sun, and she glowers at Harut before disappearing again. I shake my head and smile. Elan is doing her intimidating introduction she loves so much.

"Holy Freyja! She's one vicious-looking dragon." He backs away from her and looks at me. "I knew you were different."

Frowning, I ask, "You mean because I don't have wings?"

He shakes his head. "Well, there's that, but no. You just had something different about you. I never would've guessed it would be because you befriended a dragon." His eyes stray for a moment as he gazes over the battlefield. "And I'm guessing you're here to prove that you are worthy again." He looks at me again with a questioning look on his face.

"You got it!"

Indicating the soldier lying on the ground, the one he had been fighting over, he says, "Be my guest."

"Really?"

He nods.

"But won't it upset your leader or something?"

He smirks. "Don't worry about that. I'll deal with them." He nods again to the soldier, who groans loudly as though on cue. "Please, be my guest. Let's see if this magic that Valkyrie was talking about helps you reap souls."

CHAPTER SEVEN

With shaking hands, I approach the moaning soldier. A large gash lines his torso, exposing his intestines. There is no hope for him on Midgard, and he needs to be released from his pain.

"I can sense an honorable side to him." Staring at him, I take in all of his features. He has the harsh face of a warrior in his thirties, but there is something different, possibly softer in the lines around his eyes.

"Yes, that is correct. The angels of death target the more honorable and less ruthless souls to reap because that is what Freyja wants for Folkvangr."

I gaze over my shoulder at him. "From what they teach us at Valkyrie Academy, the Valkyries go for the savage, fearless warriors."

"Yes, that is right. You are a bloodthirsty lot."

"Then why do Valkyries and angels of death fight over warriors?"

The soldier moans again, and I return my gaze to him.

"Because if they are strong, then the Valkyries will also want that soul. Your kind is also a greedy lot."

I frown. After hearing that, I would have to agree with him. I focus and remind myself that I'm here to prove the other wingless Valkyries' and my worth. I'm not going to let an opportunity go to waste. Placing a shaking hand on one of his, I brush the hair off his forehead before resting my left palm there.

Blood is trickling down his face, and his pale-blue eyes stare up at me. The pain on his face screams so loudly that I almost feel it in my body. I concentrate hard on the magic tingling in my left arm as it moves toward my hand.

Leaning close to his ear, I whisper to him, "I release you from your pain on Earth and send you to Valhalla to serve amongst the bravest of warriors."

I wait—and I wait some more. Nothing happens. The soldier groans, and a deep twist of guilt knots through my stomach. I haven't relieved him of his pain. *How can this be?* I can't relieve him, even with magic and the right to join the Valkyries on the battlefield. But I thought that my magic could send him to Valhalla, or at least prove my right to be here with the winged Valkyries. I release a small amount of magic into him, giving it another go. He cries in pain, and I stop instantly, staring at my hands. I'm not trying to kill him—I'm trying to reap him and relieve his pain. I'm disheartened deep to my core—not only for me but also for him.

Harut squats next to me, and he places a hand on my shoulder. A strange kind of cold warmth flows through my body. "There must be more to it than what they are telling you."

"Or what they're not telling me," I say.

"Wingless!"

The familiar voice screeches across the distance, and I exhale deeply. That voice always brings trouble for me. Slowly, I turn my eyes up to see Mistress Sigrun stomping my way, her tan leather jacket flapping against her waist.

"What are you doing?"

I push up to stand, and Harut stands next to me.

Squaring my shoulders, I say, "I am entitled to be here. I won the right, remember?" I narrow my eyes as she crosses her arms and holds her chin high. "You agreed in front of all of the academy. Are you planning on breaking that agreement?"

She raises her chin some more, her blue eyes sharp. "You didn't win properly. You had help."

"And so did Rota, Prima, and Mist. They were supposed to be the only ones fighting. Instead, all of you winged Valkyries stood against us. It was only once the dragons realized that you weren't playing fair and outnumbered us that they intervened. Otherwise, it would have been our lives."

"And that would have been three lives not missed," the mistress says. She leans to the side, placing all of her weight on one hip, and her royal-blue leather pants squeak from the movement.

"Did you really just say that?" Harut moves in front of me, blocking the mistress.

"Stay out of it, angel of death." She turns to the Valkyrie Harut fought earlier. "Reap him." She indicates the soldier still moaning on the ground.

Harut blocks her path to the soldier. "No. You may not reap him. He's mine."

"Out of the way, angel of death," Mistress Sigrun demands then unsheathes her sword and holds it menacingly in front of Harut.

I step in front of the mistress and hold up my left palm. The circle on it glows. "Step back, Mistress. This is Harut's soul. It is his right. He was only giving it to me."

"If he has given it to you, then he has given it to all the Valkyries. Step out of the way, wingless." She glares at me.

I raise my left palm more, and she backs away. "What? Are you going to use magic on me now?"

A corner of my mouth lifts. "If I have to." I wave my palm. "The Valkyries don't want this soul, anyway. He is gentler than the normal soul that you need for

Valhalla. He is more of a friend and a lover. Someone with compassion. Not a typical Valkyrie requirement for a soldier of Valhalla."

The mistress stares at my palm then at the soldier before staring at my palm again. She crosses her arms and puts her weight on one leg. "Then you can have the dregs, angel of death."

Harut squats and reaps the soldier. A tinge of jealousy sweeps over me as I watch the warrior's face turn peaceful.

The mistress stares at my cape with an upturned nose. "How did you get here, wingless? It would take flying power to get here as quickly as you did."

"I came here on my dragon."

"Of course you did. Go home, wingless," she snaps then flies away, her beautiful white wings shining in the sun.

My gaze falls to the dead soldier, and I'm frustrated that I still can't reap souls—after everything I've done to get here.

Harut's concerned black eyes watch me. It's strange that one who is considered my enemy is the only friendly one here, except Elan. "Are you all right?" he asks.

I nod, even though my heart is tearing apart over another failure.

"Come." He reaches for my hand, and a strange tingling sensation shoots up my right arm, making it feel numb. It's a different sensation from what happens in the left one. This sensation rushes from my arm and through my torso, and I can feel the blood rushing to my ears.

I pull my hood over my head, and I catch a glimpse of his eyes as he looks at the intricate detail of my cape.

"You've made an interesting cape. It looks even more beautiful in the sun. I don't know how I didn't see it earlier if you were flying straight at me."

"You have me baffled. Only Elan, my dragon, can turn invisible."

The battle continues to rage around us, and I find my interest has wavered for the moment.

"Shouldn't you be reaping more souls?" I ask.

He surveys the field. "The battle is almost finished. There aren't too many souls left to reap. The other angels of death can take care of this."

We stroll toward the saddle. It's sitting strangely off to the side of the battlefield, on the invisible Elan's back. When we reach Elan, she turns visible for a moment. I clasp onto the saddle and climb up then stick my feet into the stirrups and spread my cloak over the sides, covering the saddle. Elan disappears underneath me, and I peer at Harut through the corner of my eye.

"So what do you think?"

He shakes his head. "I now know why I couldn't see you."

CHAPTER EIGHT

Frowning, I observe Harut from the corner of my eye. "What do you mean?"

He opens his arms wide. "You're invisible."

I turn to face him fully. "What?"

He chuckles. "Well, everywhere your cloak covers is invisible. I can see your face, though, now that you're looking at me."

"Are you serious?" Gazing down, I can't see Elan, but I can see myself. "Elan, can you turn visible, please?"

Elan's golden scales glitter in the sun. "Can you see me now?" I ask Harut.

"Now, I can see you. Yes." He nods. "Why don't you try it again?"

"Elan, can you turn invisible?" I ask. The golden glow disappears from below me, and the green grass of

Midgard replaces her scales.

"Yup, you're definitely invisible again," Harut states before I can ask him.

"Huh. Imagine that. Can you please turn visible again?"

Elan's glow appears in front of me again, and I climb down from her back. I stroke her side and rest my hand on her shoulder, making sure my cloak touches her scales. "Elan, can you please turn invisible again?" Her scales disappear in front of my eyes, and I ask Harut, "What about now? Can you see me?"

"No. I can't see you. I can see your face when you look at me, but if you pull your hood over your face, I can't see you at all."

"Imagine that. I've made something more important than I thought." I pull my hand away from Elan, so the scales of my cloak are not touching her. "What about now?"

"Yup. You're visible again."

I walk around to Elan's snout. "Did you know about this, Elan?"

She shakes her head. *I see our scales regularly on the ground in the wastelands, but I never thought to see if they would turn invisible when our invisible bodies were touching them.* She huffs, and a puff of smoke shoots out of her nostrils. *Can I ask you a favor?*

"Of course."

Can you ask your friend to stand downwind? He stinks.

I chortle and feel the blood rush to my cheeks over the thought of passing this embarrassing information over to him. "What do you mean?"

He stinks of death.

I gaze at Harut with confusion. *How can someone who looks so handsome smell disgusting?* I noticed an odor of rotting flesh at different stages on the battlefields, but I didn't connect it to him or the other angels of death.

"You look as though you're talking to your dragon," he says.

I forgot to tell him. It completely slipped my mind. "Yes. Sorry. I assumed that she was sharing the conversation with you too. Elan speaks in my head." I frown at her. She shared the conversations she held with me in front of Hildr and Eir in their heads, yet now that she wants to say something embarrassing, she only tells me and asks me to pass the message on.

Harut moves cautiously closer to Elan. "She does? What is she saying?"

"I don't really think you want to know," I say, trying to give him a reassuring smile, but I know I've failed.

"Sure I do." He moves closer. "I've never spoken to a dragon before. I had no idea they could speak."

"Um… well." I search my mind desperately for how to say this politely. I've only spent a small amount of time with Harut, and he has treated me well on the battlefields. Since I've grown quite fond of him, the last thing I want to do is upset him. "Um."

Elan shakes her head. *I said that you smell, angel of death. And I need you to move downwind.* Elan's voice booms through my head, and the breath catches in my throat when I look at Harut. She must have shared this conversation with him.

Harut's gaze drops to the ground, and his cheeks redden. "Oh. Now I understand why you didn't want to tell me." His shoulders slump. "Unfortunately, that's an occupational hazard. I had forgotten about it because we never communicate with other species." He turns to leave. "I'm sorry."

Holding out a hand to stop him, I say, "I don't mind. Well, um, I do mind the smell, but I'm not going to avoid you because of it." My tongue trips over the words. "Just because my friends have something wrong with them doesn't mean I'm going to turn them away. Although I would be happier if you stayed downwind from me if you smell like corpses that have been rotting for several days."

His face turns red, and he looks as though he's about to turn away again.

"I'm sorry. That came out completely wrong."

"No. That's okay. I know it's the truth. It's just embarrassing." Gradually, he moves downwind, his eyes not meeting mine.

Silence fills the air as we fidget awkwardly, and I try to think of a way to change the topic. I feel so bad, and I glare at Elan.

After a while, Harut breaks the silence. "How did you manage to get magic? The other Valkyries have talents in fighting and reaping souls, but none of them seem to have magic." He indicates the Valkyries aggressively finishing their fight. "Do all wingless Valkyries have magic?"

"No. I'm different. A beast marked me, and I've only just discovered it. It's a long story. Let's sit and talk about it."

We sit close to Elan and rest our backs against a tree.

"Actually, before we start, did I see you in the portal of Bifrost not so long ago?" I ask. "It was so strange. Heimdall was refusing to let me go to Midgard, and as he stood in my way, your image appeared in the middle of the portal and seemed to hover there for a few moments."

"Yes. That was me. I thought you saw me. I came looking for you. I was hoping that you would turn up to the next battle on Midgard, but you didn't come. So I tried to come to Asgard without permission." He chuckles. "You should be grateful for your gatekeeper. He is one tough cookie to get past." He holds up a finger and smirks. "But I did manage to spot you through the portal, and I could see you were having trouble getting past him too."

My cheeks heat when I think of him going all the way to Asgard's portal to see me. "Oh. That's sweet."

His eyes travel over my face, and the warmth in my

cheeks intensifies. I don't know what's wrong with me. He smiles then stands, and the grass crunches under his feet as he moves in front of Elan. Her golden eyes fix on him. "Can I pet her?"

"Of course."

Elan's gaze turns threatening, and he halts.

"Elan! Enough with your act already. I know you like the attention."

Her glare softens. *Oh, just a little bit.* She nudges Harut with her snout, keeping her nostrils upwind. *As long as his smell doesn't stick to me.* She flashes all her teeth in her intimidating smile.

"Elan!" I can't believe she's being so rude.

Harut chuckles. "She's a cheeky one, isn't she?" He rubs her nose. "Don't worry. My smell won't stick to you. I would have thought you would be used to the smell, seeing as you like dead animals and everything."

Elan throws her head back. *You take that back! I don't like dead animals. I like live animals. They don't stink, and the meat is fresh, not rotten.*

He throws his hands up in resignation. "Okay, okay. I get it. My bad."

The field starts to clear of Valkyries and angels of death, and the bodies of the wounded soldiers remain unmoving. A few soldiers wander through the bodies, searching for any survivors among the injured.

Mistress Sigrun lands not far from us, her face

wearing the usual scowl that she reserves for my kind. "Wingless. It's time to go."

"I'll come back shortly, Mistress." It is an effort to not sound like a spiteful brat, but I do my best to keep my voice even.

"You need to come back now, wingless!"

Grr. She makes it so hard to be respectful. "My name is Kara, Mistress Sigrun! And I will come back when I'm ready. Right now, I'm talking to my friend."

She glowers at me and places her hands on her hips before she huffs then springs into the sky.

"You have such a friendly mistress," Harut says sarcastically.

"You don't have to tell me."

We watch the Valkyries disappear one by one.

"Harut!" a voice calls across the distance. "What are you doing? You're talking with the enemy." A scowling angel of death lands in front of us, his beautiful back wings spread with annoyance, making him seem more intimidating.

CHAPTER NINE

The angel of death is standing intimidatingly in front of me, his hand hovering over the hilt of his sheathed sword. "Harut, you shouldn't be this close to a Valkyrie. They are our enemies."

Harut blocks the angel of death's access to me. "Kara is not our enemy."

Two more angels of death land next to the first, soft thuds sounding as their feet touch the ground.

"Do you need assistance, Harut?" one of the new angels of death asks. "Are you unable to defeat this Valkyrie?" Sliding metal grinding against metal rings out as he draws his sword.

Harut remains in front of me. "Guys, I'm fine. Kara is not a normal Valkyrie."

Pulling from my inner strength, I stand next to Harut. There are too many angels of death for me to fight, although I know Elan would help. "I can't reap souls. You can relax. I am not your competition. Harut has witnessed that I'm unable to do it." I remove my coat and expose my back to strike out any suspicion. "And I don't have wings. I'm different. I'm not like the other Valkyries."

The angel of death on the other side of the first moves forward with his sword drawn. My left arm twitches as the magic courses through it. I can feel it swirling in my arm, all the way up to my head, waiting for my heart to instruct it.

As though something in my eyes is scaring him, the angel of death pauses, but he looks at me menacingly. The three of them don't seem convinced and look indecisive over what to do next.

Heavy footsteps sound behind me, and the ground quivers. I realize that Elan is visible and standing over us. By observing the hesitancy on the angels of death's faces, I know her expression is aggressive and showing she is ready to attack.

The first angel backs away slowly. "The battle is over, and it's time to go. Are you coming, Harut?" Without waiting for an answer, he pushes off into the sky, followed by the other two angels.

Trying to settle the magic down, I open and clench my fist several times.

"Well, I guess that's me." Harut clasps my upper

arm, and again, the strange sensation of coldness mixed with warmth floods through my skin. It must be the coldness of death blended with his feelings toward me. "Perhaps I will see you again soon." His black eyes seem to see right through me, and heat rises to my cheeks again. I enjoy our friendship, although I also find it confusing when his handsome face looks at me that way.

I nod. "I guess I should be going, too, and see what happens when I get back to Asgard. It will be interesting to see if Mistress Sigrun honors her agreement, even though she's bitter about it."

His eyes travel up Elan. "Goodbye, dragon. It was nice to make your acquaintance."

I watch him fly off as gracefully as any of the Valkyries, and that familiar tug of envy over their glorious wings tears at me. I pull my cloak back on and turn to find Elan standing over me, watching Harut disappear.

You always have trouble wherever you go. Don't you, Kara? Never is a day boring around you. She smiles and shakes her head. *And who would have thought it would be like that? Here I was, thinking that to settle around you in Asgard, waiting for you to come and do something, would be mundane. But no, you manage to get into all the trouble you possibly can.*

I shrug and slide my hood over my head. "You're a dragon. I thought you liked a little excitement."

Living a life with you makes the dragon fields look like a mild place to live.

"What can I say? I want to do great things, and with that comes a lot of disruption in the world of Valkyries, and it looks like it is the same in the world of angels of death too."

Even though you are a complete handful, I don't mind. She nudges me with her nose. *I love an entertaining life.*

After petting her nose, I climb onto her back, hook my feet into the stirrups, and collect the reins. "I get it, Elan. I'm a handful. You'd be bored without me."

She looks at me over her shoulder and winks then jumps into the sky, heading back to our entry point near the forest. The rainbow bridge flashes expectantly in front of us, and we submit to its beckoning, allowing ourselves to be sucked into its vacuum. With a thump, we land on the solid ground of Asgard. Heimdall stands on guard in his usual position. His hand rests on the hilt of his sword, which is pointing at the ground.

"About time, young Valkyrie," he grumbles. "You've managed to annoy Mistress Sigrun again. That, I can tell."

"Pfft. What's new?" I wave a hand dismissively. "I have managed to do that many times. Seeing as no one came to grab me from Midgard, I'm guessing she said I had her permission to be there."

He shakes his head, and his brow furrows. "No. That

was the strange thing, but she didn't say that you are no longer allowed to go and help with the battles."

"That's a nice change. I guess this is one step in the right direction."

Apprehensive, he stares at Elan. "That's some vicious-looking dragon you've got there."

"Not to me, she's not."

"But her kind is vicious. You're lucky to have her as a friend."

"I know. Together, we are going to make big changes."

Heimdall peers down at me. His eyes fill with humor, and a strange sound rumbles from his throat. A moment later, he holds his stomach and throws his head back, and a large cackle bursts from his mouth. "If you say so."

"Oh, I do, and I know I'm right. Anyway, see you next time." I look at Elan. "Let's get out of here."

As we fly over Asgard, I marvel at the difference in the scene from Midgard. Here, it is so gray and bare looking, a complete contrast to the greenness of Midgard. My arm begins to tingle again, but I ignore it, as it is becoming a part of my everyday life. Maybe the tingling is because the magic is growing within me.

Elan lands within walking distance of the academy. After removing the saddle, I throw it over my arm and top it with my cloak, then I stroke her nose with my free hand. "Thanks, Elan."

She nudges me, and I leave, pondering over another strange day and the disappointment that I can't reap souls for Valhalla. It must be in our blood that all wingless Valkyries cannot do this. Even so, I still want to be involved in the battle and prove that we are useful in other ways.

As I march back to the academy, something swoops behind me, and claws clasp my back and scratch through my leather clothes. I drop the saddle and cloak and scream in pain. I spin around to see the creature flying above me. It has attacked me from behind. This is weird.

I cry, "What are you doing? I've done nothing to you, Loki. Why are you attacking for no reason?"

The zmey sweeps down again, claws first, and I yank my sword out of its sheath on my back, blocking the attack. Pain sears my side, but I don't dare drop my sword as the zmey swoops down a couple more times. I wave the sword menacingly. If the book is right, this is Loki. But as I look into the creature's eyes, I don't see a similarity to any god. The creature looks completely vicious and aggressive.

I call again, "Loki, I know it's you. Stop! Change into your god form so we can talk about this."

As I wait in hope, the creature flies down and attacks again. I'm dumbfounded. It appears as though he is trying to kill me.

CHAPTER TEN

I'm ready to scream for Elan when the zmey swoops down one more time, but then the creature flies away. I watch it disappear into the distance, speechless over what it did. My back aches, and I explore the damage with my hands. When I pull them back, they're covered in my blood. Another scratch runs up my side, but it doesn't go as deep. Blood and rips have ruined my black leather clothes. My head tells me I should head to Anita in case the creature's claws are infected. Instead, I follow my heart and stash my saddle and cloak under a large rock and head in the opposite direction.

The magic of the dark elf is a pull that I can't resist. I wander into the narrow dark tunnel that leads to the dingy little cave buried deep within the mountain. Eventually, I reach the area with the lights and turn the corner. The distance doesn't seem as far as the last time.

As luck would have it, the dark elf is sitting quietly in the corner with one of the large books sitting open on his lap. When he looks up at me, his eyes are filled with question, then he sees that I'm clutching my side with my bloodied hand.

"You need a healer, young Valkyrie."

"I can see the healer later. I'm fine."

"What happened?" He closes the book and places it on the pile.

"That's what I was coming to see you about. What do you know about Loki?"

A strange expression crosses his face, and his glowing yellow eyes seem to dim for a second. "Nothing other than he is a god and is quite mischievous. Why?"

"Because I read in the library that Loki is a zmey, like the one flying in the skies of Asgard. These marks are from a zmey. It attacked me without warning and wouldn't stop. I didn't even provoke it."

The dark elf's hairless eyebrows rise, and he stares at me. "Are you sure it was the creature that marks with magic? The one that marked you originally?" He rises to his feet and gestures to the injury. "May I see?"

I turn to expose my side to him and flinch when he touches the edges.

"It's not too deep. Let me apply some ointment." Gilroma grabs a container from the far corner, and it clinks against the other bottles as he pulls it out. His footsteps are slow as he approaches me while dipping his fingers into the solution. As he runs his hand over the wound, a strange sensation slowly courses through it from top to bottom. "That should do."

I twist to gaze at the spot but struggle to see it, so I reach around to feel it. It is healed, and I can't feel a mark like the one left on my shoulder. "Thanks," I say, confused yet not willing to question the complete recovery. "Why would the creature mark me again?"

The strange elf paces then stops and sits on a rock not far from me. His glowing eyes watch me intensely, then he speaks slowly, as though weighing his words. "I do not think this is a mark of aggression. I think this is a mark of magic. The only reason why I think the zmey has marked you again is because, for some reason, the creature wants your power to be stronger."

"What? I haven't worked out how to use the first lot of magic."

He nods slowly. "That will come with time and with more lessons from me. What you had served its purpose, and it wasn't a powerful form of magic."

"I thought it was powerful. It helped me against the winged Valkyries." I frown. "Why would it pick me?"

He shrugs. "You were marked once. Why not finish the job?"

"But it's not something I asked for. I only wanted to have wings and to be able to reap souls like the other

Valkyries. None of those came to pass. This happened instead."

"You should be grateful for what you've been given." A strange dark shadow passes over his eyes. "You may find that many of the winged Valkyries will become envious of you."

"The main purpose of the Valkyrie is to reap souls. I can't reap them, so why would they be jealous?" I ask, arms flailing. "I just want to reap souls like a regular winged Valkyrie."

The dark elf sits against the wall and crosses his legs then his arms, leaning back. The leg that overhangs the other kicks back and forth a few times as though he is deep in thought. "You know, there is a reason why you can't reap souls."

"Yeah, because I wasn't born with wings and the blood of the Royal Valkyries." I don't bother hiding the spite in my voice.

"Yes and no," he says hesitantly.

I stop pacing and look at him directly. "What do you mean, 'no'?"

"The winged Valkyries can only reap souls because Odin has blessed them."

I snap, "Yes, yes. When they are conceived, they naturally have Odin's blessing because of their wings."

The dark elf kicks the top leg some more, and it irritates me. "Not exactly."

"What do you mean?" I ask again, more sharply.

He stops kicking his leg and uncrosses it, placing his foot on the floor. "Odin blesses them with the power after they are born—once he sees that they were born with wings. That is why all of the winged Valkyries look almost identical. They change after they have been blessed."

I stop pacing and stare at him openmouthed. "Do you mean Odin purposely leaves out the wingless Valkyries?"

He nods. "Yes. But you're not a hopeless case. If you go to Odin and prove yourself, he may bless you with the gift as well. He has the power to grant this to a Valkyrie at any stage of their life."

I lean forward and hold my stomach, letting out a loud breath in the form of a sarcastic laugh. "As if that's going to happen. Odin hates me."

"No. Odin doesn't hate you. He despises the fact that you are bucking the system, going against his wishes and his dominance. He is a god who opposes change. You need to play into his ego a bit more and learn how to work him. Then he will be more likely to change."

"A difficult task, wouldn't you say?"

He nods. "Yes, it is difficult. But now I have told you what you need to do if that is what you really want. How you take it from here is up to you." He rises to his feet and clasps his hands behind his back. "Now. Let's see what this newfound magic can do."

• • •

THE END

Did you enjoy this book?
You can make a big difference.

HONEST REVIEWS of my books help bring them to the attention of other readers.

IF YOU'VE ENJOYED this book, I'd be grateful if you could spend a few minutes leaving a review (it can be as short as you like).

The review can be left on Amazon and Goodreads.

Thank you very much.

ACKNOWLEDGMENTS

I am touched by the enormous amount of support I have received from my immediate family. My husband has been a helpful first reader and at times been a wonderful motivator, with hints of ideas to help me through the blanks. The support from my three sons has also been overwhelming. They have put up with my head being in the clouds, thinking about the next plot twist or story for several years. Along with many hours spent working on my books and keeping in touch with my readers.

A big thank you to my extended family who support me being a book enthusiast.

A huge thank you to my editors and proofreaders for picking up the things we missed. My wonderful helpers are as follows:

Chosen - Susannah Driver, her editing and writing tips, and my Proofreader, Kristina B.

Vanished - Susannah Driver, her editing and writing tips, and my Proofreader, Jessie B.

Scorned - Kate Birdsall, her editing and writing tips, and my Proofreader, Vanessa L.

Inflicted - Stefanie B, her editing and writing tips, and my Proofreader, Irene S

Empowered - Susannah Driver, her editing and writing tips, and my Proofreader, Kristina B.

Thank you to all of my readers who have loved my work, and continue to read my stories.

BOOKS BY KATRINA COPE

Pre-Teen Books

The Sanctum Series

JAYDEN'S CYBERMOUNTAIN

SCARLET'S ESCAPE

TAYLOR'S PLIGHT

ERIC & THE BLACK AXES

ADRIANNA'S SURGE

~~~~~

Young Adult Urban Fantasy

Afterlife Series

FLEDGLING

THE TAKING

ANGELIC RETRIBUTION

DIVIDED PATHS

Afterlife Novelette

THE GATEKEEPER

~~~~~

Young Adult Urban Paranormal Fantasy

Supernatural Evolvement Series

(Associated with the Afterlife Series)

WITCH'S LEGACY (Prequel)

AALIYAH

~~~~~

Young Adult Nordic Myth Fantasy

Valkyrie Academy Dragon Alliance

MARKED

CHOSEN

VANISHED

SCORNED

INFLICTED

EMPOWERED

AMBUSHED

WARNED

ABDUCTED

BESIEGED

DECEIVED
~~~~~

Get updates & notifications of giveaways

Would you like a FREE ebook?

Visit https://www.katrinacopebooks.com/valkyrie-academy-dragon-alliance

Or,

Click here to get started: FREE copy of Marked

Through this link you can sign up for my newsletter and receive a FREE copy of Marked plus updates about my fantasy books, sales and notification of giveaways.

YOUR THOUGHTS

Did you enjoy this book?
You can make a big difference.

Honest reviews of my books help bring them to the attention of other readers.

If you've enjoyed this book, I'd be grateful if you could spend a few minutes leaving a review (it can be as short as you like).

The review can be left on Amazon and Goodreads.

Thank you very much.

ABOUT THE AUTHOR

Katrina is an author of several Young Adult and Preteen/Middle Grade novels. Each of her released books reaching the top 100 in certain categories on the Amazon's Best Sellers Rank – a few even as high as number one.

She resides in Queensland, Australia. Her three teenage boys and husband for over nineteen years treat her like a princess. Unfortunately though, this princess still has to do domestic chores.

From a very young age, she has been a very creative person and has spent many years travelling the world and observing many different personalities and cultures. Her favourite personalities have been the strange ones, yet the ones under the radar also hold a place in her heart.

During her last extensive travels, she spent 16 nights in a bomb shelter on a Kibbutz 8 kilometers off the Lebanese border. It was to avoid Katyusha bombs that the resident volunteers decided to name her after (she is still trying to work out why).

Katrina's online home is at www.katrinacopebooks.com
You can connect with Katrina on:

facebook.com/Author.Katrina.Cope
twitter.com/Katrina_R_Cope
instagram.com/katrina_cope_author
pinterest.com/katrinacope56
bookbub.com/profile/katrina-cope

www.ingramcontent.com/pod-product-compliance
Lightning Source LLC
Chambersburg PA
CBHW060758310726
48980CB00002B/149

* 9 7 8 0 6 4 8 7 6 6 1 0 0 *